The
Master's
Muse

**Center Point
Large Print**

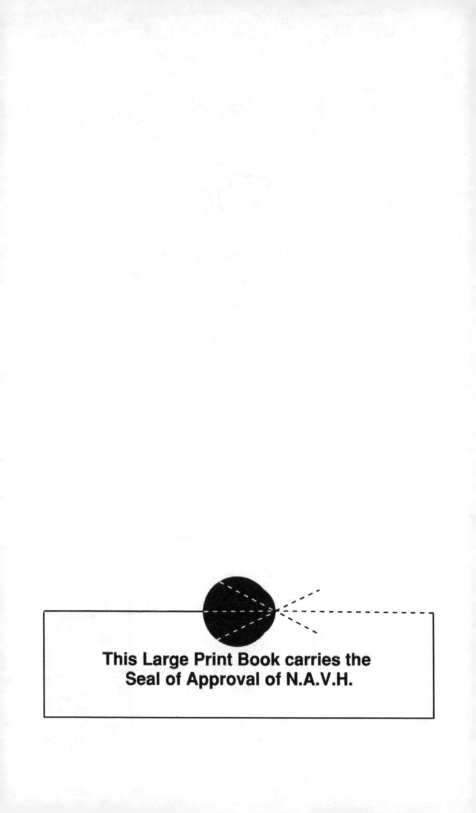

**This Large Print Book carries the
Seal of Approval of N.A.V.H.**

The Master's Muse

Varley O'Connor

CENTER POINT LARGE PRINT
THORNDIKE, MAINE

This Center Point Large Print edition
is published in the year 2012 by arrangement with
Scribner, a division of Simon & Schuster, Inc.

Excerpt from "Tortures" in VIEW WITH A GRAIN OF
SAND, copyright © 1993 by Wisława Szymborska, English
translation by Stanisław Barańczak and Clare Cavanagh,
copyright © 1995 by Houghton Mifflin Harcourt Publishing
Company, reprinted by permission of the publisher.

ISBN: 978-1-61173-503-1

Library of Congress Cataloging-in-Publication Data

O'Connor, Varley.
The master's muse / Varley O'Connor.
pages ; cm.
ISBN 978-1-61173-503-1 (library binding : alk. paper)
1. Le Clercq, Tanaquil—Fiction. 2. Balanchine, George—Fiction.
3. Ballerinas—Fiction. 4. Poliomyelitis—Patients—Fiction.
5. Paralytics—Fiction. 6. Large type books. I. Title.
PS3565.C655M37 2012b
813'.54—dc23

2012012190

For Michelle Latiolais, Katherine Vaz,
and Joel Wapnick

Prologue

$\mathcal{W}$e set our sights on each other almost from the beginning.

I cannot remember a time in my life when I was unaware of George Balanchine, the great choreographer who had come from Russia to transform American ballet. The teachers in my earliest dance classes said he was a god, a living legend. So when a scout from his New York ballet school guest-taught my class on the Cape and suggested that I audition for a scholarship, I was ecstatic. As we rode into the city on the appointed day in my father's car, it seemed my excitement carried us there.

George later said that at the audition I looked like a real ballerina already, just small, as if he were watching me from the wrong side of a telescope.

At eleven, though, I loved the audition number they pinned to my shirt like the number on a racehorse. I loved his fixed attention to my every move; little ham that I was, I danced exuberantly. At the time I didn't think much of the master in person. He looked ancient, sort of oily, with his front teeth sticking out and his cheekbones like blades. But even then I felt his radiance, his quiet power.

He didn't teach the children's classes on a regular basis. Intermittently he would materialize, snapping his fingers and marching up front—the guy to impress. Some kids got shy, but not me. To stand out, I'd go to the left when everyone else went to the right. One day I danced like a baby coquette. Balanchine said I disgusted him, that all I had done was pretentious, to please, and he sent me from the room.

Gradually, I perceived what Mr. B—as the dancers called him—was trying to tell me. You had to be inside the dance. For Balanchine, we didn't just dance to music. With the lines of our bodies and the beat of our feet, we expressed the music itself.

As he started showing an interest in me in the studio, ballet, which until then had been a fun game, became fascinating. I wasn't just the horse, I was riding it too. I think I responded to George so profoundly because he taught me how dancing took us beyond our own little selves.

Ballet linked us to other cultures and other times, through its history. And as living dancers, we carried the past into the future.

In the company, I skipped over the corps de ballet. Early on, he cast me in *Symphonie Concertante* with Maria Tallchief, his then wife and star. At a rehearsal I did a hundred repetitions of a step I couldn't nail. Maria said, "Tanny, don't break yourself over this, it's never going to be perfect." But I knew what George hoped for from me, and I was determined. She also warned that as I went along—as a girl who had been singled out—the pressure would only get worse, once I had a reputation. Add on to that stress, she would later intimate, marriage to Balanchine, and good luck.

Back then, George was enchanted by the ridiculous me clowning around on all fours like a dog, making him laugh. He was drawn to my kind of angular beauty. He was touched by my physical weakness, which he was compelled to strengthen. He liked my American nuttiness mixed with my sophisticated French blood—how I went to the Lycée and won all the word games, yet got in a fight with Jerry Robbins one night at a party and left with a couple of sailors. George giggled his Russian head off when I came back drunk and announced I was about to throw up.

He wasn't that old, really. I loved the things he said, loved the feel of his body against me, partnering me. When he proposed to Maria, she told him she didn't know whether she loved him. He had said that would come. Her girlfriends said if they married, he would do a lot for her. He did. They worked well together. At home they played four-hand piano. I can barely find middle C—but *passion?* George told someone Maria is tiger and Tanny is flower. I might buy the descriptions if he was referring to our physical types. Maria's compact and dark. I'm lighter and more willowy. But in temperament, falling in love with George, I was a locomotive.

For me, his allure wasn't separate from what he did for the dance. Balanchine brought classical ballet into the twentieth century. He created a modern language for an old form, remaking it into an art that was brash and hip, in tune with the country's post–World War II spirit. He instilled both an American and a cosmopolitan character, draining the fustiness out.

Going to the ballet was cheap in the 1940s and '50s, and to see it in Balanchine's manifestations mattered to all kinds of people. Some nights at the early performances of New York City Ballet, I thought the energy of the crowd might blow off the roof.

His technical innovations upped the intensity for the audience, and for us, his dancers, greater skill was required to produce his effects. He infused ballet with jazz and popular dance forms and an athleticism that lent weight, humor, and *sex* to ballet.

Choreography poured from him. If he was choreographing a dance and a step was too much for you, he invented something else right on the spot. He knew what you were capable of before you did. He believed in you and his belief was so flattering and motivating, you just couldn't disappoint him. You think of a ballet master as strict and forbidding. Highly focused and exacting he certainly was, but at the same time he was nurturing, joyful. He was endlessly captivated by the dance, never lost his childlike enthusiasm for its every facet. It was why his dancers were devoted to their Mr. B. He seemed to say, "You're with me in this." The work was a symbiosis. He needed our young bodies, and we needed his genius.

I don't even recall at what point desire permeated my consciousness. Because we were intertwined in the work, the art of dancing, we had that base of connection and closeness. He was more than just any man. What he wanted for me was what I wanted for myself.

I've heard people call him ordinary in looks. So-and-so used to see Balanchine around the neighborhood in his trench coat, "a nondescript-looking person." I couldn't agree. He wasn't tall, his looks were of course more vivid in his young manhood: the slightly Asiatic cast to his features, the smooth dark hair, and the black-brown eyes. In the days I took photographs, I tried to capture on film how I saw him—laughing, melancholy, austere—all the different shades and realities of him. He didn't have good skin. You can see that in certain pictures. It reminded me of how hungry and cold he had been as a teenager in Russia.

In 1950, touring in a London still ravaged by the Blitz, I roomed with Maria while George was away, and she confided in me her attraction to another man, speculating about being single. The next morning I practically flew to company class past the rubble and boarded-up windows. I catapulted on air knowing George would be mine. I was twenty-one.

The first night he saw every inch of me he kept smiling, looking slowly and thoroughly at my shoulders and down my torso and legs to the tips of my toes. I squirmed beneath this protracted examination and pretended to bite off his elbow. At that, he grabbed and lifted me with such strength my breath stopped. He flipped me from the top of the bed to the bottom, so that I lay with my head at the foot. Kissing me, looking me over and over, he smiled more.

We married on December 31, 1952. He was forty-eight, I twenty-three. At supper, as my husband's compatriots trooped in, talking nonstop and gesturing madly in their vigorous middle-aged Russian animation, I whispered to Mother, "What have I let myself in for?" We roared. I about split my pearls.

It was a joke. I adored him. It would not be for us as it had been with the other wives, I was convinced. I was the fifth wife, if you include Alexandra, his unofficial, common-law wife. George counted her as wife number two, and so do I.

After the wedding we moved into a walk-up

apartment on East Seventy-Fifth Street. Typically up at the crack of light, George would awaken me in his kimono, bearing my cup of black coffee.

Then it was off to classes, rehearsals, fittings, and performances, racing all day and night.

Early in our marriage he created the ballets *La Valse* and *Metamorphoses* for me and said on the radio for the world to hear, "I love her. I say, dear, you give me such a wonderful life, I want to make something for you."

New roles kept coming. I danced on TV and appeared in fashion magazines. My modeling thrilled George. "They want her for *Vogue, Town & Country.* Hauteur, she has the look. Then she smiles and she's Vivien Leigh, you know? Like little girl, like kitten. She has many colors, you see, like me. Real Mrs. Balanchine."

I met Igor Stravinsky and Leonard Bernstein, Tennessee Williams and Gore Vidal, I became friends with prominent poets and painters.

Then I went onstage to dance my first swan queen, crying my eyes out from nerves. I couldn't stop crying, and they literally pushed me onstage. I managed, but it was a timid performance. I had entered the vortex of pressure Maria had described.

George only said, "Better tomorrow," and he was right. I got a rave in the *New York Times.* John Martin wrote, "Dancer yesterday, ballerina today."

But with the increasing success of the company and my career, George and I had less and less time for anything else. I began to feel that I had no life. This wasn't true. The life I had was the one I wanted, but it was still hard.

When we were first married, on nights I wasn't performing we'd go to a double feature in Times Square. We sat in the balcony, where we could puff away. We loved the movies, loved one of my legs tossed over his, the "Down, girl" I knew he would say as I inched up his trouser cuff with my foot.

I was young. Voracious. I wanted to dance, but I yearned to go out on the town until the wee hours and make love until dawn, which was impossible for a ballerina. I didn't realize to what extent dance, for George, *was* love. By 1956, we began having trouble. We had been married three years.

Speaking of his other wives, he claimed, "They all left me." I answered, "Dear, you absented yourself." This just made him colder. With him, you could tell where not to go, it was abundantly clear like the lines drawn in dirt by his favorite celluloid cowboys.

We would be married for another thirteen years. But I didn't know that during the tour of 1956. Remarried and pregnant, Maria dropped out of the tour in Zurich. George reassigned her roles to the other principal girls, mostly me. To dance

Maria's ballets as well as mine gave exhaustion new meaning.

The tour of 1956 redefined me forever. Its events created a "me" for posterity that superseded anything I had been before. People would no longer think of me as simply a ballerina. My achievements would be overshadowed by the other part of the story.

There is much more to it than people know, and most of the more contains George.

The start of it swirls with a flurry of ifs—

If I hadn't been dancing too hard, if I hadn't been taxed by too many roles, if we hadn't been touring, if Mother had not come along that year, *if* amid everything else George had not let me down and I hadn't let him down.

I told him that once. Oh, I raged with ifs.

He looked at me calmly. He quoted his old nurse who told him, "*If* mushrooms grew in your mouth, it wouldn't be mouth, it would be kitchen garden."

Ifs, George illustrated, were silly. But still, one wonders.

Part One
Polio

1956–1958

Tender little hand, fingers of vapor.
—*Elena Ferrante*

1

*W*e danced at the Biennale in Venice while it was still hot, while the canals stank and rats skittered in the alleys and sunned themselves on the ledges of fountains. Then it turned brittle cold. The day we left I couldn't distinguish between the fog and the puff of my breath.

In Frankfurt, we were informed that Stravinsky had suffered a stroke conducting in Berlin and was not expected to live. Almost nothing could have upset George more than the possible loss of his artistic father, collaborator, and friend. He couldn't sleep at night, and I ended up sleeping in Mother's room to get the rest I needed for performance. Everyone felt the pall of his gloom.

Making it worse, George and I weren't getting along. I suspected that he was infatuated with Diana Adams, another dancer in the company who happened to be my best friend. I had no real evidence. My husband, far as I could see, attended to the usual sprains and emergencies, rehearsed replacements that had to be made. But I could feel it.

We called the long, late summer and autumn tour of 1956 the German tour, because of Stravinsky prostrate in Berlin. The previous year, so very different, we'd begun in Nice, on to the flowers and sea and palm trees of Monte Carlo. The grand duchess came backstage with a bouquet from the prince of Monaco. I didn't like crowded Marseille, the rough stage ripped the satin right off our shoes. From there we took the train to Lyon, where they gave us a lovely reception in the park and the mayor invited us to the palace. Florence in May was warm and sunny, and we danced on a huge stage with a good floor. I didn't care for Lisbon, we were like film stars there, the people threw belts, ribbons, men's collars to autograph, they'd clutch at our clothes, and I couldn't understand a word they said. In France it was easy for me, and in Italy too, though I don't speak Italian. In Italy I spoke French, English, and pantomime. In Stuttgart I bought beautiful cobalt-blue pottery and two feather quilts, rose and moss green. Amsterdam was exquisite, the canals, the paved streets, and the little white houses.

I thought of that tour lying awake in Mother's room throughout our stay in Frankfurt, then in Brussels, with the days getting shorter and colder, as if the earlier tour were extant, parallel, proof that happiness and ease weren't myths.

In Antwerp I spun off the stage and nearly fell in the wings, catching myself by clutching at ropes. Upright again, I was soaked through with sweat. Mouths moved on girls rushing by, but I couldn't hear them. Somebody had shut off the sound, and the girls looked like ghosts. Sounds shot back and boomed, and I started violently shaking.

George came to my dressing room, a cramped trap that had a wide upholstered chair, where I huddled, cloaked in my old flannel bathrobe. He got in the chair beside me and rubbed my arms, and I calmed.

"No more sleeping with Mama," he said. I could see he was worried about me. We had just learned Stravinsky was stable, and I tried not to link George's openness and care to mere relief.

"You don't love me," I said. He didn't answer, but he didn't leave.

In the morning I felt better. Mother said if I lost one more ounce, the audience wouldn't be able to see me. Since Venice she hovered, bringing me milkshakes thick with cream, white as her hair. It was quite strange because overall I was dancing effectively. I would drink Mother's elixir, gag down a couple pieces of steak, and go on as if my muscles weren't seizing. Onstage they revived, and in Paris I danced the best swan queen of my career.

I remember little of Paris. Ordinarily on trips to Paris I went to museums and cafés, I bought out the shops of gloves and perfume, but that year I stayed in and rested. This time Paris was a mission, saving myself, compressing myself into dancing well, showing George, proving that I

21

could go on regardless of our future as a couple, and proving to myself that I wasn't sick.

At night I lay in the bath then slid into bed and unconsciousness easily, dimly aware for a minute or two of George quietly moving about the room so he wouldn't disturb me.

On the morning we disembarked from Cologne, I discovered that I hadn't brought enough of the powdered dextrose many of us used in those days. I was riveted by the conviction that I couldn't dance without it. I asked girls on the train and nobody had any. Mother hadn't brought any extra, and as my options gave out I turned desperate. George claimed a cup of coffee would work equally well, that we girls were basically taking, "What they call? Placebo. The kick's in your heads."

I'm finished, I thought.

Arriving in Scandinavia, clammy in my coat, mittens, and hat, I thought, just get through Copenhagen, Stockholm. . . . Mother and George believed I felt a cold coming on, and with each day Stravinsky remained on the planet George acted more chipper.

We finished unpacking in our room with the brocaded wallpaper, in Copenhagen, before going over to the theater for a run-through.

"Did you pray for Igor?" I asked.

George sniffed, unsure it wasn't a mock.

"What do you mean, did I pray? I always pray."

"I mean especially hard?"

"Since when you take interest in religion?" and he picked up his keys and said, "Let's go. I'll let you out fast, you can come back and rest."

I sat on the horsehair mattress smelling of straw. "Do you pray in Russian?"

"No, Mandarin."

I tried to laugh, but it hurt my chest. I said, "Tell me a prayer."

"Come on, I will on the way over."

"In Russian," I said.

Shoving me through the door, he said, "Sure, Russian."

A car waited for us downstairs and we rode to the theater with Diana and another dancer, who hopped down the sidewalk in the cold.

"Diana!" George called. "Yvonne!" I watched, a fist in my throat, as he greeted them—beautiful, long, dark-haired Diana, and equally dark and beautiful, voluptuous Yvonne.

The Royal Opera House was magnificent, red velvet and gilt, carvings and soaring arches, a cathedral of art. George was ballet master there in his youth for a season. But, wed to the past, the Danes didn't want his ballets. George said Denmark grew the most beautiful women in the world like grass, but so what? They didn't *make* anything of them. Since George had become such a star, the Danes had invited him back. He brought us and quietly gloated.

He let me go after only an hour's rehearsal, saying I was out of *Bourrée Fantasque* for tomorrow. I would dance only one ballet for the opening and conserve my forces.

Outside the theater I did not hail a cab, I ducked away from King's Plaza, dodging a streetcar that surged through teeming people on bikes, and set out along smaller streets, searching for dextrose. Ludicrous, because how would I ask for it? Where would it be? I had decided, however, that it would save me.

Copenhagen was handsome, rather like Prague. Because of dark autumns and winters, from four o'clock on candles flickered in banks and office buildings. In the lobby of our hotel you could barely walk for the pots of rust-colored and violet mums chockablock on the marble floor. Mother had threatened to steal one of the filigreed sterling sconces. Interiors in the north, George said, were everything.

I didn't feel cold anymore. I smelled the sea. I thought of finding the Tivoli Gardens, but then I remembered they were closed. I knew Mother would worry if I didn't head back to the hotel soon, and I was reminded of stories George told me about the mother of Tamara Toumanova, his first very young star, his "baby ballerina." Mama Toumanova wore each new pair of Tamara's slippers herself, tromping about, softening them so her daughter wouldn't get hurt. Mama stood in the wings and called, "*Four* pirouettes, Tamara!" Yes, my mother, Edith, came on tour with us far too often and watched every one of my performances, but she wasn't *that* bad. She even laughed at the sign on the dressing room door of the corps in New York at City Center, NO MOTHERS ALLOWED.

Damn, Tamara could dance. She could balance forever. George made the role I was now dancing in *Symphony in C* on Tamara, and I'd heard that at the difficult balance where the cavalier circles her in the grand tour, Tamara would let go of his hand. You had to *knock* her off pointe. I had yet to let go of the man's hand, though I didn't clamp on to it anymore.

It was pleasant out walking alone with nobody watching me, nobody asking how I felt. Strangers passed on the sidewalks and laughed inside yellow squares. Soon candles were lit. At cafés people sat outside wrapped in blankets, warmed by long metal heaters. I began to see stars.

There was a statue of the Little Mermaid nearby, perched on a rock by the water. I wished I could find her. Then I recalled that Hans Christian Andersen chopped out her tongue, as if the tail were not bad enough.

I didn't see one single drugstore or grocery. You'd think in a large international city *somebody* might have a bag of corn sugar. Fatigue overtook me. I'd come to a park in a square and sat down on a bench. Cars, clusters of bicycles passed rapidly. I knew to go back, go to bed. But I watched the stars. I liked being out in the open air, free. I felt momentarily very good in my good old body. I could start over. I could do anything. I was twenty-seven years old.

The Danes saved their Jews. Thinking this churned my emotions, and I pictured the bombed buildings of Florence, the one bridge left spanning the River Arno—what was it? The Ponte Vecchio. What year had it been? 1952. Then I thought of my father, who was connected in a way I wanted to grasp to the problem between George and me. It wasn't just that Mother and Father were separated. My father was a distinguished man, a scholar and a poet. George was as fascinated by him in the beginning as he had been by Maria's father, who was marginally an American Indian chief. Father told George about Mallarmé speaking of a dancer as "writing with her body."

I always liked dancing, but I was also always a bit of a lazy thing. Poor Father coped surprisingly well with my laziness, my lack of ambition in school: "What are you doing, Tanaquil?"

"Nothing," slouched on the couch.

"Nothing will come of nothing."

"So true." What a brat, and Papa smiled mildly, continuing into his study. Despite his restraint, a father who named his daughter for an Etruscan queen had a few expectations.

When the dancing caught, he said, "Fine. Just do it well." Mother was apoplectic with joy. In Mother's St. Louis, becoming a ballerina wasn't done. She read widely, traveled, married a glamorous Frenchman, and times changed.

There is a photograph of me at eleven months in Cannes, before we moved to New York. I'm holding on to a grille at the side of our building *en pointe*. Not technically, of course, but I'm already at the barre.

We were a family whose problem was we didn't talk. Or I should say, our words were games, bilingual tennis matches. For us words themselves were too potent to trust as conveyors of emotion, of need, as if words taken seriously could kill or enslave. In fact, and this was the irony, words were everything for Father. As he and Mother drifted apart, while Mother got more involved with me, Father increasingly shut himself up in his study with liquor and books.

One night I dashed in distraught over a failed rehearsal and Father opened the study door, wafting brandy, eyes crimson in his narrow face. Swaying, but ever charming, he bashfully smiled and said, "*Ma chère*, I finished my translation of Villon tonight." François Villon, poet-thief of Father's cherished French medieval literature, though I'd had not an inkling of the project. We should have celebrated, with tea or cocoa at that juncture, yes. He could have read me a poem, I could have confided in him about my rehearsal—except Mother was finished with him. I copied her behavior, and nothing of this was discussed. The actual separation took years. I was a kid; I don't blame Mother. Some women prefer kids to men and some want men forever and the kids are a big interference, and there are other gradations, such as how personalities mesh and so on. But inside, Father and I were alike, much more than Mother and I.

I wished in Copenhagen, face to the stars, that I hadn't said, "Swell!" and hurried to my room. I wished I hadn't been schooled to be light and gay and afraid of the passion in Father and in me. I wished George hadn't fallen for me because I was funny and bright and long-legged and that, from the first, we had talked about more than dancing. I wished I had seen him more, seen Father more. *Been* more.

I wondered if Mother's coming along this year on tour had spoiled the chance of a remedy, a renewal. I worried she served as a buffer between George and me, enabling him to do whatever he wanted with minimal questions and complications.

But as Mother herself might have said, how much could one affect, control? Father lived through written words as George lived through dancers' bodies, and Father loved drink, and George got messed up as a kid in Russia eating cats off the street and replacing his absent family with music and girls.

The chill jarred me, the intricate scrollwork on a lamppost, the pristine condition of the park, its design, and the exoticism of the language I could hear snapped me back to my senses and I dropped the idea of the dextrose.

I stood like the Etruscan queen I was named for and hailed the gleaming black coach coming toward me. I deserved to be a queen, I thought, because I worked hard as a miner.

It had proved bracing, lingering outside alone, on my last walk through a city forever.

In the morning I awoke with a cold. Friday went swimmingly. George called music the water and us the fish. In his vernacular I could be angelfish, catfish, swordfish, or crab cake on a bad day. In another vein, my legs were columns, wands, whips, scissors, coltlike, needle-sharp, arrows, garrotes, and once, in an embarrassing class, he said, "Asparagus. Cooked asparagus." Oh, the trials of learning to dance.

He checked on me as I lay in the bath on Friday after the opening-night performance and gala. In relief, or out of hysteria, I tried to get him to kiss me, but he wouldn't.

"Rudolph red nose, I'm not getting sick." His eyes skimmed my breasts, though, afloat in the water, and I began to believe I could get him back. I wanted him back. I said a silent pagan prayer that Diana or whoever the hell it was would elope and grow huge with child overnight. That was the one-way ticket out of the Balanchine kingdom.

I didn't desire a child, being fully aware of George's feelings on the subject. Other relationships of his had ended over "the baby question," and anyway, having been in physical training since the age of seven, my plans for my postdancing life did *not* include labor. I thought I might lie around for a couple years and then play Joan of Arc on the stage and star in a sexy film with Sinatra.

There was the slightest heaviness in my left thigh. I lifted it from the water, testing. Champagne? The single glass I'd had at the party?

Back in the room, steam clung to the brocaded wallpaper, making the walls look swollen.

My thigh had this hitch, getting in bed.

Some said it took so long to become evident because I was strong. Others said the severity of my case resulted from my exertion during the incubation period. No one could pinpoint when I'd been infected, but George believed it had happened in Venice.

Saturday blurred. I was feverish. It is the repetition—the thousands of repetitions for each single motion you execute on a stage—that carries you through. I got through the matinee.

My back ached. I stretched out on my dressing room floor, deciding I'd stay there and rest until the evening performance. Dear Betty, our company manager, brought me a thick rug and one of the long metal heaters, a Danish delight!

I must have slept. George opened the door in pitch-dark. I knew it was him by the click of the knob, the efficient care he took doing all things, by his firm light tread, and his cologne—too cloying, I'd thought at first, then it mixed with the warming earth of him and I grew to love it.

The light. I drew my arm across my eyes.

"You don't tell anyone your plans?" he asked me.

You care? I thought. I didn't say it, too sick. I sat up. "I'm tired," I said.

"Come," he said, and, taking his warm dry hand, I stood. "Can you eat?" he asked.

I shook my head.

"Can you dance tonight?"

We stood face-to-face, his bow tie slightly askew—I corrected it—his hair less tidy than I preferred—I pushed back dark strands twinkled with silver, gathered them through the others. His charisma, his mystery, his genius, and his fame too, yes, attracted me to him, and yet more than anything it was our world together, the studio and the classes and the tours and our apartment with the stupid plants I kept buying although they got dusty and died because we'd be gone—our *world* I most loved, one running on music and muscle and, heavens, more even than that: his body. His strong lean body.

"Hug me," I said, and he wrapped me, full-body hug—our lengths together, his chin against my shoulder and head against mine.

"You're hot," he said.

"Not too." I felt better.

"Where do you hurt?"

"My back." My left leg is heavy, I said only in my mind.

"I'll get you massage tonight."

"Yes." Dear Rat, I thought. I wouldn't have said it aloud. But it was part of his sweetness, and I needed that. His parents left him as a child at the Imperial School. They shaved his head. With the head and the teeth and his sniffs and his, even then, supercilious expression when inanimate, when he wasn't consumed by laughter, dance, music—well, the kids at the school called him Rat, and he ran away. Brought back, he secluded himself, playing piano. But one day he had looked through a keyhole at older dancers, three ballerinas at practice, and he saw something interesting. It appealed to his intelligence. They looked as though they were solving a puzzle. He thought he could do it. He liked it. He gave himself to it and it saved him. So, Rat. My Rat.

He pulled back. "You'll be all right?"

I nodded.

"I'll have them bring milk."

"Yes."

He grazed my jaw with the backs of his fingers and left, and the space he had occupied rang.

I washed, redid my makeup, and crosshatched my slippers. I danced.

The next day's matinee I danced *Afternoon of a Faun*, a ballet created by my good friend Jerome Robbins—easy steps, short, you came on, and out of motion wove an impression, and the Europeans went wild. I adored Jerry's *Faun* for its atmosphere and its poetry. I stood in the wings pretending it was a hot summer day. I knocked wood and went through the door, stepping into the white silk room drifting as if from a breeze—fans blowing backstage—against the blue cyclorama of sky. Debussy's music held me, told me the manner of the ballet. Swimming through my partner's arms, staring into the mirror, the water—reflection. Such bliss: lifts, sudden surges, flicking my hair off my neck. Toward the end, Jacques kissed my cheek. My hand touched the spot. My eyes turned to him and, slowly, turned back away to aloneness, lost once more in self, and then I was going, walking those wonderful deer steps of Jerry's offstage. Soon came the applause. I listened that day. I'll never forget how that day I listened.

As I rested limply in my dressing room the sickness took me, traveling through me and pushing out of my pores, spilling heat that seemed to glow and settle like sand on the mirror, the lights, the brushes, the tube of greasepaint on my dressing room table, my costumes, those skins hanging on their glowing wires. I sank to the edge of a chair, too weak to do more than pick up my robe, could not even put it around my sore shoulders. Hearing a voice in the hallway, I called to it, any voice, told it to bring George, and he came. I said, "It must be a very bad flu." He got me changed, bundled me in my coat, hat, and mittens, but we didn't take off my makeup.

Mother creamed my face back at the hotel. I lay in the bath, I lay in bed, but I couldn't sleep. Nothing helped. Hours passed, George in and out, Mother imploring me to drink water, but I couldn't. I asked who was dancing for me tonight. Otherwise it was just ache and time and the swollen flocking on the wallpaper turning to fanciful shapes—orchid, pinwheel, a rabbit scampering onto the dresser.

George leaned over me and I nearly retched at the scent of vodka on his breath—crossing the Atlantic from Paris to New York, I was three, Mother was seasick, and I saw again her green face, her pale lips, *Oh, gods*—she rocked in the berth—*curse the odor of onion soup*.

"Do you want a doctor? Tanny?"

34

Shook my head no, no doctor, afraid of what he might find. "Sleep," I said, and at dawn it came.

Smoke. George was out on the balcony having a cigarette. Morning light, hazed by the drab day, filled the room like dirty dishwater.

What was yesterday?

Faun.

I got sick.

I must be better.

I didn't ache nearly so much.

Letting him smoke, I sat up. But I couldn't swing my legs over the side of the bed.

I pulled off the cover. I tested my toes. Nothing. Ache, though. It was still there. Flex?

Wouldn't. Knees wouldn't respond. The heavy left thigh was heavier. So was the right. Even my hips weren't mine. Wait. Try again. No response.

When I spoke, my tone was steady. I was too disoriented to panic. It was all too odd.

I called, "George, I want to get up and I can't move my legs."

2

Outside the Capitol Theater in New York once, they displayed an iron lung over the course of a week. It looked like a tin coffin out on the sidewalk. Inside the theater Greer Garson cajoled for money after the newsreels. At a freak show I had seen "Polio Boy," a gasping head

35

poking out from an awful metal tube. I didn't forget it. Pools closed in the summer, parents horrified by the scourge of our day. But always dancing, I rarely swam, just occasionally in the ocean—the Cape, Fire Island, Florida when Maria and I and two of the boys drove down for a quick trip on one occasion, singing our heads off in the car to Nat King Cole. We lolled on the beach and ate, ate, ate. Got so fat we had to go on strict diets. "Girls," said our costumier, discerning brows arched, "I didn't recognize you." And we were tan. A disaster. We had to apply body makeup on every inch of exposed skin, stacks of it over my freckles. Skating and horseback riding were also forbidden, because they were bad for turnout.

But by the midfifties polio was close to preventable in America. Salk produced his vaccine and children lined up for inoculation. There wasn't enough vaccine in 1956. Only the youngest dancers in the company received protection from polio before we went abroad.

Still, we didn't think polio. Not Mother. Not George. Not me. My immovable legs couldn't be paralyzed. Paralysis meant loss of feeling, we *thought,* and my legs wailed with sensation.

George sat on my bed and oh how I watched him, listened to him as I had as a young girl, to the god, the teacher, the man I completely trusted—my love, my darling.

"I've seen things . . . bizarre," he said. "If body's pushed, it reacts." He hadn't shaved, which alarmed me. "This girl I knew in St. Petersburg," he said, "she was dancing a lot. She goes home one night after performance, lies on the floor, and stretches her legs up on wall, for rest." I did that. I'd read with my legs up for hours. "She starts to relax," George said, "and her feet take on life of their own. Jumping like— what's that, you know, Mexican jumping beans? Hop-hop twitch all over the wall and she's lying there watching her feet, they're like chickens in somebody else's yard."

"You never told me about that," I said.

"Lasts, I don't know, fifteen, twenty minutes? Maybe half hour."

He carried me gently—everything hurt—into the bathroom and waited patiently outside. I couldn't go. He carried me back to bed, saying, "Don't cry," so I didn't.

He went to the phone, and I lay there thinking of how he used to brag about me, "She is ideal Balanchine dancer," he said, "trained up in the style. American legs," he said, "they break my heart. Small head. Light bones. In the school she ties up her legs like a pretzel and walks on her knees. Make funny. Later I have to say, no more funny, you make funny too much. Soon you play Odette."

George was speaking to someone, asking for a

doctor to be sent. I thought of how Jerry Robbins had loved me too, saw my swoons in *Symphony in C* and said, "I want to be in that company!" Made me *Pied Piper*. Such fun! Swarming onstage jitterbugging and chewing gum. George got jealous if Jerry's dances attracted more attention. Sometimes he wouldn't let Jerry use me. In Jerry's *Ballade* I played Pierrot, returned to life by a magic balloon. At the end of the ballet I let go of my balloon and watched as it floated up into the flies. On opening night the balloon drifted back down right in the middle of George's lyrical *Pas de Trois*. Thereafter, the stage manager shot the balloon with a BB gun during the pause.

When George was still married to Maria and we were sneaking around, Jerry asked where he stood with me. I liked going out with him, laughing like hell, but I told him I loved George, that maybe it was a case of George got here first.

George opened the door to Mother and the heat returned, no longer pouring from me, but contained with fierce concentration inside. I heard Mother's voice and I tried to respond, but in my mind I was climbing the steep metal stairs from the stage up to my dressing room at City Center, only they didn't lead anywhere and I fell back to the depths of a pit. In the distance I heard another familiar voice, "Places, you pretty, pretty people," but I couldn't move.

Stabbing. Sharp knives in my spine brought me up and back into the room laddered by heat waves that wavered and spun in and out. In breaks of clarity I could tell Mother and George what was happening, and seeing the artificial lights I knew it was late afternoon and I knew that my legs weren't up temporarily twitching in somebody's yard. I knew they were dead, although shouting with pain.

I was too busy riding the hurt to consider whether I was dying. The fever was too high for me to care that a doctor came. His spectacles sparkled, his touch made me cry out.

"Forgive me," he said in accented English. Just the sheet touching me hurt. Mother had torn it away to the floor and I watched it, the doctor examining me, the icy bite of his instruments and the sheet a white seething pool.

George had beautiful hands, a pianist's hands, virile Russian hands that knew how to grab a woman. The doctor was gone. George sat at the bedside, one of his hands resting close to my face on the pillow, long fingers, patterns of hair, veins, nails I knew nearly as well as my own. Mother had pleaded with the doctor to give me something for the pain. But they couldn't in diseases involving the central nervous system. My eyes drew in the opium of George's hand.

A stretcher wouldn't fit into the elevator. I was brought from the room in a canvas chair. In the hallway I thought they attempted to insert me into a cage: "No."

"Tanny," George's nasal voice cut the fever, "it's the elevator, see? Elevator in Europe."

Golden accordion door—oh, yes, I could see. "You're coming with me?"

"Of course," he said, "we all fit." I counted faces, his, Mother's, two strangers who bore me in easily; at five feet six and a half I weighed only 108 pounds.

The motion, the jolt at the lobby, each second was distinct and magnified, warped to distortion: the swaddling blanket smashed me, the car outside jumped at me—no, just the wind, a thin dog racing away.

"Don't turn on the siren," Mother said.

She understood, she and George understood, and if they understood I was not lost. They said to drive carefully, but bumps punched, and when I was carried into a building for tests, they sent Mother and George away.

The next day they transferred me to another facility. There had been serious polio epidemics in Copenhagen several years earlier and Blegdems Hospital had developed ground-breaking treatments.

Nobody said "polio" to me, only that I was quarantined until the infectious stage passed.

The squeak of the linoleum floors: *Can't you put some wax on those floors?* I wanted to scream. I saw a tall window and, outside, a gray brick wall. Coming and going, the high starched hats, crisp aprons of nurses. Blue dresses for the student nurses, the corps de ballet, white dresses for the principal nurses, the stars.

Somewhere in my delirium I remembered that we were soon to move on, and I dreaded that everyone had traveled to Stockholm without me.

A little pink face beneath her white tower of hat said, "No, madam, your mother and husband are here, right outside most of the time."

"They're waiting for me?" I could barely speak.

"They are!" Smiling, she had yellow hair.

"When can we leave?" I asked. I flustered her. Closing my eyes, I said, "Never mind." I couldn't turn my face from her, because my neck was too stiff.

The deadness invaded my arms and shoulders; it entered my trunk and strangled my lungs.

Dr. Hendriksen of the sculpted bronze hair and perfect English informed me that they had brought a respirator to help me breathe. The iron lung. I couldn't care less if I died; the iron lung the key, the translation: polio.

"No," I said.

"Nonsense," he answered, "you'll be much more comfortable."

The transfer hurt badly and I passed out. That happens. Pain grows too intense and you black out, which is solace to know. I surfaced again. "Go with it"—the swooshing—said the doctor. For seconds, frightened I couldn't breathe in there, I reacted as if underwater. I gasped, and air rushed in.

I had a collar. I faced a metal sphere. I had a rearview mirror showing the pink-and-yellow girl. "Call off the battle," I said. Thought I said? Wanted to say?

"Don't be sad," she answered. "Your fever is down."

And yes, I could breathe easier and the stabbing had lessened. But summoning all my weak might, I tested my toes and nothing moved. I could not even move my fingers.

The girl brought me notes she held to my eyes, one from Mother, *Papa is coming,* another from George, *Tanitschka, you are not to go.*

"And to read later, you have hundreds of letters and telegrams from throughout the world!"

Good lord, a fan. I asked her to remove the floral arrangements. Just like the sick one in *The Immoralist,* I abhorred them. I had to be brave; the flowers destroyed me.

The iron lung felt warm and womblike at first, but at night the bellows of my green metal bed was the breathing of monsters, a horror ballet, and I wanted out. As if George could hear me, I spoke silently, what is the point? Eurydice as you very well know cannot be saved. Sometimes the lung produced the sensation of flying, but I was the plane itself, not inside it. I soared far and fast away in the sky and into space where the sun had burned out and cold spinning planets whizzed by me like tops. Then I was outside in Colorado against the red rocks, dancing *Faun* beneath a full moon, a windswept *Serenade*, fireflies pricking the night. But in the wings in Colorado there had been oxygen tanks guarded by uniformed nurses, given the altitude, and as I danced in the lung the tanks flew from their hidden perches out to the stage—and I awoke to the real world, the squeaky linoleum and my dead body attached to my thinking head. Dr. Hendriksen kindly explained that I was already getting better and would get better yet. I replied very reasonably that I couldn't be in the lung another minute. He didn't answer. The nurses worked over me, hands in the portholes, washing my soreness, turning me, adjusting tubes, always polite, even times I muttered goddamn you, hell, fuck—the ever-elegant Mrs. Balanchine. Sometimes I did cry a little. George couldn't see me. I didn't cry from discomfort, pain, embarrassment, but from frustration. The patience I needed was monumental, and that's why they call the ill patients. I didn't have it and I was tired unto death.

Then suddenly Mother and George banked the sides of the lung. Soon they took me out and strapped on a hard-shelled respirator the size of a bread box; it looked like a turtle enthroned on my chest, and I felt hopeful that day.

Dr. Hendriksen announced to the press that I was no longer in critical condition. "But she will stay in the hospital for some time, followed by a long period of convalescence." Hooray. November 15 was the day of his announcement. Later I affixed dates to what had transpired. I danced *Faun* on October 28. The company left on Halloween into the winter of Stockholm. George and Mother remained. A supply of vaccine was flown over by the American Embassy for fifty dancers afraid they were next. The whole healthy lot returned to New York on November 12.

On the night of my diagnosis, I learned, George got drunk with Dr. Hendriksen and in the wee hours knocked at the door of our ballet mistress, Vida.

"Tanny has polio," he said. She tried to embrace him, but he pulled away. He wouldn't enter her room, rested brokenly against the wall in the hallway. I might or might not live. It was his fault, he said. For leaving Maria. For creating *La Valse*, my signature piece, an exuberant girl's first formal party at the end of which she is beguiled by Death. And he was most haunted by *Resurgence*, a dance he had constructed for a March of Dimes benefit when I was fifteen. George himself played

Polio, ominous and black-caped, who entered a classroom of ballerinas and struck me down. From my pretend wheelchair I did ports de bras so plaintive that from nets high in the flies it showered dimes. At the end of the dance I stood, cured and triumphant. "An omen," George said in Copenhagen, in his fatalistic Russian way.

Okay, George, an omen, I might have agreed. But if there is blame involved, how come *I* got it, not you?

The guilt over Maria was a religious feeling about the sacred bonds the Russian Orthodox Church ascribed to marriage. George didn't go to church much, too busy, but he had been brought up in it, and the ceremony, much like the stage, enthralled him. His feelings for art and religion remained deeply enmeshed.

He prayed for my life, and repledged himself to me if I lived.

It wasn't hard to intuit the pledge, but I no longer cared. I didn't care about anything. I was a twenty-seven-year-old dancer locked up in a broken body.

Get better? Why?

Mother sat every minute at the bedside knitting, click-click. My philandering husband said he was demolished, yet he got to *stand* there and even go out in the rain. I could see it, the harsh Danish rain dashed by the wind so that it struck horizontally at the window. Even on days it didn't rain, Mother said, the clouds sat so low they draped people's shoulders. On the days it didn't rain, Mother and George arrived out of mist and wind, dust-rain glazing their faces, thin layers of moisture and dirt. George went through dozens of handkerchiefs each week. I liked, held to, and resented the city's smell of salt, mud, and fishy water that Mother and George brought into my room. I waited each morning for it to cut rubbing alcohol, steamed wool, and hospital disinfectant, as I awaited the light that didn't come until ten, when at last it commenced its creep up the wall.

I was despondent. The worst pain was over, but the stiffness that followed was unlike anything I had ever experienced as a dancer. I couldn't sit up, could not bear to be raised or propped up by the bed. They packed me in steaming wool to break up muscular adhesions, flesh of cement.

George sat by the bed reading newspapers, asked if I wanted to hear an article.

"No."

He brought books of English crossword puzzles. Some trick. I had always done crossword puzzles. *He* couldn't do them, the Russian. He'd concentrate, scowling. "Tanny," he ventured. "Holds soup. Starts with a *t*. Six letters and I think ends with *g*."

"For god's sake," I said.

"What?"

"It can't end with *g*."

46

"Then . . . ?"

"It ends with *n. N.* Tureen."

I think it hurt George that for several days I kept a telegram from Jerry on my pillow. George was all cheer and no-nonsense. Two dancers in the Swedish Royal Ballet stricken by polio, he stressed, fully recovered and presently danced with the company. We must be patient, discern which muscles could be brought back. He thought he was some kind of polio expert. "Nerves are like carrots," he said, "start underground. You can't see anything going on and then boom, carrot's there."

Jerry wrote: *Dearest one, There is so much we can't understand that happens in life, and that we will never understand. Just know that I don't stop thinking about you. Soon, rapture, I will see you.*

Jerry had struck the right chord, and I had wanted to hurt George.

As a result of a conspiracy between George and Mother, Father didn't come. It wasn't his classes at the university stopping him, it was felt he would be too emotional.

But he called, and Mother propped the receiver up with a pillow and I heard him.

"*Ma chère*, are you there?"

Almost at once I felt more like myself. "Don't talk that loudly," I said to him, "you're cracking my ear. Transatlantic calls are efficient these days, old boy."

"Tanaquil," he said softly, "you must use your mind now. Do you understand? You must use your good mind to navigate the sharp shoals. Listen to George."

"Yes, Papa."

"He will not lead you wrong. Regain your strength and come back to me."

"I *do* miss New York."

"It waits."

"*À bientôt.*"

"*À bientôt*, Tanaquil."

Father. Home.

Letters came each morning and Mother read them to me. Jerry's missives arrived afternoons, special delivery, more to look forward to.

I dictated to Mother:

Dear Big Broadway Director Star,

We in Copenhagen salute you. George is choreographing *Apollo* for the Danes. He brags about his new find, in Georg-ese: "Body like god. Looks like Tarzan, you know? Weissmuller." And he's doing a *Serenade* for the polio fund.

PS I want to be brave, but I'm still scared.

I signed my name. The fingers of my right hand had come back and George's rubber band/pen contraption enabled a sad scrawl.

Dear Jerry,

George says he'll never return to New York City Ballet. He's being dramatic. But I count on you, obviously, to help out there if necessary. I know you're busy with your various projects, but please?

Special delivery: *Anything.*

The therapists carefully steamed, dunked, and stretched me, and I stretched Mother to her very limits. Mother resembled Margaret Dumont, the large woman in the Marx Brothers movies, a good sport, but often befuddled if tested beyond her rather limited capacities, which made for the comedy, you may recall.

One day I was able to sit up enough for a full view of my legs—my legs, which had been able to squeeze men to death, turn a floor into a Stradivarius, conquer Balanchine's wickedly fast pas de cheval, the horse step straight up onto pointe. My legs: my weapons, my wings.

They had become thin, white as snow, limp. Objects. Not mine. I shook, or anyway the parts of myself that could shake shook; my teeth chattered as if I'd been tossed from the warm hospital room into a hacked-open, ice-shrouded lake.

Mother, aghast, asked me to sit back.

I lay down, but couldn't stop shaking.

She said in her aging debutante's voice,

"Please, daughter, get hold of yourself. Think who you are, remember your stature."

That did it. I opened my mouth and howled, let it all out.

Two student nurses rushed in and to her credit Mother sent them away, shutting the door. The expression on Mother's face was one I had seen as a child during times I'd released rage or frustration she could not understand, a size of emotionalism that didn't exist in her. She appeared as if trapped in a stall with an enormous animal out of control.

Mother stayed in the stall. She came back around my bed and sat in her chair. She stood and approached the howler. Poor Edith. How traumatic it must have been for her to see me reduced to—well, basically, a screaming log.

She put her hand on my head, smoothed my hair.

Mother, orange blossoms, her scented soap. The animal heaved a few minutes more, and settled.

She had learned that it wasn't too hard to comfort me. Thereafter, if I got frantic she touched and spoke to me softly. If it was bad she sent George from the room and she and I went through it together.

George orchestrated a fabulous Christmas. As a surprise, Natalie, a friend of mine who worked in the office at City Center, came to visit. At

George's instruction she smuggled bourbon, marshmallows, and yams on the plane and George cooked an American Christmas feast in the kitchen of a Danish dancer, transporting each dish to my room. We ate early, while I had energy. I didn't mind flowers anymore and my room was packed with them and gifts from friends and strangers. I opened twenty-five gifts myself. Mother opened another fifty-nine. We joked about working unceasingly until August writing thank-you notes.

Past noon, Mother and George stepped out to give Natalie and me time alone. She sat beside me, holding my hand, my loyal, blunt, self-possessed Russian Natalie. "You're very loved," she said.

"Yes," I agreed. She brought summer days spent at her house on Fire Island, afternoons by the water, and nights of charades and whiskey. But at the bedside her face seemed to float in a faraway place that had been my life but was recast, reconstituted by the airy creature, the sylph I was now, and I couldn't get over the glints of dismay in her normally placid brown eyes. Seeing George feeding me must have shocked her.

"You're speaking more clearly," she said.

"Yes, and I'm quite a breather." The turtle was gone and I didn't miss him one bit. "I'm tired," I told her. "I'm me in the morning, but I've been through a lot."

"Oh, Tan . . ."

"Don't."

"What?"

"Feel badly. Listen. I won't dance anymore."

"Don't say that, you don't know."

"I do know. But I'll walk. I wanted to tell you."

"All right."

"I'll rest."

At night I didn't sleep well. I lay awake in the silence that broke to the sudden scurry and squeal of a gurney and its retinue rushing the halls, heel-toe and squeak of a nurse's rubber shoes. Street noises clamored and tapped at my window, disturbing the hospital darkness and conjuring visions of my old self, my shadow self I held on to faithfully: taking stairs two at a time, lingering in a pair of mules over the stocking vitrine at Bonwit's, hailing a cab.

I just did not think about dancing. If it came, I forced it from my mind. I would not listen to music. George said for now that was fine. We were improving.

Once George had told me: "You see I was dead man, and after that every day's good, like a bonus, I don't worry. Something always comes along. Also, I learn to appreciate. Do as I please." The privations he suffered during the revolutionary days, near-starvation for seven years, dancing in unheated theaters in the dead of winter, finally brought him tuberculosis following his defection. For months he had had to lie still, high up in the mountains in a sanitarium straight out of Thomas Mann. He refused surgery, and his left lung collapsed. He lost the directorship of the Paris Opera Ballet because of his illness, and wasn't healthy for a long time. He spat blood for months and wilted with fevers. He learned to work through it, to go on despite it, as he had gone on when his knee went out as a very young man and his life as a real dancer, on the stage, was finished.

He didn't mention these things to me in my alien body in Copenhagen. Had he, I would have socked him in the jaw with every muscle in my face. But I knew the stories and they existed between us.

He talked with the doctors and watched the therapists working with me. He created variations on what they did, and once he felt confident that it was safe—or maybe it wasn't, George had the assurance of a pope—we worked together later in the day putting in extra sessions, the two of us in my room, in a sense just as we had worked in the studio together before, watching each other, trying out moves, laughing sometimes, or one of us huffy, pouting and trying again, going through pain, watching pain, learning from pain, spitting pain in the eye in the endless struggle with the body we both already knew intimately.

It was with George after I'd already studied for

years that I learned to dance, really dance. Working at the school with Oboukhoff, Vladimiroff, and Stuart got me only so far, because what they taught was old-fashioned and not what George wanted in the company. In 1950 he took a couple of us and gave special two-hour classes at night for weeks: Again. Again. Stayed on us like a gnat. No. Try again. No, dear. No. Snapping his fingers. Double. On toe, then off toe, jumping, how to use our atrocious hands, how to initiate, how to show. People wanted to see what it was we were going to do. How to blow up and send gesture. It was fantastic.

In Copenhagen we again worked, toward flexibility, mobility, strength, seeking muscles to compensate for those that wouldn't come back.

At first, Mother watched us. But I think it looked to her as though George hurt me.

"Tanny, aren't you tired?" she would ask hesitantly.

George: "No, she's not tired."

"Two peas in a pod," she observed one day, "stubborn and ruthless." Said lightly, upon her departure for the hotel.

Mother was busy herself. The famous Danish firm Georg Jensen had designed a pattern of flatware in my honor, "very modern and refined." Mother embarked on posting settings to friends in New York and the members of her extended St. Louis family.

Although the doctors emphasized that it would take up to a year to see what I would ultimately be able to do, they were intent on completing the initial cycle of treatment. We planned to return to New York in April, where the next phase would begin.

One night George carried me to a chair by the café table he had purchased and set by the window and we celebrated a good day of therapy.

He opened a bottle of Château Haut-Brion, our favorite, which we had fondly nicknamed O'Brien. "Look!" he said.

"Verboten," I answered.

"Anyone watching?"

"O'Brien," I said, tasting the sound.

I couldn't quite hold the glass, so he put it to my lips and I slurped. He said, "Sexy. Do it again." I was glad to comply.

Both of us pleasantly tipsy, he carried me back to bed and sat up beside me, a luxury newly possible; we hadn't been close like that for a long while.

Then he kissed me.

Startled, I pulled away, and then, testing, struggling inside but serious too, I said, "No pity kisses."

"You kidding? I never pity-kiss in my life," he said proudly.

"Yeah, never needed to, right? You cad." He

drew me back and, leading with his full lower lip, kissed me again. I started to enjoy it. Him too, kissing my cheeks, mouth, hair. He seductively pressed his hand to my thigh.

"George . . ."

"Feels good. Tears?"

"I feel . . . like a woman."

"You're woman, all right, biggest femme I met yet."

"I take it, sir, that is a compliment?"

"Yeah, you know me."

"I know you." Who cared who it had been? Diana? Or the rubber orchid, my name for an extremely elastic and lovely dancer he was enamored by. His fuzzy line between dancing and romance clarified now. He had left the dancers and had chosen me.

"Tomorrow I bring you more treats. What do you want?" He meant heavenly food, to fatten me in the wake of the damned glucose drip.

"Let's see . . ." I dreamed. "*Pâté de campagne*, steak with wine and mushroom sauce, *fraises des bois* so little and sweet, like eating spun air."

"This I'll be able to find in Copenhagen?"

Soberly I said, "George, I have faith."

We necked. I hadn't considered that a paralyzed person might neck, and in the middle of the proceedings he said, "Want to hear dirty joke?"

I murmured—god, I was *alive*—"I thought you were wooing me."

"I am. But listen. It's good."

"From the Danes? You're going to tell me a good one from a *Dane?*"

"Yeah, never know, right? Better than Swiss."

I hooted.

"Two sailors," he said, "one girl. First guy says, 'So I take one end and you take the other.' Second guy says, 'Sweetie, we got a couple ends here, why make a limit?'"

Silence.

"Get it?" George asked.

"I'm sorry, it may be the worst joke ever."

"Oh, well, struck me funny."

My urbane, cosmopolitan husband liked dirty jokes, often including homosexuals, though he meant no malice. Too many men he cared about loved men, and yet because Jerry Robbins batted from both sides of the plate, to coin an old phrase, I had heard George ask a stagehand, "How you like dance by Jerry the fairy?" That arose out of jealousy, I'll bet. Somebody told me Diaghilev described George as heterosexual to the point of perversion. Now, *that* is extremely funny, if you think of Diaghilev: boy-mad.

But how *good* to feel ribald and alive and not sick, to slide into sleep on floods of kisses and wine.

I thought of the delight we took in each other in the beginning. Mother counseled me to forgive. Father said, listen to George. Alexandra,

George's second wife and a member of the little band of Russian dancers who escaped with him into an uncertain Europe, once told me I had to consider how they were forced to fend for themselves, to bring themselves up, almost like wild animals. It did things to people.

George's long journey to the successful late 1940s and '50s, when the company came together, had never been easy. Much more struggle followed his early days in St. Petersburg and leaving Russia. He got his real start in Europe with Diaghilev's Ballets Russes—"I would be nothing without him," George said of Diaghilev, the first great impresario. But in the years after Diaghilev's death, he again faced a precarious life. Even once Lincoln Kirstein brought George to America it remained rough for him for a long while. But all of it, George's marvelous background, the serendipity of him and Lincoln, doing dances for movies and Broadway when, at first, America didn't much care to receive classic ballet—it coalesced into a unique style and it led George to the right moment.

Postwar, it clicked. Young men poured back from Europe, refugees injected American culture with modernism, and with everything charged up, New York's fertile ground welcomed a new kind of ballet. The opening of New York City Ballet, named at its inception Ballet Society, was a scene in a scene, a thrill in a city of thrills—of abstract expressionism and Marlon Brando, cool jazz and the Beats. When we took our bows, the audience cheered forever and for six years sat at the edge of their seats, avid to witness what we would do next.

Then with the success of *The Nutcracker* it got more serious. Formerly everyone who knew anything about the arts in New York knew Balanchine, but after *The Nutcracker* we were dancing on *The Ed Sullivan Show* and George was on the cover of *Time* magazine. Things had changed. It put new pressures on him, on me, on us.

Fame: wouldn't wish it on anyone. Near-fame, that's what to wish for.

But nothing lasts, nothing stays, life is perpetual evolution.

All this I pondered, of all this I dreamed.

3

Stravinsky had slowly but steadily improved from his stroke, though in April he remained housebound in Los Angeles.

My brown hair streaked with gray, I returned to New York and entered Lenox Hill Hospital on the Upper East Side.

Home. Father. At first sight of me his seamed, persistently handsome face opened into a wide grin. Then we both burst into tears and for comfort ate the entire box of my favorite chocolate he had brought me.

He came each day wearing a three-piece suit, holding his hat with the snappy red feather, and, finding a place for it amid my bouquets, he read to me in his French-tinged tenor. The mints and aftershave didn't mask alcohol vapors, yet I didn't smell them at every visit and, good grief, *I* would have needed a couple of drinks to see me.

"He's writing," I told Mother, "he's standing for full professor. I wouldn't exactly dub him a raging alcoholic."

"*Did* I?" she asked. "I am pleased he is doing so well." But she wouldn't see him. Their visits were scheduled to never coincide.

I depended on Father's visits. Other than Father, Mother, and George, I didn't want visits. I dreaded and yearned to see Jerry, who was gone on vacation but would soon return. I hated the idea of most people seeing me and I didn't care to see them, particularly dancers.

George wasn't with me as much. He hadn't returned to the company, but he had gone to Los Angeles to see Stravinsky, and back on the East Coast he was busy at our weekend place. Before we met he had bought a parcel of land in Weston, Connecticut, with his Hollywood money. After we married, we'd put up a small house, and we had begun chopping away at the grounds in our city dwellers' attempts at beautification. Now

George was seriously making the place "nice for my wife," although, according to recent plans, I wouldn't get there in the near future. Released from Lenox Hill, I'd travel south to Warm Springs, FDR's famous polio rehabilitation center. Eleanor Roosevelt had extended a special invitation, and inquiries convinced George that Warm Springs, "more on the lines of a fancy resort," would bridge the transition between the long hospital stays and resumption of an ordinary life. Whatever that might mean. "Still, we'll work hard," George said, "get help if we need. Most of the best therapists are here in New York." To the Associated Press he said, "She will work endlessly, she is a dancer, she's used to it."

Endlessly.

It.

Didn't.

End.

I had plummeted psychologically. George interpreted my mental state as a plateau. "So what?" he said. "Happens."

Christ, he could be blithe. Sure I could sit in a chair now, feed myself, messily, and I could be wheeled around in *the thing*. First time I saw it, I blanched, felt illogically that it didn't look sound and would easily tip me onto the floor. In New York they had new lighter wheelchairs, compared to the stalwart Victorian wood chairs in Denmark. Except for trips necessitated by tests, I stayed in my room. If I couldn't get out on my own, I'd sit here and rot. Some days I thought I'd go stark raving mad. And I *certainly* didn't want strangers staring at me.

Then the opinion of the Lenox Hill doctors of what they called traces, muscular possibilities—during this period of evaluation—wasn't promising.

George breezed in late for the discussion of the first test results, trailing Lexington Avenue: I felt the cold air waft off him, and I could read the energy of the street in his bustle.

"Why didn't you wait?" he asked. Irritably, he whipped his hand from his cuff and glanced at his watch. "I'm eight minutes late. Why aren't they still here?"

"They didn't have much to say," I said.

Shrugging his trench coat off, taking the leather chair—quite a room I had there, for a big shot—he sat quietly, crossing his legs. "So?"

"My arm traces don't look too good," I said. "That puts into question whether I'll have the strength for crutches."

"Who cares about crutches? You'll walk on your own."

"Crutches and braces *lead* to walking, George."

"Not necessarily. We'll use those parallel bars."

I was silent.

"What?" he said.

"They're not too keen on my leg traces either."

"Tanny, the evaluation has just begun."

I picked up a dance magazine from my bedside table, folded to the incriminating article that had incensed me more than the doctors.

I read aloud, " 'The family suspects she won't walk again.' "

He got up and grabbed it. "Who brought you that drivel?"

"Do not stand over me glowering, George."

"I am not glowering."

"Yes, you are."

He sat down again. "I didn't say it."

"Who, then? Mother?"

"Nobody." He skimmed the article. "Nothing's in quotes. Conjecture, that's it," and he tossed it into the wastepaper basket, same as he tossed away most reviews. Then he picked up and admired a nosegay of violets and said, "Pretty, who from?"

"A fan. I ripped up the card. Take them if you think they're nice. They're for Le Clercq, not me."

"You change your name?"

"Shut up."

"No. It's homage."

"It's pity."

"I'm out and about," he said, "and what I hear is concern and respect. The pity part is in your head. You are too prideful."

"Don't you dare lecture me," I said. Out and about, I thought, out and about.

"While I'm at the podium, Blue Fire"—his

name for my angry eyes, which hardly ever intimidated or threw him, what did?—"remember, if I listened to doctors I'd be dead."

"You weren't paralyzed."

"No," he answered, still unfazed, then stood, came and kissed my forehead. "I'll be back later. . . . Why aren't you up?"

"I don't want to get up."

"Well, at least turn your head and look at the tree. It has buds."

Of course, I intentionally didn't. I counted cracks on the ceiling and got so bored I started hoping a nurse would come in and do something to me.

Then a big golden coin of sunlight touched my right hand, and I turned my head to the upper branches of the plane tree filling my window, its pronged buds prancing and bobbing in a breeze. Light played with them, and a leaf of newspaper flew up from the street on a gust, meandered in air, stroking the branch, and drifted from sight. I had entered the tree, my attention pulling me through the glass—why, I could have been me at nine, leaning out of my open bedroom window, living in *that* tree. I imagined the nine-year-old me joining the tree. In the eternal moment she wasn't confined to a human body at all.

Jerry and I shared an avocation: photography. Ballet and photography utilize shadow, pose, and pattern to achieve an effect. As a break from the rigors of dancing, taking pictures relaxed me. I got interested at a modeling gig in the country. Going over the contact prints with the photographer, I observed the part played by natural light and how near-perfect pictures were spoiled by a single flawed detail throwing off the entire composition. I disliked dance as a photography subject, because of dim lighting and constant action. When I photographed dance, I took quieter shots of people talking at rehearsal or resting around the piano. I liked doing portraits in daylight best, and they were most often of George or Jerry.

Jerry had sent me informal shots of gang members in Spanish Harlem, studies he took for *West Side Story*, his new show. While I was in Copenhagen he had chalked up another big Broadway hit with *Bells Are Ringing*, but it didn't engage him, not as the gang show did. He had helped out at New York City Ballet, *but the counts in the faces of the corps girls drove me nuts,* he wrote. *You danced to music, not counts.*

You spoil me, Jerry, I wrote back. And he had, since his first telegram in November.

In our letters we admitted how nervous we felt about finally being together in person again. He called and said, "If it's too hard I'll go out for a bottle of scotch and we'll get smashed." But then there he was, the same as always, a shortish, balding, great-looking guy, forty to George's fifty-three, arms filled with an enormous Snoopy.

We talked for hours, his dark gypsy eyes aglitter. He softened me up enough to agree to a trip in *the thing* to the hospital roof. "How'd you get permission?" I asked. The roof was off-limits.

"Star power, baby," he said.

And the *sight* from the roof was the loveliest gift I'd gotten yet: New York 360 degrees around me. The park, jagged buildings—the Chrysler, the Empire State piercing the jumbled horizon— a silver thread of the East River visible through the commotion of water towers, spires, streets, tiny cars, trucks, and bugs of people on terraces, swathed in the hazy gray green of a city spring and punctuated by honking, an underscore distantly roaring, practically playing Gershwin for just us two.

I smelled motor exhaust and in about thirty seconds felt grit on my armrests.

Jerry squatted beside me, and I planted a loud smack on his lips.

He'd brought his Leica, and photographing the view he hopped, jumped, leaped over vents, caged glass domes, warped bunches of tar-paper roofing, and he then put down the camera and demonstrated dance phrases from *West Side Story.*

He stopped abruptly, rushed to me, and sat in

his white pants on a filthy ledge. "Tan? Was that insensitive of me? You feel bad?"

"No. I guess 'cause it's you."

But he didn't get up again, just sat staring at me.

"I liked it," I said. "It'll obviously run forever and if I can get sprung from Warm Springs I'll—

"What?" I said, interrupting myself. He watched me intently, as if he hadn't heard.

"You're fabulous," he said. "From right here"—he framed me with his hands, peering hard—"there's nothing but you and the sky. You're against the sky at the top of the show and that's just so *you*."

"Oh, Jerry . . ." I was a crippled girl in a terry-cloth robe. "Thanks for not saying anything about my gray hair."

"What are bottles for? At least you've *got* hair."

I laughed, and he replaced the camera strap over his head and asked, "May I? Wow." He didn't wait for an answer. His face in the viewer, he said, "Are they blue? Green? Gray? Who are you today, princess?" And despite myself I posed, imagining myself out of the chair and attractive.

"Your eyebrows are dark as ever," he said. "You ever notice we have the same eyebrows?"

"We've got good eyebrows," I agreed.

"Lost twins?"

Next day, he brought me the contact sheets and a loupe. I would always be the old Tanny to Jerry, and my gratitude for his delusion was boundless.

But I had to employ all my acting skill to cover my upset at images of my bent hand holding my gray-streaked hair off my thin neck, the bony pale of my face, at how more than ever I needed a costume and makeup and how much I regretted the photos. One, though, a wistful profile, was Jerry's favorite, and he had already cropped it and blown it up.

From that angle, and with a bit of skilled help, I was a young beauty gazing at vast, still-yet-to-be-discovered life, out of bed, enraptured.

"Your eyes are eerie there, aren't they?" said Jerry. "Transparent like glass. Love it."

The truth about Jerry and me was that one night the previous summer we had gone beyond friendship and flirting. On a beach in Fire Island while George obsessed on another woman—everything about him shouted it, and we couldn't stop our version of shouting at each other, disagreeing and nitpicking and quietly sighing in exasperation was our modus operandi.

George would get miffed with me out of nowhere and it made no sense; his responses and his weird behavior were screens for what he really wanted to say.

It was late June. We were supposed to go out to dinner, but I said I wasn't hungry. I sat on Natalie's deck alone in the dark. Leafy trellises sheltered the deck from the road, which came alive every so often with people laughing holiday laughs, going off for trysts, drinks, adventures. Moonlight touched the leaves, rustled and flattened by wind. I heard George come out of the house and cross by me to the gate and open the latch, and wait. I had assumed he'd already gone on with the others to dinner. I felt the ticking moments, empty of what we could have done or said and didn't. I felt our inadequacy to the situation, our inability to be for the other what the other needed, open gulfs—our silence composed of my husband's chameleon nature, his cloudy essence, my youth and exhaustion and scattered yearning. Waylaid by grief, I was willing to grovel, to become anything he desired, and yet I thought, why? I had already done what he wanted—danced, loved him. I had no life but him.

I thought, tough! You asked for a feisty broad, mister, you've got one, and if you are under the impression that a better girl than me exists, you'll learn. The latch clicked; he went out.

I dashed into the road and found Jerry at a bar by the beach, dazzling in white T-shirt and jeans. A cigarette hung off his lip and two beautiful boys sat at his table, attempting to regale him. He quickly turned, in love with me still.

Down by the water, I unburdened myself. I was usually careful. Discretion came with the territory of my position as Balanchine's wife, but I had to talk to someone. Jerry was one of the few people I could trust. He and George had a competitive but incredibly firm relationship in the work. Jerry brought the company edge and George gave it class, it was said, an incorrect oversimplification, but illustrative of George's high European past and technical knowledge of music, whereas Jerry couldn't read a score but had this snazzy and burgeoning American popularity. They enhanced each other and, smart men, they knew it; artistically, nothing could set them on bad terms or keep them apart for long.

I talked urgently to Jerry's welcoming silence and, holding hands, we walked away from civilization. Then the sound of the ocean excited my sense of adventure, and I knew what I wanted. We stopped. He pulled me close.

"In the surf," I whispered, "like Deborah Kerr and Burt Lancaster." He smiled, led me to a sheltered spot, and we descended to the sand and made love on our jackets.

"Tan, you are the one," he said later. Putting his finger to my lips: "Don't say anything." And it was rotten but with Jerry still on my skin I wanted George. I wanted George more than anyone in the big lonely world.

While I was in Copenhagen Jerry and I alluded to the night on the beach in our letters, but Mother was taking dictation. At first I could barely read his letters myself, and as months passed and my recovery wasn't quick, wasn't sure, didn't follow the plot that everyone predicted, I recalled my one night with Jerry as if it had *almost* happened. If in spite of myself I remembered the genuine loveliness of being with him, it hurt more: all that wonder and possibility ruined by what would come.

4

May 24, 1957
Warm Springs, GA

Dearest George,

There is no need to rush here. Mother has settled me in and I've picked up the signs (Mother's gained weight and you've lost) that you both need a break. So do me a favor and don't go down with the ship. (Ha.)

It's beautiful here. It's quite a trip from Atlanta, way out at the end of a country dirt road opening into a colony of white-painted brick buildings skirting a lovely courtyard with a colonnade designed by the late Dr. Roosevelt, as the patients call him, in the same style as what Thomas Jefferson did for the University of Virginia.

I eat in a real dining room with white-jacketed waiters! (Next stop, Sardi's.) There's plenty to do, movies, etc., but I'm here to work, and work's what I'll concentrate on.

My spirits are high. Most everyone is in the same stage as me, the first year of rapid improvement and good news each day. Besides, the population is smaller because of the Salk vaccine: fewer children—we send up prayers of gratitude for the diminishment of suffering, but also for the more adult country club atmosphere.

The famous Pine Mountain springs are buoyant but, alas, they aren't curative. I do therapy in an indoor pool. No braces for now, they've decided. We're strengthening. Also, I'm learning tricks of the trade: how to shift from bed to the chair by myself, etc. Very exciting, REALLY, I want to do EVERY-THING by myself.

When you come bring 1. my blue chemise 2. *The Turn of the Screw* 3. the rest of my jewelry (we dress here) 4. All of Agatha Christie 5. more pictures of you and me, but none dancing.

Eat caviar.

Je t'aime,
Tanny

My room had carved woodwork and a marble fireplace. Just the escape from hospital rooms accomplished wonders. My left arm was strong enough that I could get around alone in my chair, now praising its lightness, tooling along the ramps connecting the various places in Warm Springs where I needed to go.

I stopped wanting to hide now that I was living among other polios. Like me they were prideful and independent: polio toughened the temperament. If it hadn't, I guess we'd have been dead. We were compulsively determined and constantly busy—out of necessity to adjust and get as far as we could, and out of the wisdom of keeping thought at bay. I learned bridge and participated in tournaments. I read and did crosswords and gossiped with the others about the affairs that seemed to erupt everywhere here. Most people didn't know much about me, while others respected my need to be one of the gang. George flipped over the news that I was learning to play clarinet to increase my breathing capacity. And when I told him about a polio from Wisconsin who laughed uproariously in the Warm Springs movie theater as if in mime, since his laughter was only detectable by the up-and-down heave of his shoulders—he had lost his diaphragm muscles and couldn't make a sound—George was fascinated. The physical and the kinetic intrigued him in dancing and beyond.

George and I tended to communicate by phone, because he never was comfortable writing in English. He had beautiful French, but mine was childlike. Father decided that I should strive for improvement *there* and sent a complete set of Balzac.

Typical, Mother said dryly, instructing me to put the box at the back of my closet. She sent Colette, in English, *much* more appropriate for a young girl.

I enjoyed being fought over by Mother and Father, by George and Jerry (inadvertently), by the more sophisticated patients at Warm Springs, avid for stories about the poets, playwrights, and painters I knew. Preternaturally cautious about anything personal, they didn't ask about dancers or musicians.

Jerry was a writer like me, and along with clippings I sent to amuse him and the light touch with which I constructed my letters, I confided a few of my anxieties: I couldn't quite comb my hair (though Mother had seen to it that we got rid of the gray), and if I couldn't do that, would I ever hold a camera steady again?

Jerry, I'm starting to fear that my traces are teases, and can you believe I'm hoping for surgeries? In my case, nobody's even suggested surgical reconstruction. I say I'll do anything and they just shake their heads, yes, they know. We go on with our swishes and swirls in the pool.

But I am learning to do more every day. I tell myself, think about that.

Jerry confided his anguish about naming names to HUAC in the early 1950s, writing, *I betrayed my country, my friends, and myself.*

He hadn't spoken to me about this. I knew he had briefly joined the Communist Party—the only political organization back in the thirties that wasn't anti-Semitic and truly cared for workers and the poor—and quit when the party revealed itself as totalitarian. I knew he resisted the pressure of the House Un-American Committee for years, until the subpoena prompted his drastic decision.

> Jerry, I'm so sorry. Why didn't you tell me? I had no idea what you were going through then. You didn't say anything. You have to reach out, you know.

George made his appearance in June. He grilled the staff on the reasoning behind my therapy. They had decided on a conservative approach with my legs to avoid injury of unaffected muscles. My upper body was coming along well, but it could be years before we knew the extent of the damage in my legs.

Years, I thought. Plural? But how many years did it take to achieve an ideal arabesque? And how often had George rebuked me, "No more lousy sixes!" We struggled heroically to accomplish my clean entrechat-six, a jump in which the dancer beats her legs six times.

If we had to go slow with my legs, he figured, we would concentrate on the suppleness of my trunk and neck. "I want your beautiful posture back," he said. "You will sit in the chair like my queen."

I grinned widely, ready to acquiesce to anything. He captured my hand, chivalric, and put it to his lips.

Given his interest in anatomy, and science in general, George would have better appreciated his stay at Warm Springs had he been left alone to quietly quiz people, patients and staff alike, about their experiences and expertise, instead of becoming the center of attention himself. This happened most often in the dining room at meals. Despite his thorough conviction in himself and his abilities, his celebrity rather annoyed him, apart from what it could get for the company. But he was able-bodied, and therefore fair game for inquisition. People wheeled up to hear about Hollywood and Jerry Robbins—who would come, but in a flash, so no one got to him—and how George picked kids for *The Nutcracker*, and was Ed Sullivan as stiff in life as he seemed on TV? One woman asked how he liked dancing for the czar.

"Czar Nicholas, yes," George answered politely. "I was small boy. Czar sent royal carriages to take us from school to the theater, nights we were in ballets."

"What did they look like?" asked the woman, a

smart lady from Texas with hands gnarled as claws.

Patiently he explained, sniffing and blinking, his tics telegraphing to me his discomposure. I imagined him peacefully manipulating her fingers in an effort to comprehend the distortions.

He bowed, and hurried back to my room, where—and this was George therapy—he busied himself organizing my shelves and closet, measuring space for the bookcase he'd built in the shop with Willie Mars, a local man on the staff who had driven him to Warm Springs from the train station. George had taken a course in woodworking. He liked to cook, iron, and mow the lawn at the house in Weston. As a choreographer he considered himself a craftsman, and from this attitude came his statement, "I don't create, I assemble."

It was not disingenuous. He fixed the broken latch on my lacquered antique Chinese jewelry box and I thought about his care of the pianos back at the studios. He was always the last to leave rehearsals, clearing ashtrays, shutting lids over keys, and stacking scores, as if the pianos were people and his personal responsibility too. His loves were concrete. He had lived through adversity into appreciation of what was definite, present, or, as he said, *today.*

"When you going to try?" he'd ask a hesitant dancer. "What about now?"

Another George homily: "Nothing ethereal about ballet. It's bodies in space. We don't dance spiritual feelings, because there is a body onstage that must move."

We hit the mats to regain my dancer's posture in one of the smaller wood-floored physical therapy rooms, sweating like pigs in the southern summer. We would set the exercises while he was here, and I'd do the repetitions myself. No mirrors. "I'm mirror now," he said.

"You weren't before?" I asked incredulously.

"I mean I more want you feeling it, dear, and it isn't to see, we're not making picture for audience but three-dimensional moving sculpture." Frankenstein monster, I thought, amused and inspired, usually, by George's God complex.

We attacked my inability to pull over from back to stomach using my torso and stronger left shoulder alone.

"Look, I will lead and you feel," he said. "Follow the motion."

I did; I still couldn't do it alone.

"Okay, then I train therapist to be me for after I go," he said.

We'd work fifteen minutes, rest five, another fifteen, another five—timing calculated in consultation with the doctor. During rests I'd scoot off the sticky gray mat, lie flat on the cooler floor, and watch George sitting against a wall, watching me, acknowledging the debacle of my body: how odd, how multifarious are the aspects of human experience, and how extraordinary that a person carrying half of her body as deadweight could yet throb with energy, life force, and a will so insistent that why—and what is the metaphysical reason behind this?—couldn't she get up and walk? We knew why, of course, down to our toes—pardon the pun—but the fact remained thorny, hard to fathom and approach. The thoughts in our eyes, realer than words, fell away as we plunged into work again: into the literal body.

I ached at night. As an antidote to my aches and the possibility of running into inquisitors on the main campus, we frequented Willie Mars's cottage down the road and drank vodka George brought from New York with Willie and his wife, Sophia, on their porch as the night cooled. We were marooned in a dry state and liquor was banned from the hospital grounds. Nobody obeyed.

"Those patients are cagey," Willie said, "get hold of the local moonshine, if need be."

"I wouldn't know where to get it," Sophia said, "and I've lived here my entire life."

"I keep you innocent, sugar," said Willie.

"Innocent, ha!" she retorted. "Point is, those folks aren't only resourceful, they can charm squirrels out of trees."

"Birds," Willie said.

"Squirrels, 'cause they're bigger," Sophia overrode him.

The trees dripped moss over red soil, and hoot owls blinked glowing eyes from high branches that sheltered the yard. The Deep South was novel to me. Like Willie and Sophia, most of the staff members were locals and some of the kindest people I'd ever met—and they moved very slowly, another impression of the South that proved valid. But who among us had any pressing appointments?

Slow, quiet, could be a pleasure. George and I took the double swing on the Mars's porch, my back against cushions, my legs in his lap. The motion of the swing soothed, the rocking creak of Willie and Sophia's chairs creating with the swing's chain a restful syncopation.

Yet Sophia's remark about the charm and resourcefulness of the polios nettled me like an itch, too rah-rah about how special we all were. Sophia was a dark reedy woman with a surprisingly big voice; she should have sung opera. Willie was lighter and stocky, and his sharp widow's peak rather comically matched his pointy goatee. Of the pair, Sophia was clearly in charge.

"They're resourceful because they have to be," I said to her. "Charming? A few. A lot more are merely insistent, like mules."

Sophia threw back her head and laughed her big

laugh. "I've got something for you, missy," and got up, real slow, and went into the house.

"One more," I said to George.

"No, you're in training."

"Liar, you're afraid you'll run out before you go back to New York."

"So we get moonshine. You'll use your insistence."

"Sophia is attempting to lure me into occupational therapy," I told him. "Half a shot, come on." He succumbed.

"Her doctor prescribed occupational therapy," Willie said to George, and, nodding at me: "*She* wheels in bold as you please, and asks Sophia, 'Is the intention to occupy me or to train me for a new occupation modeling clay pots?'"

"Bad girl," said George, and he swatted my knee.

"It was a perfectly straightforward question," I said. I hated clay and baskets and anything else I expected in that room, where Sophia ruled.

Sophia, however, obviously wasn't put off, relating the story to Willie as hysterically funny.

"I don't care for explaining ballet to reporters," George said to Willie, "but is part of my job. This one"—me—"said to a very nice man asking her one easy question after a show—"

"Don't tell," I said, feigning regret.

"She said," my husband continued, "'I don't give a shit, I'm going home to soak my feet.'"

"I'd been under torture," I told Willie, "by *him*."

We fell quiet, breathing in the potent odor of second-bloom magnolias and counting the beats, for my part, of the silences between the vibrating sobs of the cicadas.

"It's for my hands," I admitted to George. "But I'm only interested in making you tie clips and cuff links," I quipped. "Sophia says metal work's too advanced."

"If is for your hands you must do it," said George, rubbing my feet.

"For once, darling," I said to him, "could you be unpredictable?"

"No."

Sophia emerged from the house with a large paper bag. She pulled up her rocker and brought forth brilliant yellow and cerulean-blue strips, half an inch wide, of a dense fabric with a satiny sheen that fell in waterfalls from her palms.

"Well?" she asked.

"They're gorgeous," I said.

She gave me a bunch, and as I fingered their smoothness and resiliency, she said, "I thought we'd weave place mats."

"On a loom?" I said.

Sophia chortled. "Uh-uh, by hand. We can do them in rows and knot them off, along the theory of knitting."

"I can do this?" I asked her.

"Yes, and in the end you'll have them to keep or give as gifts."

"You should have seen Sophia and her catalogues from Atlanta," Willie told George, "searching away."

I was touched.

"I knew you'd want something challenging and unique," Sophia told me.

"And glitzy," said George. "Tanny's Fifth Avenue girl."

"I got that," Sophia teased me.

Back in my room, I pictured the colors, bright stripes in the dark, my fingertips recalled the satiny smoothness, and I felt excited about getting started. And I wanted to weep because of the hoards of people who had to expend so much energy helping me, using their own precious life force to keep me going—why, George, pushing me up the steep path over tree roots and rocks, could have been training himself all these years for the strength to haul me around.

"Hot?" he asked. Each night he bathed me. I was learning to get into a bathtub myself, but I couldn't yet, and getting out sounded harder than Everest. I thanked my lucky stars and every saint I didn't believe in that I'd mastered the toilet bit, but I couldn't bathe. I had come to know I could fight the bathing and render myself and everyone involved abject, or I could accept it.

"Pretend you are Cleopatra," George said. "I'm

slave." He pulled back the coverlet and put the rubber sheet on the bed, and then I slowly shifted from the chair to the bed and he helped me off with my dress, my brassiere, and my underpants. With George, I always wished I were prettier, but half of me was nearly pretty, and if he wasn't too tired he seemed to take sensual pleasure in running the sponge over me, dipping it back in the water, the motion bonding us in a new way.

There hadn't been much hanky-panky—George's term, he got a kick out of American slang—since he'd arrived, but the bathing, the bookcase, the exercises on the mats were also actions of love.

"Czar's wife," George said, "Empress Alexandra, never washed her hair herself. Not once."

"And look at the price she paid for that," I said languidly.

"I'll make you pay," George answered, "tomorrow."

Pay in work. In our early days, I was an expert seductress. Tired or grouchy, next thing he knew we'd be flailing about. "You want to kill me?" he'd say.

"Yes, kill with love."

"What I get, I marry young girl."

Our first night together was a scream. He could be extremely prudish and failed to conceal his surprise that I wasn't a virgin. At that, I couldn't stop laughing.

"Don't laugh," he said tenderly, "I would worry about you with somebody else."

He toweled me off while rolling the rubber sheet back, his arm muscles taut and pronounced as he completed the slow procedure, his manly hawkish face a study in concentration. I loved the vertical dips in the topography of his cheeks, crevices more than lines that ran from under his cheekbones to just above his jaw; they were similar to my father's and unusual in the faces of American men. George had dimples too, but only if he smiled broadly, and seeing them was a big reason I worked at making him laugh.

When I was dry on the cotton bedding again, he powdered me for coolness, pulled the top sheet to my waist, stripped himself, and went into the bathroom for a shower.

If only I could hang up his plaid shirt, crease his trousers—well, I could. Shifting my weight to my left shoulder, I scooted to the edge of the bed and reached for the chair; hooked my arm around an armrest and wheeled it close. It took bodily rearrangement to point myself at the proper angle, but I gave the deep effort and seated myself without falling—I was covered with bruises and tried to avoid adding to their design. Now! George had finished the task of setting up my room properly. Everything was at wheelchair-level, and furniture against the walls. Naked and happy, I hung up his shirt and pants, tossed his underwear into the hamper, and set his turquoise and silver American Indian bracelet on the mantelpiece. Maria's people had given him the bracelet and he cherished it as a symbol of his American citizenship.

I was about to retrieve a pair of clean briefs from the bureau when he opened the bathroom door, a towel wrapping his waist, and looked for a second about to holler, "Tanny! You are all steamed up and sweaty again. Besides, now in the morning you will be weak and sore and spoil work!"

I threw him a goofy smile, what else could I do?

He appraised the situation and, collecting himself, he said, "Thank you, dear."

A rush of sheer terror charged through me at how much I loved him.

He left. It had been sensible and mature to encourage him not to stay long, to recommence his life in New York and prepare for my eventual release from Warm Springs. But I missed his touch, his care, his company, and had I *been* Cleopatra, I never would have let him go.

Our exercises produced good results. I could turn back to front within a month, my shoulders grew stronger, my balance improved so impressively that the therapists brought out the leg braces. No crutches, just parallel bars I held on to as I stood in the braces a little longer each day. By August I had learned to scale Everest successfully, hauling myself from the bath and into the chair like a seal.

In late August, a letter brought news that Stravinsky had fully recovered and was in New York rehearsing a premiere for the fall season at the Philharmonic.

That day in the occupational therapy room I wove a place mat furiously—don't think, I inwardly chanted. He is Stravinsky! I had ten whole years as a principal dancer, ten good years. I had inspired Antony Tudor and Frederick Ashton and Merce Cunningham and Jerome Robbins and George Balanchine.

George, you're with Stravinsky right now, I thought.

Don't think. Why shouldn't he be? Could be they were eating and drinking together and having a whale of a good time. It was nice to think of somebody having a whale of a good time.

Only one other inmate was present in OT, a teenager on crutches painting at an easel, which would have been easier sitting down, but why would he sit if he could stand, even awkwardly? I understood.

Soon it would be fall. The ripe fragrance of late summer filling the room from the open windows reminded me of the studio much more than of school. I'd quit school and studied with a tutor from the age of thirteen. I used to tease George by saying, "My body, my body, what about my mind?" It seemed awfully ironic that again, even after I couldn't dance, my life had to be so much about my physical self.

If the heavy late-summer fragrance reminded me of the studio, it meant sweat, rosin, and woolen tights, and thinking of it brought along the memory of roses I had cradled onstage during curtain calls, drenched like a racehorse.

Don't think. But it came, the hollow backstage full of dancers stretching and jumping, the orchestra tuning up, the heave of my chest as I stepped into the light and just went, like a jazz musician, flying on sound and my body that somehow did not let me down onstage, that did as George said it would do. How I loved the strut of *Western Symphony*, and the huge black feather hat I wore. I was so good in hats. I thought of my straw hat—designed from Greta Garbo's in *Camille*—in Jerry's *The Concert*, where I was a girl so enthralled by piano playing that she doesn't notice her chair grabbed right out from under her bottom.

Sophia returned from her bihourly trip down the hall for coffee and sat beside me. "Hands sore?" she asked.

"Yeah."

"So stop."

"I'll finish the row."

The chicory mixed with her perfume, gardenia. I'd miss her.

Reading my mind, she said, "I heard you might be leaving us soon."

"They're talking about it," I said.

"I hate graduations."

I kissed Sophia on the cheek.

"Why, thank you, Tanny," she said. Then the teenager called for help and she got up.

I loved graduations. Sure, I would miss her, but I couldn't wait to go home. Phone inquiries led me to believe I could get better therapy for my current needs in New York. Besides, the South with its de facto segregation and still active Klan had begun to grate on me badly. If less blatantly, New York was also benighted, but in my world of artists, people were closer to getting it right. Right before I got sick George had hired Arthur Mitchell, black and from Harlem, and in response to the complaints of two mothers of corps girls, George dismissed the young ballerinas. Matricide, I thought, would have been a fairer and surer method of alleviating the problem.

George had brought Arthur into the company to partner me. *Don't think.*

I finished my row and, waving to Sophia and the kid, wheeled out of OT. I went down the hall and into the elevator glaring my don't-talk-to-me-I'm-not-in-the-mood look. Had anyone granted me one wish six months ago, I'd have been cured and a good enough balancer to dance Princess Aurora. My one wish now was for privacy. Please.

In the courtyard, intense heat dispensed with the need to keep anyone off. I was instantly slick, my muscles oiled and loose. I longed to sit in the sauna at Monsieur Louis on East Sixty-Third and I longed for a manicure and a decent haircut. From the light, the columns blushed copper, and the roses tumbling down from the arbor seemed to drip the gold leaf painters used. The flagstone patio burned my bare foot when I took it out of my slipper and tested a stone with a toe. Apart from my room this was the one place, in the blazing month of August, where I could be alone.

Forgive me, God, if you exist, which I doubt, but I was sick of cripples. Sure, many were interesting and *admirable,* but en masse I'd had it. The therapeutic benefits of living in proximity to others worse off had long since diminished. And with polio, as with war victims, I saw a few so damaged in body or mind they wobbled my own precarious sense of stability. I wasn't Gandhi. I was not even a celebrated dancer any longer, someone with enough distance from suffering to witness it out of the compassion of equanimity. I was out here raw and alone, just hanging on, hanging over the fire by my chipped fingernails.

Not long ago a troll in a handmade wheelchair

showed up at the train station uninvited. Polios arriving on the train unaccompanied and unannounced weren't unusual, especially at the height of the epidemics once word of FDR's hospital spread. Destitute people. Desperate people from desperate families, who'd chosen to abandon damaged kin. The patients were dealt with on an individual basis, often transferred to other hospitals where funding and space could be found.

But this troll carried a fat satchel of cash. Evidently his family had saved up for years to send him here. He was beyond help, if much help had been at all possible in the beginning. His torso bent far to the right and nearly fused with his right hip. The right arm was useless and withered and he kept his elbow tucked into his belly, out of the way. I am grateful I couldn't see his legs, just the tiny feet dangling. His neck, left shoulder, and left arm were bullish from compensation, bulging, red, and powerfully fast as they shoved him ahead in the chair.

He was given a new chair and allowed to stay for a week. But they could do nothing further for him and, needing the bed, they told him to keep his money and return home.

The night before he was to leave he sat in the dining room unable to eat, as he had voraciously since he'd materialized. He had probably never tasted such food, sat in such a grand room, seen clothes like ours—his were rags; he'd been given a fresh outfit too. He hadn't by anyone's guess seen a girl as beautiful, lively, and adorned as fourteen-year-old Caroline, who, in the egalitarian spirit of Warm Springs, was seated that night beside him at his table.

From my adjacent table I couldn't hear what she said to him. Maybe she didn't say anything and simply chattered, as was her habit, to the table at large. I was, though, watching him when he did it, as I always watched if I saw him anywhere—I was surely responding to his energy more than his ugly visage. He pulled back that tremendous left arm and hit Caroline in the face, knocking her and her chair to the floor.

People screamed. Willie and two other men on staff were at Raymond's side—that was his name, Raymond—and escorted him from the dining room so fast that I don't know if Caroline screamed. Somebody else quickly carried her away, and after a long shocked silence her chair was put right.

Raymond waited all night at the station alone for the train that would come in the morning. It turned out he had hit her with his open palm. She was mortified but not hurt. He could have killed her. He didn't. But the grim sadness of the attack burrowed deeply within me.

The courtyard empty of people could have been the palace garden in *The Sleeping Beauty*, under a spell. In reverie, I saw a ghostly me rise from my chair, a semitransparent Tanaquil walking across the courtyard and over the grassy hill in the distance, going home to New York. She'd walk until she got tired and then hitchhike the rest of the way, until the mighty George Washington Bridge loomed in the distance. In the city she changed clothes in her old apartment, the one above the liquor store she had rented before marrying George, grabbed her bag of rehearsal outfits and shoes, and headed straight off to class. She found it just starting, Diana, Maria, Allegra, Nicky, and Arthur lined up at the barre. "Hi!" they said brightly, as if I'd been gone for a couple of weeks.

Diana whispered to me as I took my place, "Pretty good, Le Clercq. Best trick you pulled yet."

George, in a western shirt, was nonplussed. "Yes, then," he said, by way of hello. "Now we begin."

King Robbins hit town the first week of September, driving up in a powder-blue Ford convertible packed with a picnic hamper and a cooler of white wine.

"We're off," he said, as he whizzed me away.

"You weren't mobbed?"

"I swept into the office and got permission, then I swept up to you in my movie-star sunglasses and nobody dared."

The wind tossed my hair, stung my eyes under my own sunglasses, and farther out in the country the scent of scrub pines complicated the top notes of grassy warm dirt.

It wasn't as if Jerry were John Wayne, but people knew he was my friend, and rumors, like brush fire, zipped through Warm Springs.

"Don't come back tomorrow," I said, "if anyone saw you."

"I'm only here for the day," he admitted.

I'd waited all summer for him. I scolded him if he didn't call or write often enough and he hung his head, I imagined, and expressed remorse with lavish gifts, but he didn't come.

"Tan, don't give me the silent treatment, we're together now. These last months have been impossible."

"We're together now," I agreed. "And I know it's a bitch getting here. Thank you."

"Well, don't thank me," and he reached out and held my hand, driving one-handed to our destination, a shelflike field surrounded by shadowy valleys and low hills beyond.

He spread a blanket and carried me over. Resting against a sturdy oak, drinking wine, I said, "Ecstasy." He sat beside me, one outstretched leg crossed over the other.

I had been in a funk when he arrived and warned him, "Do *not* bring the camera."

"You look fabulous, you know," Jerry said.

"Fabulous not yet, but better."

"So what's wrong?"

"You asked." And I paused. "The social worker said I could go home and George said he wasn't ready. He said to keep me here as long as they can."

Jerry was rendered momentarily speechless. George did that to people.

"Well, Tan, it took him awhile to find the apartment, then he had to move, and he's doing the stuff out in Weston—"

"I know what he's doing in Weston."

Jerry's lowered eyes said I was right.

"Oh, god, he's put his head together with Stravinsky and who else?"

"Don't you want George to go back to work?" Jerry asked kindly.

"It's just"—*damn it, I would not cry*—"why is he keeping it from me?"

"To spare your feelings?" said Jerry.

"My feelings? What about my feelings about being here for my birthday *and* for the polio anniversary? Also in October, you may recall."

"I recall," he said softly. "Here, baby, get drunk."

"You too," I said. We sipped in silence. "People have lives," I said, "I know. In the future I too shall have a life." His caring, his wine, gentled my tone.

"How's the walking?" he asked.

"Harder than hell. But on my feet, it's just like

this—" and I held my glass to the expansive view and inhaled the fresh air. "You have no idea of the difference in perspective between a sitting position and standing."

"I'll bet."

Father had told me that Kant defined our ability to stand as the human spirit's victory over nature; elevation, then, leaping and defying the air, equaled the profoundest embodiments of beauty. "What about you?" I asked Jerry. "What's impossible other than your impossible career?"

"I'm in love."

"Oh, that explains the summer. I understand."

"But he's young, I mean very, and I don't know if it's me he likes or if he's only smitten by the personage."

"You love him?" I said.

"Yeah."

"Then don't be a dolt, Jerry, just love."

We ate the ham sandwiches and potato salad and blueberries sopped in cream and a couple of chocolate bars I tried to save for later and couldn't, and, sunburned and contented, we drove back and whooshed up to my room in our sunglasses and I played him the clarinet.

"Okay, I'm a bust," I said. "But look," and I demonstrated how far I could expand my belly. "Diaphragm breathing, like singers and actors do. It's completely unnatural for dancers, with all our pushing up from the gut.

"Here," I said excitedly, putting aside the instrument and wheeling to the bureau. I took out place mats wrapped in tissue paper for him to open.

"I'm speechless," he said. "They're exquisite."

I memorized him, sitting on my couch beneath the art print of Vermeer's *The Little Street* Mother had sent me—old Delft, depiction of luminous everyday life, and the beautiful contemporary man in the foreground.

"Yours have been done for a month," I told him. "But I decided you couldn't have them."

"Unless I came."

"You did."

"Come over here and sit on my lap," he said.

"Why?" I wanted to make love and knew he didn't, and it would have been wrong but I didn't care, desperate for the delusion that I wasn't pinned to a chair. Poor bug, poor butterfly.

"Just let me hold you," he said.

"Okay." I went, and he scooped me up and his body enclosed me; I brushed my face against his ear, his cheek. I kissed his nose.

"Why are you, you?" I said.

"That's a question my mother's been trying to figure out for forty years."

"Why do you have that horrible New York accent?" I asked. We laughed. It wasn't really horrible, but I'd said that to him once at sixteen.

He ended up spending the night on the couch.

The train wouldn't leave until morning and the hotel was a long drive away. I had food sent to the room and we talked about old times, how I'd nearly kicked out his teeth dancing *Bourrée Fantasque*, how appalled some had been at Jerry's *The Cage*—murderous girls and dead men—while nobody questioned the sacrosanct second act of *Giselle*, where dead brides come out at night from their graves and dance men to death. We talked about Palisades Park the day I got scared riding the Loop-the-Loop and buried my face in his chest and bit him and then wanted to ride it again and bit him again, I was a beast.

"I'm sorry," I said, "I'm like an old person, reminiscing."

"You're not the old person, I am," Jerry said sadly.

"Tell me about yourself, your love, your trip to Italy." It hadn't been all work and the angst of early love over the summer. I knew he'd spent three weeks in Rome.

"You know," he said, "you can always come stay with me. There isn't enough room at the apartment, but there is at the house."

"Tell me everything," I said, ignoring his offer.

We didn't speak of the night on the beach at Fire Island.

In the morning he left at dawn. "Be brave as you can," he said, "and if you can't, then spill it at me. And come stay with me anytime."

Yeah, right, I thought.

"Bye, doll."

"Bye. . . ."

I wrote him, *the days and evenings before me seem unbearable, impossible to live through, but then one always does—it's the one sure thing, isn't it? Until you die.*

I'm reading Shakespeare. Heigh-ho.

5

*T*oward the end of my time in Warm Springs I started dancing each night in my dreams, and the dream-dancing helped to sustain me. I became whole, which gave me a rest from the constancy of my brokenness.

Then, shortly after November 11, 1957, the day I returned to New York, the dreams faltered. I arrived at the theater to find that I didn't have any shoes, I rushed from one ballet to another and couldn't get my hair up—anxiety dreams like I'd had occasionally while I still danced. But these were different and in a sense worse than the fever dreams in Copenhagen because they were unrelenting. My arm didn't transform into a bludgeon and nobody chopped off my feet. Stages, thankfully, did not writhe with snakes. But I kept falling and awakening, catching myself. The dreamscape of juxtapositions, of me in my old body but in surroundings altered enough they were incomprehensible and uncontrollable, and the fact that this was what each night was, wore me down.

Sometimes I cried out and woke George: "Nightmare," and he was unfailingly attentive, putting a cool cloth on my forehead. Sitting awake beside me until I could go back to sleep, reading to me if I couldn't. Maria had told me that while they were married George had nightmares about Russia, about the aloneness, the fear, cold, and hunger—the death he had witnessed of an exhausted horse that expired in the street and the starving people running with knives and hacking the horse's flesh off to cook and eat.

George assured me my nightmares would pass, but many nights we lay together waiting for dawn.

We had a new apartment in the Apthorp on the Upper West Side, near the company's new school and the studios, an apartment selected by George for its spaciousness, sunlight, and beauty. Before I arrived he moved in and arranged everything. He had snuggled my dozens of pairs of street shoes into quilted bags and hung them against the doors of the roll-in closet in our bedroom—tennis shoes, oxfords, mules, sandals, and the elegant heels he had bought for me in all of the beautiful old metropolises of Europe.

The Apthorp takes up the block on Broadway between West Seventy-Eighth and Seventy-Ninth and extends through to West End Avenue. Built in 1879, it recalls a Renaissance palazzo, with gold-crowned iron gates and a central courtyard. Our five white-painted rooms had thick civilized walls and enormous windows. The two grand pianos looked quite at home. To decorate, George purchased a French chandelier, an antique weather vane, three glorious clocks, an Audubon American eagle, and a sofa and two chairs he placed in what we just had to call the parlor because these pieces, ornately carved and covered in blue Italian silk, resembled those of the swanky houses of ill repute in western movies. Because we could no longer go to the movies—too many steps—he promised we'd go to the drive-in come spring. For summer, he had built ramps out at the house in Weston.

On top of everything else he had spent the fall supervising the preparation of the company's repertory and choreographing four major ballets.

Antony Tudor said that just to think of Balanchine's energy made him slump to the floor.

George was everywhere at once, teaching, making ballets, casting, coaching, and running the company's daily operations, doing our laundry, shopping, and cooking, dashing home to prepare lunch for me.

From the minute my plane hit the tarmac I was also busy. For months, apart from the disquieting dreams, I didn't have time to brood. I had batches of welcome-home notes and requests for visits. One couldn't say no to the intrepid Gene Kelly, and I couldn't put off any longer friends and acquaintances I had shunned while at Lenox Hill. People who genuinely cared wanted to see that I was all right, and I missed them. George said that with friends strong as mine who were dying to put me into cars and take me places, I had no good excuse not to go out. But it wasn't so easy. Planning ahead was imperative. I had to call and find out whether I could get through an entrance, let alone to the facilities, in a wheelchair. Many public places were impossible.

I kept busy, though, planning and doing as much as I could. Father and two dancers took me to Central Park and autumn leaves fell in my well-cut hair. I altered my wardrobe. Full skirts were in vogue and were roomy enough for a wheelchair. I emphasized sweaters and scarves to counteract the cold I was susceptible to.

George and I had Thanksgiving dinner at Jerry's house in Snedens Landing with Jerry, Jerry's lover, Mercutio, and his dog, Billy, a Brussels griffon.

"Did you pick out your name yourself?" George asked the lover.

"First name or last?" Jerry said, teasing much more than George.

It wasn't unusual for dancers to change their names. Jerry did. But funnier than the name

Mercutio was that the lover, serving the side dishes as Jerry carved his spectacular turkey, had kept his last name with it, Schwartz.

"Tell them why you didn't change it," Jerry said.

And with dignity, Mercutio—gleaming in candlelight, black eyes and hair glossy as patent leather—said, "I wouldn't dishonor my family."

"They'll be with you, baby, in lights," Jerry said.

Unfortunately, George, I knew, wouldn't rate Mercutio's odds for success very high, pretty and dignified though he was. The young dancer had a long head and neck and nearly simian arms, but he wasn't tall. George labeled this type of physique "tragedy, a tall man from only the waist up."

Mother and Natalie helped me shop for Christmas, driving me to navigable stores in New Jersey. I tackled the welcome-home mail. Hardest were those that prayed for my "swift return to the stage." What to say? You had to assume the person meant well and put it off to lousy writing, which Mother said was not a crime.

Jerry offered to take me to the ballet.

"No," I said, "and don't ask me again."

George was fine with this. Given his monumental assurance, he didn't need ego gratification from me. He'd mention work, but drop it if I was disinterested. He'd never liked to talk a lot about dancing away from the studio anyway, preferring respite. Our pre-polio talk had centered on dance because we were doing it together. George wasn't an artist either to suffer in creation and was therefore without any need to vent creative pain. He'd study the score and make a piano reduction—he had trained in composition after graduating from the Imperial School—and decide on the mode of dance appropriate to his vision of the music, and the rest happened in the studio. He worked off the particular dancers in front of him and if they got stuck he figured, in his words, "Something will come along." It always did. I'd heard that while choreographing *Gounod Symphony*, George said at a blocked spot, "Okay, we pray to Gounod." Composers were gods to him, his pantheon, and he served them.

The living god, the father, Stravinsky visited that November, before the premiere of *Agon*, the third full-length Stravinsky/Balanchine collaboration. I sat at the window watching Broadway for him, and at precisely five minutes to eleven, his scheduled appointment, he stepped onto the traffic island, paused by the benches and took from the pocket of his long coat a paper he peered at closely through his dark glasses, checking the address, and continued ahead, an apparition in a homburg hat, Igor at seventy-five returned from the dead. Excitement bubbled up in me.

"He's coming!" I called to George.

"Hold him at the door!" George shouted back, busy fussing over tea sandwiches and macaroons in the kitchen. Champagne chilled on ice, in case Stravinsky requested it.

"Tanaquil," he said in greeting, not much taller standing than me sitting down, and, pressing the round dark felt hat to his breast, he kissed my hand in his most courtly manner. Oh, now click your heels, I thought happily.

Apparently George didn't want to miss the reunion, coming quickly to us as Igor proclaimed in his rusty-hinge voice, "Your beauty is undiminished."

I didn't miss the pride shining in George's eyes. "Notice her beautiful posture," he said. "She always had nice strong back."

"Yes," Igor agreed.

"We sit, we sit, please," George said joyfully, twirling with motion, taking Igor's coat, settling us in the parlor, arranging his feast on the oblong table. I suppose Igor and I were both apparitions, two of my husband's lost loves about to consume an early-afternoon tea.

"How is Vera?" I asked Igor.

"She could not be better. She sends her express love and demands that I telephone this evening and tell her about our meeting."

"Inform her of my express love as well," I said.

Stravinsky was too fastidious to inquire about the details of my health or to speak at length of his

105

own. Shoptalk ensued, which I didn't mind. It recalled other occasions Vera wasn't present and I mostly listened to Igor and George and learned; *Agon* intrigued me, despite myself. *Agon* is Greek for contest, protagonist, and agony, or struggle. Danced in rehearsal clothes against a blank gray drop, and plotless, the extreme stress and intensity of the choreography arose to complement the density and pulse of the music. But as George maintained, his so-called abstract ballets, though free of linear story, always derived not only from music but also from living relations.

The central pas de deux danced by Diana and Arthur presented partnering less suggestive of romance and more of the precariousness of relationships. It contained breathtaking balances, watchfulness, and called up questions about identity, separation, and recombination. Diana's very white hand against Arthur's dark one as they danced was in itself a brilliant enactment of the racial tension going on in the culture at large.

Stravinsky talked that day about the struggle between music and choreography. George responded, "Absolutely! Struggle means to be together."

When I finally saw the ballet, years later, I thought it was perfect for Diana. I wouldn't have danced it so cautiously, and caution and care were the elements here that set off the feats of balance and threw into prominence the sculptural shapes.

I didn't have to see it to glean that another aspect of the "living relations" was auto-biography, George's and mine.

He hadn't chosen me over the dancers or vice versa. He had chosen to do it all. Not that I'd seriously entertained the notion that he would quit New York City Ballet for good. Decades had gone into getting the company and expanding the enterprise. George himself was that line in the Yeats poem, *How do you tell the dancer from the dance?*

He claimed he didn't know himself except as a dancer. Trouble was, I didn't know myself much outside of that context either.

We struggled ahead, he at a manic pace, I in a deliberate, seemingly poised fashion during the days and then breaking in two with dreams at night.

The holidays passed. It got cold. I hated winter and my legs were extra sensitive in the cold.

"So put on more clothes," George said.

"More clothes? You know how long it takes for me to put on the usual? Christ's sake, it's like dressing a corpse."

His face shut. "Please, dear, don't say that."

"You know what I mean!" He was unmoved. "I'm sorry," I said.

Atrophy. My muscles could not maintain warmth, and circulation was another problem.

Busy with the company and chores at home, George didn't work with me on therapy anymore. I dutifully exercised on a mat, but maintenance rather than improvement had become the goal. My right hand had continued to improve and I could write easily again, but the arm remained weak and the legs did nothing. A massage therapist came once a week and did not touch my legs, focusing on my upper body.

"I don't know what we're saving," I said to George, referring to the cautious treatment prescribed for my legs by the Warm Springs doctors. "I don't know what we're waiting for. I want to get really aggressive so the muscles, such as they are, don't shrink entirely away. If I hurt something, this elusive something that might someday assert itself, so what? How much more could I be hurt?"

George said to wait for the New York doctors' opinions, the ones I had contacted from Warm Springs and saw after the holidays.

The evening of the third expert, the third to examine me, question me, and tell me that we should expect nothing further, I sat at one of my window posts, the one behind the pianos overlooking Broadway—the view of the street and the sidewalks and the island where Igor had appeared, pausing to check our address. There was no snow, just iron cold. The trees were stiff with it, witchlike. The trusty streetlamps were beacons in the dark and the headlights of cars and traffic lights valiantly fought the winter, cutting open the night. The commercial signs across the way always looked comical to me, and they did now: "Oh, people, come buy our wares before we're all dead." Commerce wasn't valued in our family, the Le Clercqs were never practical types. We honored beauty. George too.

This doctor today, a gruff and old though not grandfatherly man, had said, "What did you do in the leg braces?"

"I stood."

"Did you walk?"

"No."

"Never? A step?"

"I stood a bit longer each day."

"How many days?"

"A month."

He put down his pen, aligned it beside the desk blotter, and said, "Mrs. Balanchine, there is nothing for you to walk with. My opinion is that the braces were brought out for moral support, but I don't see any reason to continue with the charade. You're an adult. We adults"—so confidential—"prefer to know the score, don't we?"

"Which for me is zero to zero?" I asked.

Gramps laughed, mistakenly admiring my sense of humor.

You should have seen his face when I refused to shake his hand good-bye.

I couldn't predict what George would say. His response to the first two doctors was to draw up a one-year plan to replace the six-month plan of last April. My therapy in the one-year plan, however, had yet to be determined.

Why did he build the ramps out in Weston? Building ramps in the autumn at a place I probably wouldn't go near until the following summer? I might have been walking by then. It occurred to me that he knew long ago, and that I knew too. His key turned in the latch. I had left the hall light on for him but I sat in the dark. He hung up his coat and, pulling a chair to the window, he joined me.

"Nada," I said.

"I see."

"George? Are they right?" He could inspect a child's arch and know if she had a chance at a career. He observed a little girl's proportions and, with a glance at the mother, gauged the mature length of young legs. "George. Please."

"Look at them," he said, staring down at the sidewalks, at the people with hung heads, hands shoved in pockets, a man slashing the air as a cab passed him by. "They are walking and they're miserable."

Hurrying home from a rehearsal for dinner prior to a performance one evening, George slipped on ice, banging his hip up and spraining his ankle.

Mother moved in to take up the slack. The housekeeper, hired to clean twice a week, came for a couple of hours every day. I thought I would scream from the crowd and the absolute evidence that George was exhausted and could not do it all.

"Listen, I wasn't careful," he said.

"You're always careful."

"Whatever you do, don't romanticize me."

"Fine." I thought maybe his falling was an unconscious wish for a vacation.

He lay on the couch, face in a book, oblivious to the activities in the apartment. "No big deal," he said, "I catch up on my reading." He started with a volume about the Basque region. I found it amusing that he liked to read about travel since, except for good restaurants, he stayed at the theater working wherever he went.

"I've already been everywhere," he would say.

And he told me, "Don't worry about my energy. I don't get tired anymore. Young people wear themselves out from confusion. I know exactly what I want to do."

Other books in his stack concerned polio and physical therapy, but I didn't ask about them.

Some nights I didn't sleep a wink because I couldn't relax, I hadn't done anything except sit in a chair. I would always sit all day in a chair. In the fall I was buoyed by the novelty of my return, decent weather, and the conviction that I would get out of the chair if only I worked, kept the faith, and did not become foolish about the dancing, because there were other things I could do, and could not do now.

George had learned speeches from Chekhov in school as a boy and he still recited them for comfort. He did one for me in a wakeful dawn, the speech of a girl, an orphaned governess in *The Cherry Orchard*. She's nebulous, a figure in the background of the frenzy playing out between aristocrats fighting for their estate and a cunning peasant who wins. But she gets her little solo onstage to tell her story. She recalls her parents and for a few lines she is almost with them again. Then she speaks the fact: I am alone. I have no one. The language is stripped—in Russian too, not just in English, George said—it is not sentimental, and its starkness actualizes the girl's real but largely invisible pain, a pain she must somehow live with and hold. I memorized the speech and recited it too.

Mother left. George returned to work. The calendar turned over to March. People asked to visit. I said yes to Jerry and Diana and Natalie and my parents, but I was subdued. George hired an ex-student from the school, Carl, a muscleman and health food fanatic, to take me wherever I wanted to go. Carl was a mannerly person with shoulders like sides of beef, hulking enough they appeared—and felt—as if he could put one against any opposition and smash it. Seeing Carl was to regain belief in the physical, and he cheered me.

I announced to George that I would cook.

"Oh, yeah?" he said doubtfully.

"I've ordered five cookbooks from Brentano's," I told him. "I'll get my ingredients delivered. You're good at Russian, but I'm doing French. I may let you assist."

This pleased him. He spoke brightly about this year's plans for the traditional Russian feast he always prepared at Easter. He was quite an accomplished cook, though our everyday fare was simple.

Not anymore. I did sauces especially well. George called afternoons to check on the dinner menu.

We ate my cuisine on trays—watching westerns or science fiction on TV, the highlight of the day.

The press dubbed George a phoenix and but for the cooking I was idle, silently watchful of a decision that started to rise.

I made it through Easter, an actress still. I reassured George on the outside that I was adjusting, while inside the bleakness I felt just got worse. People had always praised my dramatic flair as a dancer, and in 1952 I did *A Candle for St. Jude*, a television play. My role was a dancer but I had to speak too—sweet love scenes and scenes full of tension. Such fun, telling Madame,

"No, the solo is wrong! It should be sharp, like anguish." And we had to dance straight up, given no room to travel in the small space of the TV studio. I loved the challenge.

Now I took sleeping pills and stopped remembering dreams—dead to the world. Then the pills stopped working. I went out in my chair with Father and looked at the crocuses peeking up from the ground. Another year.

Father said we would go to the Cape this summer, he'd carry me down to the water and waves would wash over my feet and legs.

I waited for an appropriate gap in George's flurry to broach my decision to him. At last one weekend waiting as he flew around the apartment from the kitchen to the hall closet, about to go out, I said, "I need to talk to you. Tell me when you're available today for half an hour?"

He laughed. "Tonight! After dinner." Tonight was dark at the theater.

"Well," I said, "it won't be relaxing."

Poor husband. It hit him that I wanted to talk, directly and seriously, on a complex and personal subject. No one, even Mother and Father, shied away as George did from confrontation. It was why he depended on his assistants and why, gentle and mild-mannered as he intrinsically was, he could be abrupt.

As a kid I was a dreadful gabber, and in class I went through a period of gabbing nonstop to a girlfriend. We didn't listen to our teacher's corrections and made fun of her if she turned her back. She sent us to George, who was so pained to have to interpret for us what we had done, to impress on us that it was terrible. He sounded grieved, not angry, and we cried buckets.

"Talk now, then," and he sat down on the bench by the umbrella stand.

I was in my chair; he acted patient and appeared composed. But his position right by the front door—through which he could easily bolt—undid me.

"Damn you," I said. "Why do you have to add to the difficulty of this?" I was crying and I felt incredibly guilty, but what could I do? How could *I* bolt? Only one way, baby, as Jerry might put it.

"Tanny, Tanitschka, dear, come," and George knelt, grasping my hands and pressing them fast against his cheeks. "There is time, I have plenty of time." But how could I? I'd intended to present it calmly, show him that I had arrived at it rationally, thoughtfully.

Oh, to hell. I had tried not to involve him, considered all manner of harebrained schemes. Getting Jerry to take me to the top of the Empire State Building, wheel to the edge for the view, say I have a yen for a hot dog. Jerry would vanish and I would go over, boom, the chair and me, only what about the pedestrians on the street? How many innocents would a hurtling chair murder? And in that scenario, Jerry would spend the rest of his days in a straitjacket raving.

"Talk to me," George said.

I smelled his cologne and my eyes traced the line of his aquiline nose. Only George had the steel and the understanding to help me.

"I want to go, George." I stopped crying, rinsed by the cool of decision. "I could have continued without dancing, but not without walking. I'm sorry. I've tried. You've been honorable and devoted . . ." and now he would have to assist me in this?

He dropped my hands and eased back to sit against the wall, drawing his legs up. He lowered his forehead down onto his arms resting across his knees.

"Dr. Wilson gives me weak pills," I said, "intentionally. I'd have to store up for ages. You could go to your doctor for something strong. You could find out what it would take. You wouldn't be implicated. Mad wife consumes husband's prescription—"

"Stop," he said.

"I'll just go to sleep," I said quietly.

He looked up, not at me, he couldn't. He spoke to the edge of the gilt mirror on the opposite wall. "You are young. You are strong. In six months, you will be stronger."

"I can't wait six months."

He breathed heavily from his one good lung,

and said, "I won't insult your intelligence by telling you the many things in life you will still be able to see and do. Not dancing. Not acting—" I hadn't mentioned acting, he knew. "It will get better," he said.

And us? That was part of it. Who he was and who I had become. As often as I saw improvement ahead, I saw wasting away, bitterness, and abandonment. He couldn't sustain it.

"If you were me, what would you do?" I asked.

"If I were you I wouldn't have made it this far."

"Why not?"

"You're stronger than me."

"Don't say that, don't tell somebody in my position how strong they are, it's burdensome and dismissive—it doesn't become you."

"I'm spent," he said.

"I know."

"I mean of words," he clarified. "Energy's endless, as long as there's life. You think there isn't any more and there isn't. And then there is."

I gave up. But in the morning I asked him again and he said yes. Give him a week.

For Christmas 1952, just five years earlier, George's gifts to me were a camera, a designer handbag, a Steuben vase, and a proposal of marriage. Yes! He was a good deal older than I was, didn't I want to think about it? There was nothing to think about. He chose the date of our wedding, the thirty-first, New Year's Eve. He wanted to start the New Year married. Two books contained all you needed to know about life, George said, *War and Peace* and the Bible. I skipped the Bible, but I devoured Tolstoy. I read it twice back-to-back when George and I were first in love.

The seven days I waited to die were strung like glass beads catching light in a window about to be flung up. I watched the free, endless air, and phrases and scenes from the book reopened. Like Prince Andrei flat on his back dying in battle when, for the first time, he sees with his entire self the blue and white of the sky, the open dome over this scrap of earth.

Two characters speak of preexistence and eternity. If they are immortal spirits, they also existed before they were born. All is one, past, present, future, and good.

That I was young didn't matter. I'd had what I wanted, dancing and George. My dreams healed. Each night I danced beautifully again, I was the leader of the Bacchantes, killing Orpheus with my powerful legs once more.

In that week George, understandably, though reserved and courteous, grew distracted, and his expression was stern. We went about our normal activities. Mother asked me at lunch the fifth day what was wrong.

"Wrong? Don't I seem well?" We sat at my post

in the kitchen, at the table by the window overlooking the courtyard and the gurgling fountain, just filled.

Mother shrugged. She'd aged. Her hair seemed thinner, bosom flatter, the lines by her mouth more harshly etched. This I observed but I didn't allow it to penetrate, to destroy my resolve.

I talked to Papa on the telephone.

One night I cooked George an elaborate dinner. He came in and saw what I had done and said he couldn't eat it and went out for a hamburger.

How he possibly worked every day I didn't think of.

Saturday came again, the week finished.

"Do you have it?" I asked him.

"Yes."

"Tonight."

"No," he said. "Tomorrow. You sleep on it. If you feel the same in the morning then we'll go ahead."

I slept restlessly and awoke to birdsong. From the bed I turned to George, dressed, sitting in sunshine at our white-painted oak table, pen and notebook before him, puffs under his bloodshot eyes. He had opened the curtains. Our bedroom was huge and feminine, French country, masses of pillows and flowery fabrics, all of it, and also in the rooms beyond, intended to bring me a measure of peace.

"Hello," he said, this man who sheltered me, as

much as he could, from what had so hurt me. In his mouth, his eyes, in the tiny tremor that shivered over his expressive hands, I saw the boy who had lost his mother twice—first when he went to the Imperial School and missed her to despair, then when the family moved far away and he never saw her again. I saw the young man who had left his beloved Russia. Who had endured the loss of one of his Russian dancers, his dear Lidia Ivanovna, who was found drowned in St. Petersburg under mysterious circumstances. Lidia of the mischievous eyes, stout for a dancer, could jump like a flea. After all his misfortune it had to be topped off by mine.

"Lie by me?" I said.

He got up and sat on the side of the bed and took off his shoes. He eased down beside me smelling sour, of fear sweat, my elegant man. I felt the warmth radiate from his body. We watched the ceiling, and I watched our lives playing there. I thought of the speech from Chekhov I'd learned.

"'I haven't a real passport of my own and I don't know how old I am,'" I quoted. "'I always feel that I'm a young thing.'"

"'When I was small,'" George recited, "'my father and mother used to travel about to fairs and give performances—very good ones. And I used to dance *salto-mortale* and all sorts of things. . . .'"

"'And when Papa and Mama died,'" I said, "'a

German lady took me and had me educated. And so I grew up and became a governess. But where I come from and who I am, I don't know. . . . Who my parents were, very likely they weren't married. . . . I don't know.' "

" 'I know nothing at all,' " he said.

" 'One wants to talk and has no one to talk to. . . .' "

" 'I have nobody.' " Silence—traffic, voices reaching us from the street.

"I can't," I said. "I'm a coward," I lied.

"No," he said softly. "It's life force. Immense in you since you were a child." He sat up, putting my head in his lap: "Girl," his gentle hands in my hair. One day at Warm Springs he told me that without the body God gave me and took away, I couldn't have danced as I had, but without my vibrancy, which remained, I couldn't have danced as I had either.

The poet stopped talking. The general had drawn up a five-year plan. He had been plotting and writing for hours. I don't think he knew what I'd decide. He would still have gone ahead with his planning. I always believed he had the pills. That he would have given them to me.

"Breakfast?" he asked.

I nodded. Then I was alone.

Part Two

Being Russian

1962–1969

Time heals all wounds: this does happen to be true.

— *Tanaquil Le Clercq*

1

$\mathcal{H}$igh summer 1962, the house in Weston: Diana's old mud-green Chevy chugged up the drive, spraying gravel and voluminous clouds of dust that shrouded the delicate plantings along the hill, then, voilà, they reappeared. The tailpipe scraped as Diana ascended and I laughed.

They stepped out, my friends, Diana and Natalie, and approached me at the table on the grass, Diana in round amber sunglasses and a pert straw hat, loping, a lovely giraffe, Natalie short and ample, hair bare to the sun, in a midnight-blue satin sundress, the impractical Russian.

"Kisses, kisses!" cried Natalie, extending her plump arms. There were kisses all around, and Diana folded her long self into a chair and lit one of her Lucky Strikes extravagantly. "My feet are terrible today," she said.

She'd been dancing a lot and was injury-prone, but that wasn't it.

I poured glasses of mint tea as Natalie said with a smirk, "Oh, why?"

"It's hard work making a baby," Diana replied. "I don't get enough sleep."

Natalie took from her own bag a brass flask and spiked her glass and mine.

"Why must you do that in front of me?" Diana asked.

"Diana," Natalie answered, "revel in the glories of the dance and leave the little mercies to Tanny and me."

"I do adore taking nips without retribution," I said. "Natalie, you're as dark as a cordovan loafer."

"I bask on the beach with my girls," she answered. Her kids were fourteen and sixteen and obsessed by their beauty.

"I'm slug-white," Diana complained. "I can't wait to get pregnant. I need time off. Do *not* tell George that we're trying," she warned me.

"What, are you mad?" I said. It was bad enough when Diana got married, pragmatically, though, I should say, to Ronald Bates, one of the company's stage managers. This reassured George that Diana would not be swept off and away.

"Where is he?" Diana asked. "Where's Eddie?"

"Mowing the grass," I said.

"Why does it take both of them to mow the grass?"

"They're men," Natalie said. "They confer."

Eddie Bigelow was George's faithful lieutenant, an ex-dancer and a trusted assistant and confidant. They were practically tied at the hip. George assessed, ordered, instructed, while Eddie, his rangy frame bent and listening, performed all biddings from the master. I liked him anyway.

"This afternoon," Diana said, "one of them has to go into town for gas—or can they siphon it from your car? Isn't that possible?"

"I've no idea," I said.

"Me either," Natalie said.

"We're bone-dry," said Diana. "How we made it here is miraculous."

From the first hint of warming we were in Weston for weekends, then weeks, and starting at dawn George and Eddie attacked our seven acres, mowing, spraying, fertilizing, watering, mulching, pruning, staking, planting, and transplanting. Before the polio, I helped sink the rocks and plant ferns at the edge of the property. Before George and I married, our paradise was a wilderness. Together, we planned the house, a modest one-story prefab that suited our needs. Our lives revolved around the outdoors in Weston. If it rained we groused and checked windows and listened for silence and dashed outside between downpours.

Natalie complimented the full-blown roses, in beds along the driveway, roses I tended. Planting, I supervised. I had day lilies, irises, and for spring fat fluffy peonies that are so happy and inspiring during the season's cool days.

Diana inquired about the heavenly smell wafting from the house. We were having cold chicken drenched in a coriander sauce, an herb we used almost by the bushel. The sauce cooled by the sink; the herb garden in full light under the kitchen window beckoned.

"Come," I said to Diana, after Natalie went inside to phone her daughters back in New York. We crossed the ten feet to the herbs and Diana knelt down beside me as I pointed out our favorite. Together we fingered the heads, the lacy flower cluster of white tinged with mauve. The leaves of this crop were feathery, like dill. Sometimes they were as coarse as carrot tops.

"Spicy," Diana said, pinching the leaves.

"If it's especially hot and humid they stink," I said.

Diana's scents—smoke, soap with a tinge of apples, the spray in her hair—mixed with the bouquet of the herbs as we hovered over them, and I knew again. I knew in my cells. I knew in the chambers of my mind where I most knew George, my memory of how he drew nearer to me at the beginning of our liaison. Too insecure and too loyal to instigate or even agree to an affair, Diana would not have needed to. Not because George was a cunning seducer. He wasn't at all. His insatiable thirst for women was always there and they were always there and out of the many gradually one would come forth, would appeal, and the thirst welled up in him and almost by osmosis in her, and with little to no machinery the deed would be done.

His touch in the studio firmed, the interested

light in his eyes grew acute, and then came the hallway conversations. Thrilling, or it had been to me. I imagined Diana's frown of slight realization, of alertness, and how only later she would open her eyes and think, what am I doing in bed with George?

In his youth, women just flocked to him. By the time he married me, number five, it had become a bit sad, a bit funny, George and his women. Of course, I didn't see it like that back then.

"How *is* Ronald?" I asked Diana. "You know . . ." and I practically wriggled my eyebrows.

"Oh! Fabulous. Why do you think I married him?"

Truth was she married him partly for me, and if she hadn't yearned for a child to distraction, I'd have hated her for it.

Natalie clambered out onto the steps and in her lush contralto cried, "Georgi Melitonivitch!" Her use of the patronymic recalled George's father, who'd recently died. Informed by the doctors that to save his life they would have to remove his leg, he said, "I? I? Never. Death is a beautiful girl. She will take me in her arms. I look forward to the experience." George had been impressed.

Diana unfolded to her full height as we turned to the men coming over the field, beyond the edge of the house. Busy lecturing Eddie, George ignored Natalie's greeting. Diana placed her hand on my shoulder and I felt so glad to be able to love her again, now that it was over, and, watching my husband in his old polo shirt, his battered work pants, my stomach warmed.

What a glorious day! The mountain ash trees George put in everywhere for their bitter, bright red-orange berries cast down the sweet shadows of noon. The lawn was a crazy-quilt carpet, just-clipped, its juice on the air.

Today we were five for lunch, a meal George and I seldom ate alone. Mother came often, Father, Jerry, dancers and assistants, our Russian secretaries and teachers from the school. I'd become a not too infrequent visitor to the school and the studios.

One day in April, George, without warning, brought a young dancer to the apartment. "Teach her *La Valse*," he said.

"You're kidding me."

"Why would I kid? I forgot."

"The choreography?" I said.

"Yes, details," and he pressed his hands together, raising his eyes to the firmament, as he did, settling something. "Okay," he said, "I've got to get back."

The scarlet-faced girl muttered her name and, without much choice for either of us, we set to work. Thereafter we worked in a studio with an accompanist. I liked Patty, a smart dancer who understood that she shouldn't dance it fey. *La Valse* is heady atmosphere, the excitement of a kid at her first fancy party. When the masked figure offers her the black clothes, she must be sincerely drawn in. The dance looked entirely different on Patty than it had on me, since she's short. But I believe we retained the essence, the purity.

Patty McBride was one of a fresh crop of dancers brought into the company as the decade turned. Every ten years or so, George remade the ranks. It wasn't just due to people retiring, it was part of his genius to anticipate change, to refashion his vision to meet new eras and new expectations.

"It's my job," he said in a characteristic understatement, "to entertain."

With Madame Duskaya of the roped pearls and exotic shawls, who had been a countess in prerevolutionary Russia, I redecorated George's office. We installed a couch, hung curtains, reorganized files. I polished the old brown upright piano George used to compose little waltzes in his office, when he was in a good mood. But if the door shut and dark dissonant chords rolled down the hallways, everyone knew to steer clear.

As he turned into the yard George's monologue ceased midsentence, his face opened up like a child's—fifty-eight and still youthful. His thinness worried me—how so thin with the plenitude of summer?

"Girls!" His smile chased off his perpetual tiredness, the networks of lines weren't there anymore, and he looked handsome as Gary Cooper.

Kiss, kiss, and kiss, kiss, and my husband and I retired to the kitchen, refusing offers of help. It was small in there and we worked together like a well-oiled team. George had lowered the countertops. I carved the chicken and he chopped our luscious tomatoes and hummed to himself as the basil bled and the olive oil bathed the mélange in the Italian blue, white, and red ceramic bowl.

"Tomorrow we put up the shed," he said.

"Yes? In one day?"

"Maybe three. We have precise plan." He picked up a spoon to taste my coriander sauce. "Salt," he said, going for it.

"No," and I snatched it away. We nattered in opposition a minute and I won and then we were ready to rejoin our guests. I felt as if we'd indulged in a quickie on the cluttered floor of our blue bedroom.

We were slobs in the country. The kitchen was the site of continual commotion, of preparations and cleanups and tasting from sunup to midnight. It looked forlorn to me tidy, for it never achieved that state unless we were leaving.

Platter in one hand, bowl in the other, George paused, catching and holding my eyes. "Hello, you," he said.

"Hello, you, back," I said.

He kissed me—kitchen kiss, of conspirators, partners, as if the backyard were a stage and we were about to go on.

In the doorway he sighed and told me to bring napkins. Eddie, whom we had allowed to set the table, had forgotten the napkins. I grabbed some and heard George say, "Diana, put it out."

"You're a chimney for years," Diana replied, "and as soon as you quit, I'm a pariah."

I smoked on occasion myself. Once, catching me, George said, "So kill yourself."

"Just taking a small hit off death," I answered. Then: "I have appropriated. I've borrowed. Who said that?"

"Some jackass," said George.

I about doubled over in my chair, laughing. He still had the power to utterly charm me, and I for him, much more than in the year or two before I got sick, and in new ways. What we had been through together ran like a live wire between us. He had seen me regain my zest for life, seen me bloom again, as he liked to say. He encouraged me to go to the ballet and I found when I did that it wasn't so hard. By the 1960s the casts were different, and I'd lived the dance from such a young age that it would always be important to me, even if I couldn't dance myself. I learned that I enjoyed coaching and was good at it, and being able to discuss new ballets with George brought us closer. I was off the stage, but back in the world of ballet where I belonged.

I wheeled down the ramp to the long wood table and parked in my sunny spot. There was crusty French bread and for dessert orange jelly. George held forth on his mother's garden, a city block long. "Not for fun," he made clear, "but to eat. Potatoes, carrots, beets, peas, green beans, eggplants—"

"And cabbages," I said, "for sauerkraut." We nearly subsisted on sauerkraut, particularly in the cold months.

"Mama made sauerkraut by filling a barrel with layers of cabbage and caraway seeds."

"But if she pickled it . . ." I said, annoyingly, interrupting again.

George conceded, smiling.

"She pickled them whole," I said. "They paled, became translucent, and looked like giant tissue-paper roses."

"I saw pickled cabbages," said Natalie, "I remember them."

We ate, the leaves rustled, the crazy quilt dappled, the blades of grass seeming to breathe. Eddie scratched his crew cut, which would soon thin, revealing the broad dome of his skull.

How many days like that together, in summer, in Weston, how many eternal days?

Back in New York in September, Diana showed up at the Apthorp bearing a mountain of yellow roses. They'd been delivered to the theater for me, five dozen of them with an unsigned note that read, *To Tanaquil, the sublime, ballerina assoluta forever.*

"The lesson," I said to my friend, "is to get out early, then you're a legend."

Mother hurried in from the spare bedroom she was putting to rights. "It's that adorable poet again," she trilled, "I can tell." Like me, Mother was in second bloom. As I improved and adjusted, she rested, got plump and rosy and giddy again. She bustled about, finding vases. Mother loved how a few people still made a fuss over me, and I didn't mind—her loving, their fuss. I played along.

At the ballet Jerry carried me to our mid-orchestra seats on the aisle and I pretended I was a royal, as George had suggested—feet mustn't touch the ground. Why not? I couldn't think of a better metaphor, and it helped. The work of the getting there—the time to dress, the station wagon with room for the chair, how my muscleman hoisted me, like a sack of potatoes, for the transfer to the car, how we'd do it again at the theater, discreetly from a back entrance, and go up with the chair in the freight elevator—all that by now was rote, as rote as it could be. I'd remind myself of my first apartment over the liquor store. Barely furnished, with a couple of trunks for tables, it looked like a dressing room.

Now there was time for everything: the fascination of the ballet itself, flowers, love, how the days opened out long and bright like a scarf.

"Any news on the baby front, Diana?" Mother asked.

"Nothing," she said dejectedly, lighting a smoke.

"Come into the kitchen, girls," Mother said, "I'll make us a fattening tea."

"It won't help," Diana said. She ate all she could and just danced it off. Mother's theory was that more flesh on Diana's bones would bring on the *infanta*.

We ate éclairs and Diana drank tea with four sugars. My big ginger cat, Mourka, licked icing off Diana's finger.

"Come up, boy," she said. He purred in her lap. "You see, I love cute things, small things," Diana said.

"He isn't that small," I said. "Best keep your hand away from his mouth."

Mourka had come to us from a broken home and had behavioral problems, notably biting. Soon he'd be a star, appearing with George on the cover of *Life* magazine. I'd publish a book about him.

"I don't want to go to Russia," Diana said mournfully, stroking the cat.

A thaw had begun in the intellectual and cultural

climate between the United States and the Soviet Union. The State Department pressured George for a tour until he had no choice but to go. "It's ruined," he told me, "what's the good going back?" He believed he'd be kidnapped and forced to stay. As he prepared for the tour he got gloomier by the day.

"If Natalie weren't coming," Diana said, "I couldn't face it."

"Neither could George," I said, relieved that I wasn't going. I sometimes went along on tour in the States, when logistics allowed.

As if on cue, Mother, the contented divorcée and an advocate for other wives' devotion to their husbands, said, "You should go, Tanny."

The buzzer rang.

"More flowers?" Diana quipped.

It turned out to be Carl, my muscleman, an hour early to take me to the dentist. How disappointing to find that after becoming a cripple one still had to go to the dentist.

Mother brought Carl to the kitchen. Blond and monumental, he filled a chair to capacity—how they didn't break under him astonished me—and drank juice with protein powder. "Who sent the flowers?" Carl asked.

"That adorable poet," said Mother.

"It wasn't him," I said. "I would have recognized the handwriting."

"Carl," Mother said, "is there any reason why

Tanaquil couldn't travel in Russia with the company if you went along? Would you go?"

"Sure," Carl said. "We could check with Mr. B."

"Mother, does it not occur to you that George might feel less encumbered without me? That under the circumstances, he doesn't need me to look after?"

"Nonsense," Mother replied. "You'd be a comfort."

I rolled my eyes at Diana, who said, "I have to get back. See me to the door."

"Do you feel fat?" I asked.

"No."

"Thank you for delivering the roses. You don't know who sent them?"

"Not a clue," she said, and left.

I admired my bursts of yellow, my spacious living room. New York was good in the fall, I had things of my own to do, and if Mother talked to George for two minutes he'd disavow her of the idea. I was terribly down on Russia at the moment, and not only on the Soviets.

It was Natalie's fault. She'd recently called one day insisting that I should get George to fire Madame Karinska, his longtime costume designer.

"I can't tell you why," Natalie said.

"Oh, yes, you can, you're dying to," I said. I couldn't resist gossip, but I had a bad feeling that day. I loved the wardrobe department, where banks of women sat at machines and nobody spoke any English—Russian, and all of the languages of Eastern Europe. As a dancer I'd found being up there relaxing. George liked to visit Ducky, the Englishman in charge of men's clothes, in his little closet. He'd have a cup of tea from the kettle that Ducky always kept on, and hear who was sleeping with whom, who'd gotten kicked out of her apartment, and everything else. Ducky, the font. During fittings Madame Karinska, a Russian times ten, mostly spoke of herself, telling how beautiful she had been as a girl and what good legs she'd had as she measured, draped, pinned up, and peered at our bodies. She kept a cereal bowl of blue dye in her bathroom. She'd go to it every so often and run the blue glop with a toothbrush through her gray hair, so that the waves hugging her head were usually wet and cobalt. We'd comfort her. We'd defer to her always. "Never get old," she'd say, "never leave those who are dear to you and admire you. You'll end up in a place where no one remembers who you were."

"You're not old," we would say. "You're *brilliant, we love you*."

We fed her ego quite well.

And now, Natalie said, Madame opined in her lair, in the dim light that seeped through the old coated windows, amid the whirring machines and the checkerboard, lilting and guttural and somehow musical words that flowed from the sewing women, "The poor man, his wife is a millstone around his neck. What will become of him? How can he work?"

I felt shot. I had to restrain the urge to shoot back, because in a sense it meant absolutely nothing. People gossiped, of course. Madame would probably drop to her knees and wail for my forgiveness if she heard I knew. More probably yet, she just didn't think, and that annoyed me.

"She's just being practical," Diana reacted when I told her, "in a ghoulish sort of way. The Russians, you know how they are."

Natalie was incensed that I thought we should just leave it alone. "She lights candles by her icons for you to walk, and then this!"

I laughed. "Well, on to plan B, I guess, after the icons didn't work."

But it bothered me; it felt black. It felt like the mornings I woke up and thought I was in my pre-polio body. Then I'd remember, and would have to decide all over again to get up and be who I was now. It was temporarily crushing, but more than that it was a thoroughly private affair between me and my soul, and to know of the disloyalty and the bad faith made it feel dragged into light and unconquerable.

Silly, I said to myself. I was no one's pathetic figure, nobody's lightning rod. I understood the layer of bitterness striping the hearts of the émigrés, turning them false, grandiose, sniping, self-pitying, maudlin. From childhood on I'd experienced Russians, the teachers, one dismissing another with "No," flick of the hand, "not from Imperial Ballet." Or another saying, "You know what he did back in Russia? He swept the stage!" I'd used to think it quite funny. Kolya, a friend of my husband's, was the snob of snobs and the *most* outrageous gossip. If George couldn't get out of a bad mood, the best method of dealing with it was to get Kolya to the apartment. Put the two of them in the corner and let them jabber away in Russian and pretty soon George perked right up. Indisputably, many of the émigrés were splendid people, tactful and dignified, George's two Russian ex-wives, and the teacher I most admired at the school, Madame Doubrovska, with her beautiful carriage and her keen eye and kindness; she'd written the most sensitive letter to me in Copenhagen. As for Karinska, the fishwife, you had to consider that whatever she was, she did her excellent work day after day, getting up as George did, as I had to, so that whatever was black in her was not the entire story.

Who I was now: there was nothing else for me to be. I could not have predicted, before, how dancing would equip me for my nonwalking life. I had constantly, endlessly learned the enormous task of trying to dance. I remembered a picture of myself in a magazine sitting backstage on a box, towel in hand, looking as though I had lost my best friend.

I knew how to just go on. To ignore pain of whatever variety, including verbal assault. If it felt impossible, still I must try. George had seen the connection between my old and new lives all along. He was a very wise man. If he thought me a millstone, he would tell me himself. It was not in his nature to dissemble. He loved me. The other women meant nothing.

I'd remained cool on the phone with Natalie, saying, "Oh, tell Karinska to go put more blue in her hair," before I hung up. Then I chain-smoked five fags and wheeled frantically through the apartment pulling out drawers, in search of a pair of sunglasses I decided I'd lost.

But at length I opened the windows and let out the smoke. I exercised on my mat. I had gained further agility and strength in my upper body. I did not work the legs. You have to have muscle to make more muscle. There has to be a way to resist, and there wasn't. I'd found, though, that after the first two years, the atrophy had ceased. My legs and feet were thin and limp, but because I'd been paralyzed as an adult, unlike babies and children with undeveloped muscles, my legs and feet weren't left as visibly altered as they could have been—thin, smaller, not withered, not twisted. There were much worse fates than mine, those who were forever left in iron lungs or, in an entirely different scenario, people with spinal cord injuries who lost sensation and most of their functions. Polio mercifully spared me *feeling,* in the end taking only my legs and partial capacity in my right arm.

I exercised in a spacious sunlit room opening onto another room, emphatically able to be here alone, to do for myself now as needed. Mother might move in while George was away, but not necessarily.

Shiny and slick with sweat, I pushed myself up into the chair to go bathe. Powdered and dry, I brushed my hair in front of the bedroom mirror. I did my makeup. I dabbed on Chanel No. 5. My hair was thick again, my eyes bright. I was thirty-two years, eleven months, and a day old.

I was brave, but cautious. George talked despairingly about Russia just stopping: "Just froze. Terrible place. There, is like the twentieth century never came." I knew what happened to handicapped people in benighted times. I pictured an army of blue-hairs lined up in Red Square, measuring tapes draping their necks: "Obsolete!" they would shout. "So be off!"

October 2, 1962
Moscow

Dear T,

Happy birthday! I'm sorry you may not get this until next year. Hope you ate something delicious and drank a good wine. Write to me about it, so I can fantasize. George is a wraith. He says we're all bugged and speaks in a whisper. He can't sleep. Evidently the radio goes on by itself in the middle of the night. The time difference and the uncertainty of the phone connections are driving him mad. "I just want to talk to Tanny," he tells us with soulful and plaintive eyes. I'll be honest, T, he really isn't well. When we got to the airport in Russia he took one look at the lights and the cameras and rather than smiling or anything, he drew himself up and got cold and severe. They asked him how he felt to be back in his homeland and he held up his passport, staring them down, and said, "I'm an American." That's how it started.

On the positive side of the ledger, we are so far a great success. The Muscovites like me and Arthur for obvious reasons, and they like Jacques because he is a big rugged American. They have trouble with the name. (One newspaper explained, "French people, Russian people, Chinese people, Puerto Rican people all live together in America in a melting slop." Translation compliments Natalie.) But they are extremely respectful to us as dancers. Some audience members come night after night. Men wait in droves outside the theater doors for Allegra. She's popular in the way that you always were, our resident femme fatale.

My ankle's been giving me trouble but so far I've only been out for a matinee. You were right not to come. The accommodations are a nightmare, the size of a stadium and guaranteed to confuse and disorient, Kafka's *Castle*.

Maybe in Leningrad George will do better, old stomping grounds and all that. Oh, dear. Don't worry. We're doing our best to see he's okay. Lincoln does the diplomacy thing when George is in a state of collapse in his room.

Hugs/kisses,
Diana

October 17, 1962
Leningrad

Dear Tanny,

Now it's a missile crisis. I do not understand your state department. We were informed that if anything happens we are on our own. Hearing this information, George was serene. In America he believes. He says it's the Soviets driving him to despair. This makes no sense, Tanny. If it comes to the crisis we're in the middle of Soviets, yes?

We did the MEETING WITH THE BROTHER. Catastrophe. He is a nice man, George's brother Andrei. Lighter and milder and a successful composer. George looked forward to seeing him I think. Then Andrei, first off, has to say George is too influenced by Stravinsky. The end. Finished. No hope. Andrei leaves for a minute and George says, "They destroyed Shostakovich, Prokofiev, did you think there'd be anything worthwhile in someone as slight as Andrei? The man's a buffoon."

We go to Andrei's apartment. He has a nice young beautiful daughter, George's niece he likes very much. But Andrei must pull us into a room and play for us his music, one record after another. George sits as if he will die with his head in his hands. Never once he looks up and he doesn't say one word. I think I will grow old in that room. At last Andrei quietly puts away the music. Later I say to George, "Couldn't you have said something?" and George said, "No, I could not."

Then we plan a trip to his childhood home. He gets excited. "Natalie, I'll show you this and I'll show you that." But in the town there is nothing there. It is flattened. One block of apartment buildings, and this is all. The house of George's family is a Communist museum. This could be a joke, but it isn't. Now no one can tell him feel better. At the Kirov they scream for him after performances and won't let him off the stage. He makes wan smiles on his face. He is tired and undone and last night he wouldn't walk in front of the curtain.

Four weeks to go. New York seems very far away.

Love across ocean,
Natalie

October 30, 1962

TANAQUIL stop GEORGE IN STATE OF COLLAPSE stop FAINTING SPELLS stop ARRIVING NY FOR REST stop

LINCOLN

Eddie deposited George the next day with me.

"Hi, Tan," Eddie said, looking worse for wear himself. "I'm holing up in my apartment to get over the jet lag. I'll pick him up in three days. We've got to fly out again Tuesday morning. Bye, George."

"Bye, Eddie," George said, without turning to him.

I had on my cream cashmere pullover, delivered from Bonwit's, a gift from George. Poor lamb, he looked like an idiot child standing there, didn't move, gaunt in his trench coat. I took his hand, a fistful of bones.

"Darling, take off your coat," I said.

"I'm fine, dear. I'm home."

I got his coat unbuttoned and led him to the long glass-topped dining table, where I'd put out

a spread of his favorite hors d'oeuvres—
zakuski—and opened the bottle of O'Brien he'd
sent.

"It was for your birthday," he said with
disappointment.

"Oh, no, I saved it, George. I wanted to drink it
with you."

"How lovely," he said, looking over the table.
But after a sip and a bite his eyes got glassy and
I helped him bathe and put him to bed.

I set fruit and a carafe of water on the bedside
table, but he woke only twice in two days, to
shuffle to the bathroom. Sometimes he was so
still in sleep that I put my face close to his to feel
his breath. I lay beside him at night in the weak
glow of a kitschy Statue of Liberty plug-in night-
light I'd gotten him as a joke: "Your beacon!" But
it wasn't a joke to him, we had the original one
for years, and when it stopped working I searched
everywhere until I found another, since he
refused any replacement. He grew attached to
particular little things that anchored him, I think.
I lay cozily in the creatural warmth of being with
him and having him safe.

Here, he always talked about Russia and
immersed himself in its news. He missed Russia
powerfully, but I knew he had no regrets. I
wondered about the dreamscape in his mind as he
slept, a grim strip of film spooling by of what
Russia had become, of dead land, dead eyes, dead

music and dance, and ghosts that arose of what had been, of horrors, of beauty, of extremes shifting so fast they were stunning and could hardly be held in one mind. Of experiences that could never be adequately divulged by one person to another, though once in the night his mouth worked as if he were trying to tell me.

I worried too about his responsibilities. There he'd been in that huge, battered, unfathomable country, working as usual nonstop. But if I brought it up he would maintain that this made him strong.

"What else would I do?"

"How strange you are," I whispered to him. "I love you." And I kissed his temple and thought he smiled in his sleep.

On Monday morning as I put on coffee in the kitchen I turned and gasped, seeing him standing suddenly in the doorway.

"Good morning." He grinned. "You forgot I was here?"

"Good morning! How *nice* to see you."

"I am all right, dear," he said. "I don't know what they told you. I needed rest. I needed to be with my wife."

"And you are," I said. "May I make you breakfast?"

He insisted on washing and shaving first, and then he came back. He couldn't eat much but what he did eat he relished. I cleared the dishes;

149

he patted the Formica kitchen table like a good loyal dog, saying he'd missed it. I drew him to the window and showed him the nest occupied by a family of wrens, pressed up against the iron curl protecting the gutter.

We were reminded of the red fox that darted across the green grass of our yard in Weston, and of last New Year's Day, awakening at the house on the morning after our anniversary to a doe and her fawn in the snow.

"People I knew had no money, no rights," he said. "I had to arrange for them in Moscow a special performance. It was loss and the past everywhere. The past is where I don't want to be."

"No," I said. His sister had died in a German bombing raid during the war. His parents were gone. I told him what Natalie wrote about Leningrad.

"I thought that to stand again on the stage of the Mariinsky I would like," he said. "But I see it better, how it was, from here."

He had described the opulence of the blue and gold theater and the size of the stage, the lavish box for the czar; the majesty of *The Sleeping Beauty* he had been in as a child—real fountains poured real water down the grand palace steps on Aurora's wedding day, real horses paraded in feathers and velvet blankets; that stage a miracle world, blazing with light. I believe he created this other world, in various permutations, in each of his dances, and they contained the awe, the inner reaching he felt as a child in *The Sleeping Beauty*. He'd felt indescribable ecstasy. He started to work very hard. When he saw what the work could produce, he wanted to work very badly.

"I am fortunate man," he said, "only because I came here. I have good dancers. Better and better. These girls, half of them would throw themselves into the orchestra pit for me."

I laughed. "I know." The women were his riches. "Did I ever tell you about my fall and the DAR?" He loved fallers, girls who took chances. It seemed that these new ones were all catching on. But nobody liked to be injured. I hadn't cared. I must have known somehow that I didn't have long. I almost always danced full-out. "I really did not ever tell you this, George?"

"No."

"It was at Constitution Hall in D.C. The stage was extremely slick, but we were forbidden to use any rosin for fear of wrecking the DAR's floor. Well, in the finale of the last ballet I fell with a resounding thud right in the middle of the stage, spun around once on my tutu-pants, and, reeling, struggled up to my feet. 'Just imagine,' they said to me later, 'the last time Margot Fonteyn danced here she fell down in the exact same spot.' "

George sparkled, he laughed, the dimples came

out in his cheeks; and then he looked at me oddly, his laughter fading.

"Dear?" I said. "What's wrong?"

"Nothing is wrong."

"They said you'd been fainting."

"It is nothing. I only feel warmer and tired and I go out. It will not happen again now."

"But you could have hurt yourself."

"No, Tanny. I'm a good faller too." Then he lowered his head and started to cry. It was the first of two times I would ever see him cry. I didn't go to him, didn't want to embarrass him, and in a minute he stopped.

He spent the rest of the day in his office at the theater and at the school, his bulwarks, and we had dinner at the Russian Tea Room, much nicer than the real thing. In the morning Eddie came again to take him to the plane.

I thought it might be good for us to plan a trip out West when he returned. We could go in late spring between the winter season and the summer tour. I wrote to him about it immediately and he telegrammed back to me, *YES*.

He'd crisscrossed the country by car while he was working in Hollywood in the 1930s, and he went again with Maria in the forties. He loved the vast spaces, big like Russia but unspoiled and free, the America he'd heard about in Europe. He liked western films after seeing the farms, mountains, canyons, and deserts beneath the voluminous skies; liked the blocky mysterious pueblos, the bright filling stations, the little towns and the sad hotels out of *Lolita* that could have only come about here.

We'd gone together first in 1950, with Mother as chaperone. Oh, the sophistication, I'd thought, of the *lack* of sophistication, how George reveled in it was infectious, inspiring, modeled a certain kind of attention I understood for the first time, as I hadn't before, and absorbed into my own psyche.

Then we went again in 1954, both of us exhausted from the tension of the first *Nutcracker*, the cost of the tree that nearly sent Lincoln over the edge, and my Dew Drop, a victory but a part I thought might kill me. Dew Drop came at the pinnacle of George's obsession with me as a dancer, and he pushed me hard in the role, to pyrotechnical feats. When I worried he said, you let me worry, and so I did.

In the rush to the opening Jerry and George sat in the costume shop sewing on sequins. Jerry asked George how he could be so relaxed.

"Soon Tanny and I will get in the car and drive west, and the weather will be good and the food will be good."

He sat there like Buddha, Jerry said.

The minute we left the city George whistled and hummed. Halfway across Pennsylvania I came alive. It got warmer in Arizona, almost like spring. Well-being pulsed through me, and nearing the desert one day we stopped at one of those filling stations—it gleamed in the sun like a toy. Warmth tickled my skin, the dry air stretched my lungs. If I'd been a singer I would have sung! In perfect contentment, the glorious equilibrium between the outside and my inside, I made a preparation in fourth position, turned one pirouette, and with my bag tucked under my arm did soutenu turns, saut de basque, and a high, light piqué arabesque.

I dropped a coin into the Coke machine and looked back, and there was my guy, watching me over the hood of the car.

2

In 1963 New York City Ballet received the largest single-source donation ever made in support of dance from the Ford Foundation. Expansion began; plans commenced for a new home away from City Center; and a new dancer, Suzanne Farrell, came to the fore.

I dreamed her before I saw her. I dreamed of being inside a house burning down. The kitchen to the right of me sizzled, collapsed, the living room to the left—gone, and I heard the back porch creak from the lapping flames and the rafters crash to the ground. As if it were nothing I walked through the fire in the foyer and escaped unscathed. I brushed myself off, and then in the distance I saw a girl with long brown hair standing in a pool of white light.

In reality she had the same hair and was nearly as tall as Diana. She had my small head, my legs, my flexibility and fearlessness on the stage—a kid from Cincinnati.

By the 1960s the company was almost entirely fed by dancers from the school, girls who'd come up in the style as I had. George seldom brought in adult dancers by then. Violette Verdy was one, a technical whirlwind and an actress who provided contrast to George's corps of girls who had no projected personalities, these kids like Suzanne who danced bigger, faster, and sharper than ever. To them, the authority of Mr. B was indisputable. If he'd been revered by the New York ballet world when I started working with him, by the time these kids came, he was a nationwide star.

Scholarship students were selected for the school from other parts of the country. Diana was a scout. She wasn't impressed by Suzanne in Cincinnati, thinking her graceful but weak. Diana told her that if she ever came to New York they would audition her again. The girl's mother set off immediately with Suzanne and her sister, all of their possessions in a U-Haul trailer, moving into a single room with a single bed in the Ansonia, a resident show-business hotel that had seen better days. They were sort of the Joads—

the itinerant family in *The Grapes of Wrath*—of New York City Ballet.

Suzanne danced for George and he liked her right away. He put her into the school and then into the company the following year. 1961.

Looking back, I am fairly certain that Suzanne began to get under George's skin during the trip to Russia. One would never have thought. The girl couldn't jump. She had bad knees and not a jot of talent for allegro dancing. Those limpid blue eyes in the pale pretty face didn't know what the hell you were talking about most of the time. In conversation she missed out on references to practically everything, as if she'd crawled out from under a rock. She was just a kid. But then, I'd been just a kid. In childhood, a horse had trampled one of her long feet. But she had line, she had musicality, and those were the qualities George most appreciated. And beneath the baby fat there was this outrageous will. She never looked at the audience, saying, "I dance for God," and it didn't even sound pretentious because of her absolute conviction.

So there was the youth, the beauty, and the temperament, how she snapped up any challenge he threw at her, making him see that he could do anything with her—she was saying, teach me to dance, I'll listen. And she arrived at a time of reinvention, of regeneration for George, for himself and for the company, which were the same.

156

We would never go out West again.

Philip Johnson was commissioned to design the New York State Theater to Balanchine's specifications. City Center had always been wanting, with its poor acoustics and sight lines. The wings were so minute that Marie-Jeanne, a principal ballerina of the forties, hit the wall as she leaped from the stage and knocked herself out cold. George's ambition to put on the large productions he had known in his boyhood could be realized only on a much larger stage, and to fill that new stage he needed big dancing.

He had never liked nice polite "English" dancing, as he called it. He wanted us to travel. I'd always been known as a girl who ate space. People dubbed me the prototype of "the Balanchine dancer." But the physical type, the big dancing—it was all an apotheosis of what had been there for years.

His off-balance dancing was worked out initially on Maria and in dances as early as *Ballet Imperial* in 1941. But then came the money and the stage and, with them, Suzanne.

It was uncanny that Diana found her. Uncanny that in April 1963, a week before the premiere of another Stravinsky ballet, Diana learned she was pregnant. Her doctor ordered bed rest for the first trimester and Diana was out.

"She stabbed me in the back!" George hissed.

There was no calming him down. He barricaded

himself in his office and barely spoke at home.

I saw his point. I'd been to a rehearsal. All his choreography was worked out for individual dancers, but this one was so specifically made on Diana—stripped down to balance and nervous intensity to a degree that I couldn't see it on anyone else either.

Jacques was to partner Diana; Diana was mortified to have let George down—but secretly ecstatic—and Jacques thought Suzanne was very good, so he and Diana cooked up a plan. Lying on the couch in her apartment, Diana taught Suzanne her part, while Jacques danced it with her. They broke down for Suzanne the complicated rhythms.

Suzanne didn't tire, didn't pant, didn't sweat or go red in the face. She was sort of a space creature, Diana said.

They convinced George not to cancel the premiere and brought Suzanne to him with three days to go. He thought she wasn't bad. He worked with her. He brought in Stravinsky and Stravinsky said, "Who is this?"

"Suzanne Farrell," said George. "Just been born."

Movements for Piano and Orchestra took its place as a significant work. Suzanne danced the premiere effectively, her pale face still, her brow furrowed slightly in concentration. She had an unusual manner of diving deeply into penché arabesque, almost in the Russian mode with earthy, exaggerated pliancy, and as I watched her she put me in mind of American showgirls—their size, their austere sexiness. I could see why he liked her.

She learned fifteen ballets over the next months, including Diana's other roles. She was eighteen, George nearly sixty.

After the dark Russian autumn and Diana's betrayal that turned to a fresh start—"God took Diana and gave me Suzanne"—George was ebullient and unstoppable. People hadn't seen him as excited in years.

Every evening following classes and rehearsals, George trained our yellow-and-white tomcat, Mourka.

"No, he trained me," George insisted.

One night the cat stalked the kitchen, head hanging heavily as a lurking tiger's. "Look," I said, "if he weighed four hundred more pounds, he'd eat us."

George absently rolled his paper napkin into a ball and tossed it at Mourka to distract him.

Mourka leaped, twisted in the air, and batted the napkin back. George tried it again this way and that, watching Mourka's responses.

The training sessions came to include cat treats and were regularized. Hearing his master's key in the lock, Mourka raced to the door, sat at the ready, and, at the shake of the treat can, leaped.

George feinted left and right like a boxer and Mourka hopped back and forth like a Slinky in somebody's hands. Those small motions built up momentum for more major jumps, which grew various and spectacular, achieving multiple spins and great heights.

"Stay in the air, Mourka, *stay*," George said.

"It's a bird, it's a plane, it's Super Cat!" I cried.

At our dinner parties we pushed back the furniture and put on displays. Mourka lived for them. His burly chest swelled, his muzzle pushed forward, his green eyes dilated to black disks. George got very nervous before the performances. It was funny how important they came to seem to him. But everything was important to George.

Mourka in contrast kept his perspective and didn't get nervous. For the kitty the upset occurred at the end of the show. He couldn't just curl up in his basket after the glory, couldn't shake the adrenaline that had coursed through him during those concentrated minutes. What was real life in comparison? How could he rest? He mournfully traipsed the apartment as we cleaned up and got ready for bed, and this was why I decided to produce a book, a picture book with plenty of action shots. There had to be more for Mourka to *do*.

Of course it was careerist and nepotistic. We were assured of a book contract by the *Life* magazine cover: George Balanchine and his cat, the man crouched beneath the high-flying feline, Mourka *en l'air.*

In *Life*, Balanchine joked, "At last I have a body worth choreographing for."

Once again in George's good graces, Diana flew out to visit us on summer tour in Chicago. No longer confined to bed, Diana still had to be careful, and we lounged around playing cards and dissecting performances, living off room service. George was often in New York fulfilling commitments and we didn't see much of him.

"We're naming the baby George," Diana said. "Georgina if it's a girl."

"You're not," I said.

Diana gazed at me over her cards.

"You are," I said.

"He's given me everything I am as a dancer, why wouldn't I?"

"He'll like that," I said.

"Damn, no more ice." She went out to the hall, leaving the door ajar, and I heard her say, "Suzanne, what are you doing?"

"Taking a walk," Suzanne said.

"Through the hallways?"

"Yes."

"Here, then," Diana said, "fetch us ice." To me she said, "She's walking the hallways."

"I heard. Tell her to come in."

Suzanne stepped up to the doorway.

"Thanks," Diana said. "Why don't you go out and do something interesting? We're in *Chicago*."

Suzanne shrugged. She wore an unflattering white cotton shift that made her pale skin paler; a headband had slipped halfway down her brown bangs.

"Hi, Suzanne," I said. We'd met. "You play cards?"

"Oh, yes," the girl answered, shyly baring her small teeth. I felt for her, isolated and lonely on tour, proving herself, forging ahead without any clue if she was doing things right. Who'd want to be young again? Inexperience was such a burden to live through. Ballet was a fine life for a young girl, really. Other girls your age studied for tests and went through traumas at sock hops, trying to talk to pimply boys who had nothing to say, and you learned to be forceful and skilled and traveled the world seeing other cultures and spending time with fascinating older people who wanted the moon for you.

"Come in, then," I said to her. She was family, like a distant cousin. "You know gin rummy?" She nodded, flushed with excitement. Diana replenished our iced teas from the pitcher.

"Tea, Suzanne?"

"No, I'm not thirsty."

"Have you been to the art museum?" Diana

asked, and Suzanne shook her head and studied the hand I'd dealt her. "You should," Diana said.

"I like to play cards," Suzanne said.

"What else do you like?" I asked. Suzanne's blue eyes rolled up at me, deer caught in the headlights. "You like the Beatles, Suzanne?" Wider eyes, panic.

She recovered. "Yes," she said decisively. "Yeah, yeah, yeah."

"You sure? I thought it was no, no, no."

"Tanny," Diana said. "Ignore her, Suzanne."

"Sorry," I said to Suzanne's complete incomprehension. "I didn't do anything except dance and think about dancing for ages and ages, but since I stopped I've developed all of these interests. This summer I'm absolutely *obsessed* with quantum physics."

"Right," Diana said; Suzanne smiled a weak smile.

"Did you like science in school?" I asked her.

"No."

"Me either. My opinion is I missed nothing."

I won, won, and won. We talked ballet. Suzanne had idolized New York City Ballet from afar: "It was so *alive*." She'd danced in her living room with a Jacques d'Amboise dummy and couldn't believe he partnered her now. Diana told Agnes de Mille stories from her days in *Oklahoma!* I described stuffing my child bedroom slippers with Kleenex for toe shoes. The three of us laughed at our similar experiences learning toe, hanging on to the barre forever and gingerly rising, getting the feel.

We purchased a grilled cheese sandwich for Suzanne, and then she had to lie down and rest before her performance.

"That was wonderful of you," Diana said in a certain sentimental tone.

"Well, it was of you too. What are you saying?"

A beat, and Diana said, "Nothing."

"Wonderful as in big of me?" I asked.

"No."

"No, really?"

"Why are you angry? I don't—"

"Because I don't dance, have babies, those sorts of normal things, and yet I'm magnanimous?"

Diana's lips quivered.

"May I have a scotch?" I said. I wheeled to the window and Diana came in a minute and handed me a glass and sat down on the ottoman nearby.

"I never even *wanted* a baby," I said. We were on the twentieth floor, and late-summer daylight saturated the buildings, altering the raw facts, the harsh cityscape. I gripped the glass. "What's wrong with me? I don't do this. Why am I doing this?"

"You can," Diana said. "You don't have to be Atlas."

I swallowed scotch, felt its heat trace my veins. "When I learned I'd never get out of this chair, I used to have panics. I had them in bed too in the beginning. I felt when I was agitated inside—good or bad agitation—that if I couldn't move, go with what was going on inside me, I would explode."

"I've imagined you feeling that," Diana said. "But I wouldn't have been able to find words for it. It's amazing how you can."

"For what it's worth," I said. "Well, it's worth something. You learn how to sublimate, to channel energy differently." I looked at Diana's familiar profile, her short, dark, wavy hair.

"I don't get panics that much anymore," I said, "but not being able to walk is hardest with George. I can be with him sitting or lying down. We were both such *fast* people. He still is. I was always rushing after him, and he after me. Remember my shoes? All of those shoes George bought me?" She nodded. "I can't wear any of them. They're relics. Do you want them?"

"We don't wear the same size," she said.

I finished the scotch. "I would give anything if I could dance with him once more. Just once, that's it."

I changed the subject. "Have you felt the baby yet?"

"No, but I listen too hard. That's me, listening too hard, trying too hard." She laughed. "You know what I think about myself? I think that while I'm straining, listening, trying, waiting, life is passing me by. I'll wake up someday and a voice will say, 'Sorry, lady, you missed out, it's over, the curtain's down.' "

I laughed with her.

"Aren't we philosophers," I said. We watched the colors deepen outside, very present to life and each other. Soon, Suzanne would get up and dance.

George and I were spending less time together. Work ruled him, and my independence felt necessary—essential. I loved being Mrs. George Balanchine, privately and publicly too, I admit. But I didn't want to be his appendage. I worked on the cat book and coached. I planned a trip to England and France for the following year. I cultivated my long-term friendships and was open to new ones.

Jerry and I took a day trip to Staten Island.

"There's life outside of a theater!" he exclaimed on the ferry.

"You bet, boy," I said. He stood beside my chair at the ferry railing and wind whipped the cables, they snapped and rattled the chains; my hair slashed my face—God, I loved sensation. I felt my being rush out of myself and flash over the choppy waves, bolt into the sky, skim the bridges, soar over the tankers and barges and tugs, touch the skylines, and then, as if it had been on a long cord and was now tired, it reeled back and nestled into my body, calm and contented, and I sat happily with my friend.

"What do you see in the clouds, doll?" Jerry asked.

"They're silvery, like antique mirrors." The ferry bobbed on the swells, the crisp air carried motor oil, salt, and tar. Gulls with ragged feathers chattered and called. "Here is this island," I said, "that's been sitting there my whole life, and it may as well have never existed!" It transformed from watery gray to green bluffs, trees, rocks, the wharf emerging, people's faces taking on features and expressions. I had read up on the island's history and spun out a running commentary as we explored. We drove around all day, got drunk at night on Chianti, eating spaghetti in a ramshackle wood structure without any sign near the terminal.

"It exists," Jerry said.

"Definitively," I answered.

At Warm Springs, Sophia had cautioned me, "You're a polio and you'll always be a polio. You'll live your life to the hilt and woe to anyone who tries to stop you."

"Sophia," I'd said, "don't you feel my enthusiasm may also derive from who I am as an individual?"

Sophia lifted a shoulder and replied doubtfully, "Could be."

But I believed—and believed it more as I got

older—that even the most extreme forces that shape us are only one cause of who we become. There are five stories to one story, turn it to one and it's false. They are all false independently. Life and causality are a braid that gets more intricate as one goes along.

Shortly after my illness Jerry had left New York City Ballet. He claimed everything he had done for the company was for me and without me it wasn't the same. He continued to work on Broadway and occasionally in Hollywood. But he remained haunted by his testimony for HUAC. Ironically, his celebrity was the reason for his subpoena, and he named names fearing that his affairs with men would be exposed and wreck his career. But his naming destroyed others' careers, and he was hated for it. The world lauded him, people hated him, and this was Jerry's particular burden.

His treatment of dancers, the lengths he went to in getting the performances he wanted, were legend. He had always been insecure, edgier with his dancers than George ever was. I didn't know two men more different, one supremely confident and the other impossibly insecure. Dances flowed from George. Jerry overanalyzed and doubted his every invention, although most of what he came up with was usually, right off, extremely good. When he made *Afternoon of a Faun* he couldn't decide until the last minute whether he wanted us facing the audience or facing stage right. Drove me nuts. In the end George and Jerry both produced significant work, but Jerry suffered for his, and in time the suffering seemed to intensify, rather than lessen. I heard nonstop gossip about Jerry's behavior in rehearsal rooms, which were of course *filled* with people, making the situation for someone as nervous and conspicuous as Jerry even worse. But hearing things saddened me, given the gallant man I knew.

The first time I had braved the ballet in my new incarnation Jerry met Carl and me at the freight elevator, poised in his tux, his complexion strikingly dark against the white shirt. Carl pushed me out in my gold lamé gown with the décolletage and my hair in a hundred-dollar chignon intended to give me the confidence of a goddess.

It had. But as soon as I got there and what I was about to do became actual, I felt I couldn't. My breathing quickened. I started to hyperventilate.

"Let's go home, Carl," I said. Here was dashing Jerry, my squire, and Carl with his physique women's eyes tracked as if he were pastry, employed by my husband to cater to me, and I felt like an absolute flop, but I couldn't do it. I wasn't afraid of the dancing, it was simply appearing. I'd been undone by the premiere of me. "Bad idea," I said. "I'd go if I could but I can't breathe, oh, shit, what's going on?"

"Slow, steady," Jerry coached me, wresting the chair's handles from Carl.

"Jerry, what are you doing?"

"We're going."

"Stop," I said. "Turn around, we're going back. Carl!"

But against Jerry, Carl didn't stand a chance. He walked at my side, a hulk of concern.

We got to the stairs, beyond which the chair couldn't go.

"Listen," Jerry said, facing me, "you think there isn't drama and excitement in a beauty who can't walk? Play it. Come on, like George said, you're the queen. You're almost *killed* and you're prettier than Lana Turner."

He picked me up out of the chair and cradled me against his chest. "Think *Being Beauteous*, baby." My Ashton dance. I soared in the air; five guys held me aloft.

"Knock it off," I said. "You don't have to pull out the repertoire."

"Why not?" We reached the main doors to the theater. "You ready?"

"Heave ho," I said. "How's your lower back?"

And we entered and went down the aisle as heads turned and didn't stop until we were seated and there was applause. I waved and smiled, and at the curtain Lincoln brought roses to me, and George blew me a kiss from the stage and Jerry beamed and Carl reported what he had heard during intermission, without censorship. It wasn't bad, not as I'd feared. I felt free that night, lucky, reborn.

George insisted that I wouldn't like the first dance he made for Suzanne.

"Oh, why?"

"Nobody likes anything different."

"Really? Aren't you being contrary?"

"No. I did *Prodigal Son* and nobody liked it. I did *Apollo*, guy says, 'Young man, when did you see Apollo walk on his knees?' *I* said, 'When did *you* see Apollo?'" Delighted with himself, George laughed. "Now for those ballets, they whistle."

"Tell me about the new one," I said.

"It's Russian character essay, it's miniature in vein of Kasyan Goleizovsky. I picked the music and it came to me." Goleizovsky had been a choreographer and an early mentor of George's in Russia.

"Go on," I said.

"Simple dance," George said. "Young man is troubled. Young woman comes to him and they dance and then again he is alone."

George did all kinds of ballets, his best-known neoclassical works, but also story ballets, extravaganzas, and mood pieces. But he was right, not about my opinion but about the opinions of others. Most of the reviews of this short dance, *Meditation*, accused him, the cool modern master, of Russian schmaltz.

A *New York Times* critic wrote: "The dance is an unabashedly sentimental image of a man recalling his lost love." Many were shocked that Balanchine could be so blatantly romantic and emotional.

I saw nothing hackneyed about it. I liked its soft naturalness, how it unfolded in one unending stream, and Suzanne for all her lack of technique danced it with sweep, understanding in her movement that the dance was a single idea—though this objective opinion, this considered opinion, was arrived at well after the jolt of the premiere. Seeing the dance in the flesh was something else. I attended the performance with Jerry. As the lights dimmed there was the typical extra edge of anticipation, more throat-clearings and program-flipping.

The curtain opened to reveal Jacques, Suzanne's champion and my last partner—we had danced *Faun* together—on his knees, his face in his large hands. Suzanne stepped out of the dark in a white chiffon dress, her hair loose across her bare shoulders. The piece rode an aching violin, the music Tchaikovsky, who was, with Stravinsky and Mozart, the composer George most esteemed. The partnering was sinuous; the ballet essentially a long embrace. I felt, sitting and watching, how George would have held her, making the dance, and I knew that although she'd been prepared in adagio classes for handling by a man, she had not been prepared for the prolonged physical contact, the intimacy of rehearsing a classical pas de deux. George pushed the male dancers aside and worked with the women, demonstrating, better at partnering, stronger and easier than the young men. As I watched the ballet, I thought: So he yearns for her but can't have her, except in the studio. Or she might have stood for me when I danced—or for all mortal women, all loss, including the primal loss of his mother. But as it went on I didn't believe that because of the pitch of the adoration and grief. There was no distancing effect; it was raw and immediate need; Jacques lifted her face-to-face and raised her up, holding her by the shoulders against him, and she wrapped his head with her arms. I pictured George watching her, from his customary place in the wings downstage right.

The lights came up and I chatted and smiled, friends and acquaintances feigned nonchalance, and in a back booth at a steakhouse—Jerry and I didn't tackle Sardi's that night—Jerry said, "I don't get it. What's great about her? She has no technique."

"She will," I said.

"Why does he have to—" Jerry scowled. We were artists, and as worldly sophisticates anything went, right?

"Go ahead, Jerry. There isn't much you could say that wasn't already said." I saw it clear: the dance was a tribute to George's inspiration, a public announcement.

"It's disrespectful to you," he said.

"Except for getting his kicks in the studio," I said, sounding hard—I didn't care—"and a couple extracurricular flirtations, there hasn't been anyone but Diana." Then, pensive, I added, "He was gone on Allegra, but she resisted him."

Jerry shifted uneasily. "I haven't heard anything, Tan. They aren't seeing each other."

"I don't care what he's doing in private, well, I do care, but tonight was public. Yes, it's disrespectful, I'm sitting there—I didn't think he could shock me. He has." Tamara, Alexandra, Vera Zorina, Maria, me, the five marriages, each to his prima ballerina at the time. Everyone knew this.

"Have you met her?" I asked, my inflection telling all.

"No," he said. "What?"

"Forget it. She's nice, she's *sweet,* and I like the damn dance. Oh, why isn't he a pianist?" I thought of Carl, reading the newspaper outside in the station wagon in the cold. "I should go," I said.

"It'll burn itself out," Jerry said. "It could just be dancing. He's getting older. . . ."

No, dancing threw gasoline on the flame, and

I hadn't seen any evidence that maturation, in his case, changed him; getting older only hurt him.

"I still demonstrate jumps sometimes," he'd told me wistfully. "Two minutes ago I could fly." He had looked so sad. I had tried to reassure him, reminding him of what Patty McBride said just this year about his dancing: that his demonstrations for her were more beautiful than what she believed she could ever do. But lost in regret, in a reverie of the past, he didn't hear me.

There was agency in my contraction of polio. George didn't know. He assumed I'd been infected in Venice because of the timing, the heat, and the unsanitary conditions. I myself didn't think of my secret, the incident—*what I had done*—or it would have destroyed my resolve to proceed. I wouldn't let myself think of it for a long time. But then, other things happened and it bled to the surface. As I got better, but things got harder, it bled.

At first, when I got sick, the rest of the tour was going to be canceled. But it was decided to continue. In Copenhagen as I lay fighting to breathe, the company waited to board a train for Stockholm. Solemnly, each dancer was given a paper explaining that I'd been infected and describing symptoms. If anyone had these symptoms they were honor-bound not to get on the train. They waited outside in the freezing cold reading their papers. Once in Stockholm, they were instructed, they should report any symptoms that appeared. I imagine the words they spoke to one another as soft and excited and frightened. They were worried for me but more for themselves. It was dramatic and terrible. Everyone boarded. In Stockholm their nightmares would have begun. The serum arrived and they were inoculated. There were no symptoms but one, a dancer in *Firebird* raised his arm to salute the princess and it wouldn't come down.

A few minutes later it did. A mild case, perhaps. Most people with polio never knew of their infection, felt only that they had a cold or flu. The severity of the individual cases depended on the immune system, among other causes—but that was something else I allowed George to understand: for his pushing me on the tour, for his wandering, I was exhausted, I was vulnerable, and this was only partially true.

Some of the dancers waiting on the train platform reading their papers in the frigid air knew, remembered the night in Venice that neither Mother nor George knew about.

We'd performed, and I raced with adrenaline taking off my makeup, puffing a cigarette, and it was hot. I wouldn't sleep if I went back to the room, and George might not be there. I'd wait up, we'd quarrel.

So when Shaun, a fellow dancer, dashed by, I called to him, asked what he was doing.

"Well, we're going out," he said. Cute guy from Bay Ridge, a sweetie, a whole lot of fun. He was one of my retinue in *Being Beauteous*. He used to crack jokes to me in the air about my weight and I'd squash my lips tight not to laugh. After my marriage I had run into Shaun the next day at the theater, which was abuzz, and he had said, "Is it true? You naughty, naughty child."

I called, "Where are you going?"

"To the Grand Canal for gondola rides!"

"When in Venice," I said. "May I come?"

"We'd love it."

We had to get properly lubricated on wine at a hole in the wall. Hot, the sweat glowed on our faces. Eight of us, five girls and three guys, laughing and stumbling through the narrow and winding alleys, one of us reading a map by the flashlight and shining it up at his face, a proper ghoul, his nostrils lit red and his eyes dark pits.

"Shine the light on the walls," somebody said, "you see they're marked, that's how we'll know where to go."

The walls sweated. I saw them dripping under the light, but I discovered, touching the stone in the hot night, that it was cold, clammy.

Venice of pestilence, vapors, of cholera and malaria, of looted cultures, a city of jewels built of blood. I had seen pictures before I first saw it, but none did it justice. One couldn't imagine anything so theatrical, everywhere I looked was a stage set, every scrap constructed, artificial, no foliage, only statues and carvings and glaring color rising in mist, getting larger and more insistent until you were in it and you might as well have been inside the mad dream of a doge, a medieval city reeking of pillage and vengeful gods—within the immensity of Santa Maria della Salute's high dome I believed for the first time in the primacy of crushing power and the nearness of obliteration.

So night, my head hot, my feet sore, and I tasted the wine and smelled fishy water, a dank fetid smell.

How we even got there, I don't know. But we tumbled out of an alley and the black water flickered beneath the half moon, where gondolas creaked and rocked in the canal.

We hired two. Shaun sat beside me and I said I felt sick and he yelled, "Help! Let me out."

"I'm joshing you, shush."

Out to the end of the island, we were under a spell. I felt the menace and the magic—the slap of the water, dankness, glitter of moon on a hand, the dipped oar, the shiver of light on the lagoon.

The stage sets of Venice receded, became little humps on the horizon as we neared the open sea. I floated hazily in the dark.

We quietly talked.

"God, we're way out."

"It's peaceful."

"I don't feel drunk anymore."

"Do you think we'll drown?"

The Italians called to each other, and we turned back.

At the turning: "What is the water out here? Is it salt water or fresh?"

Our gondolas drew close.

"Who speaks Italian?"

"Nobody."

"Well, what do you think? Is it salt water or fresh?"

I put my pointer finger into the black water.

I tasted it.

I declared, "Fresh."

Showing off, making fun, not thinking, one of those moments of carelessness that we all have and don't pay for.

But how could I?

Dip of the finger.

Fresh.

3

I brought up nothing to George on the night of the *Meditation* premiere. I came home loopy on a couple martinis and we played with Mourka on the bed. The next morning was one of those when I awoke and thought I was in my pre-polio body. I heard George clank pots in the kitchen. It all came back. I couldn't face him yet, and I went and drew a bath. I watched the gushing water, thinking of how much I didn't want to go through a Diana phase again. It hadn't been *so* awful when George and I were estranged and I suspected them before I got sick. But when I was better and we were supposedly mended as a couple and it started once more, less than a year after I wanted to kill myself, it was dreadful, confusing—how could he love me and do this? I kept thinking, no, not with Diana. We had been close from the time she came to dance with us in 1950. Mother, Diana, George, me, and Nicky Magallanes, one of my partners and a nice *unassuming* person, formed a clique, sharing houses on tour and vacation. People called us the Royal Family. Diana and I danced together and chummed around backstage. We alternated the same role in *Serenade*. One day George rounded us up and lectured us about our entrances. "The two of you are doing it all wrong," he scolded. "You are sneaking onto stage as if you were dancing *Giselle* or *Les Sylphides*. I want you to roar out onto stage like lion." I'd sidle up to Diana in the wings and silently roar. She'd make like a big cat and pounce.

The bathwater was cold. George came to the door and called through it that he was going to work and was I alive?

"Yeah! Nice day!" I drained the water and turned on the hot again.

Get out of the iron lung. Get out of the bed. Walk, and if you can't, sit in the chair and don't die.

Know what I hold in reserve, darling? Death. I can still get out of this. But I wouldn't do it over you. I already *didn't* do it over you, and for what?

I got in the bath and thought about people he'd hurt. Women—lots of them. Men—who were in his way or were growing older. Sure, facts were facts, but compassion would have been more appropriate than disdain and dismissal in the name of his vision, his needs. Needs. Didn't everyone break apart with desires that couldn't be? And I didn't buy the cult of the genius. I had known *good* geniuses. One. Maybe two.

George's treatment of Lincoln had always disturbed me. Tall, brilliant, rich, young Lincoln Kirstein wanted ballet for America. In 1933, the year he brought George from Europe, there were only two companies in the entire United States. Lincoln supported his choreographer through box-office deficits and canceled tours over the fifteen long years that passed from Balanchine's arrival to the establishment of New York City Ballet. Lincoln took George to the doctor, did budgets, publicity, and drained his own trust fund. In the late forties his mother kept the company alive, and as late as 1952 Lincoln had personally raised money to keep it going through the following year.

All the while Lincoln wished to create. With his literary gifts, he wanted to write librettos. With his erudition in visual art, he hoped to coordinate scenery. But Balanchine needed only his dancers and music, and what he wanted was just to continue, basically alone. Lincoln was no impresario like Diaghilev, and his efforts and passions were cordoned off into administration and fund-raising. He was too sensitive not to feel the underside of Balanchine's gratitude—a slight contempt. Lincoln said there were no disagreements between them because they never talked about anything.

Lincoln pursued his artistic interests on the side, but he had breakdowns, getting worse through the years. Lincoln and his wife, Fidelma, lived in a town house near Gramercy Park. The living room looked like a miniature ballroom, its gold-draped walls hung with paintings and drawings. Fidelma, a gifted painter herself, also had breakdowns. Lincoln's parade of young men were houseguests; Lincoln abandoned Fidelma in foreign countries, pursuing flings; Lincoln escorted a young boy to the opening of New York City Ballet's first summer season in Saratoga Springs. I did not at all appreciate seeing this type of commonality between Fidelma and me. I looked up at my beautiful pink roses on the ceiling above the bath, wallpaper George had laughed at because with the steam it would peel and fall off. But it hadn't, not in over six years. It irked me that certain people dismissed the length of my marriage—twelve years. *If it weren't for the polio he wouldn't have stayed, it was over before she got sick.* But to stay when I first got sick was one thing, to remain was another. If he had remained with me since 1956 out of nothing but duty and noblesse oblige, I was out of my mind.

That night he came home late and sat reading the paper. Mourka lay at his feet like a slave.

He'd already read the reviews in the morning, and for him the ballet seemed old news.

"I think I'll move out," I said.

"Hmn?"

"I'm moving out."

"Oh, to where?"

"Europe. Paris. I've always wanted to live in Paris."

"Don't be ridiculous."

"Why is it ridiculous?"

He lowered the paper. "You have no friends there, and I cannot come."

"No? You wouldn't transfer the theater for me?"

"Not the State Theater, no. You should have asked me four years ago. I like Paris myself."

He went back to reading and I left it alone. I hadn't the faintest idea of what to do or feel.

Mother, however, weighed in vociferously on the subject. She had her own ring of spies for information, ballet mothers she'd known forever. They'd been on the phones discussing Suzanne.

Mother called shortly and gave me a full report of how she had dealt with the gossip.

"Oh, no, I said, nothing *about* this is wrenching for Tanny. Ballet dancing is for the young. Mr. Balanchine is a ballet master and he must bring on the young. Tanaquil, as a former prima ballerina"—she'd get in the dig for the mothers of the corps dancers—"understands this implicitly. She approves of Suzanne. If she didn't, he would find someone else. It's a *marvelous* marriage, they talk about everything, and he depends on my daughter's opinions."

The tactic was to deflect the possibility that anything other than dancing could possibly be going on with Suzanne.

"They are so happy," said Mother. "Would that we all could be as happy as they are. The secret is they are compatible. As a former star, she knows what is important to him. She has wit and insight. But she no longer dances so she also has the time and energy for him. Truly, he is the centerpiece of her life. Men need that. They want that. Don't kid yourself, men need it much more than we do and you can multiply it in the case of a man of stature.

You can believe me, I know. I have been close to Mr. Balanchine for twenty years and I know.

"Of course, many men of stature desire young girls. Once, Mr. Balanchine did. But even powerful men get older, life moves along. With Tanaquil Mr. Balanchine has the best of both worlds. My daughter is still young and beautiful, and yet she isn't a naïf. He is a man of vast culture, a grand seigneur, and he has found his perfect partner."

"The centerpiece of my life. . . ." I said into the phone. Unbelievable.

"Isn't he?" Mother said.

"Is my life a table?" Interesting that I got mostly Mother's side of the conversations. I deduced the pride she took in sending new gossip out on the airwaves.

"There have been other ballerinas and this girl won't be the last," she said in a more genuine tone, one that penetrated the clichés, if not the shrewdness. "But he is your husband, and if the two of you are going on, you have to allow for his eccentricities."

"Tell me I didn't just sniff a euphemism."

"You didn't. It was only a dance."

"I'm bored," I said. "Why are we talking?"

"You aren't bored, you're worried. You needn't be. *Everyone's shocked.* Throughout your career people loved and admired you. The audience took to you with warmth and they haven't forgotten.

People still feel this for you. Even these catty women were pulling their punches. You are admired and George knows it."

"What are you saying?"

"Since the Ford Foundation grant, George has a new gravitas. He is aware of it. He wouldn't jeopardize his reputation."

Would I scream? "I have to go," I said. "I can't stand scheming and gossip. My head hurts. I'm getting out of New York. I'm moving permanently to Weston."

"No, don't!" she cried.

"God! I'm not serious! Good-bye!"

Christ! I'd had it. George was a choreographer. He'd made a dance. He had a crush, if you could use the word *crush* for a fifty-nine-year-old without laughing. The object of his crush could dance, and that hurt. But I liked my life. I happened to love this particular fifty-nine-year-old, daft as it was.

I decided I'd go ahead and use Suzanne's cat, Bottom, as Mourka's love interest. What the hell, it even struck me as funny. In the book's large cast of feline characters, Diana's Phink also played a part. The photographer shot Mourka's tricks and adventures in the apartment on our homemade sets. Suzanne had adopted Bottom at George's request. Directing her as Titania in *A Midsummer Night's Dream*, he was bewildered by Suzanne's inability to caress and sweet-talk

Bottom, the donkey Titania falls in love with. "Haven't you cooed to a baby?" he asked her. "A dog? A cat?" Evidently she hadn't, and Bottom the cat was a research project.

Suzanne didn't dance the opening of the New York State Theater in April 1964, Maria did. Life settled down. I stayed the summer in Weston and George came out weekends. He arrived late one Friday night in a foul temper, denouncing a ballerina he had promoted to soloist who didn't listen, fretting over a score. He threw up his hands, telling me that Allegra was pregnant again.

"Any woman can have baby, *I* make her Brigitte Bardot!"

At two o'clock in the morning, knocking back vodka, he slathered an English muffin with an inch of butter and caviar he'd brought from the city, saying he hadn't eaten since dawn.

I suggested that he was working too hard and should stay at the house all week *some* week.

No, no, must teach. These girls, they ran out of breath, they weren't filling the stage Russian-style, and he had to get up early and go into town for a new lawn mower. He didn't trust Eddie to do it alone.

I went to bed, leaving him roiling in the kitchen. In the morning getting my slothful self into motion, I saw that he and Eddie were already gone. They'd watered the flowers and herbs by the house, so I went back inside and chained myself to the desk. It was a small kid's desk I'd set in the corner of our blue bedroom under a calendar marked with black *X*s. Each day, to verify my requisite three hours, I slashed off a square with an *X*. *Mourka: The Autobiography of a Cat* was complete, though it would not be published for several months. I had begun a ballet cookbook. I solicited dancers for recipes and embarked on writing contributor profiles. The yeses kept rolling in and the book had ballooned.

I couldn't focus. I stared out the window at trees, watching the light intensify, dissolving shadowy clots of leaves and bringing forth detail; I considered lunch. The front door sounded and clatter chopped up the silence and in a few minutes turned into Eddie's heavy steps.

He stood in the bedroom doorway paled, the red of his Irish complexion gone. His long arms hung puppetlike, drooping. He pushed at his crew cut with the back of a hand.

"What?"

"I'm taking George to the hospital. He hurt his finger with the new lawn mower. I read the directions, I told him be careful, don't touch anywhere by this hole. We started her up and he put his finger right in."

I found splatters of blood all over the kitchen. I cleaned the counters and floor, frustrated that I hadn't insisted Eddie take me along.

Three hours later they came back. George's whole left pointer finger was bandaged. He had cut off the first joint. His beautiful pianist hands, what had he been thinking?

He wouldn't talk. He sat on the lawn wrapped in a cotton blanket in the summer sun and refused to take any pain pills. He didn't want water or anything else. He didn't want dinner.

"Why don't you come inside and lie down?" I said as the light faded. "It's buggy out here, you'll be eaten alive."

Implacable, he didn't move, alone with his pain and sealed off from me.

At one a.m. he still hadn't come in. Under no circumstances for as long as I had known him had he ever apologized or said he was wrong. His behavior might show he was sorry, but he wouldn't surrender the words. Today felt similar in how he spoke with his silence that he *refused* to explain, if an explanation existed, refused to share his grief, and the grief was so palpable in the yard that it cast a vibration. The humming thickness declared there would be no discussion, no regret or worries expressed, no comfort received.

My opinion was that he hurt himself because he'd been driving himself, but equally because of guilt, being divided between Suzanne and me and therefore careless—he hadn't listened to Eddie. If he had once told me that he knew exactly what he wanted to do in his life, he didn't anymore. And back at home from the hospital he may have felt he didn't deserve my comfort, or I wasn't the one who could soothe him.

I couldn't sleep. I concentrated on the soughing trees I loved, trying to take my mind off the whole awful situation. It wasn't a still night, but they didn't sound the same or I couldn't hear, couldn't concentrate.

He had gathered my trees, stuffed them deep into duffel bags, and carried them off.

In fall, the release of *Mourka* necessitated that I emerge from obscurity and give interviews. *Dance* magazine published an article, "Bright Victory," accompanied by a photo of me in the garden, admiring the daisies. I talked to the *New York Post* and the *Herald Tribune*. Usually I invited the reporters to the apartment. I'd give a tour and serve snacks in the kitchen while I answered questions.

Mourka sat, as he liked to do, in one of the kitchen chairs with the posture of a person, legs splayed, paws resting on his big exposed belly. I would tell how he came to us scrawny but developed a taste for asparagus, potatoes, peas, and sour cream.

As we discussed the polio, since that was what they'd come to hear, I'd get the big question: How had I arrived at my acceptance of no longer dancing?

It's because I was lazy, I said, dancing got harder as you got older. I acknowledged that I wished I'd been left with a limp instead of a wheelchair, described how I exercised daily; if I didn't, my brain didn't work and I felt like a sofa. I said I liked fashion. Before, I couldn't wear anything nice. Going from fittings to rehearsal to performance had been an all-day striptease.

But apart from my effortful levity, what should have been the happy time of *Mourka*'s release was marred by a sense of foreboding. My dread, of course, had begun when I first became aware of George's infatuation with Suzanne at the *Meditation* premiere. That marker in my life had occurred just weeks after President Kennedy was assassinated in November 1963.

The day of his death was cold and gray in New York. George had called home and said to have Carl bring me to the Empire Hotel coffee shop. A group from the office had agreed to commiserate over drinks, and I should be there.

The tenor of the decade, which was up to then in American daily life indecipherable and had seemed a continuation of the fifties, was with Kennedy's murder writ bold: ahead lay years of upheaval and pain. Every American alive at the time was imprinted by the drama of those years. I've thought that George, who was so sensitive to environs—this despite his singular vocation—

was not only imprinted by the events of the sixties but was impelled by them.

George felt that when Bottom the Weaver is transformed into an ass in *A Midsummer Night's Dream*, he experiences a revelation. Bottom reports upon his awakening into our world:

> *The eye of man hath not heard, the ear of man hath not seen, man's hand is not able to taste, his tongue to conceive, nor his heart to report what my dream was.*

He had experienced a reality he could no longer grasp, it was as if he had seen the kingdom of God.

Reality is not here on earth, George liked to say, and yet the earthly entranced him and he hungered hugely for it. It is difficult to describe such a complicated man.

4

*W*ith the genesis of the cookbook the apartment grew festive. A college student I hired tested recipes in the kitchen and I played scullery maid. Dancers brought samples of their concoctions. Others insisted on supervising while I attempted to follow their "easy" instructions for masterpieces that had been in their family since the *Mayflower*. We entertained more because of the excess of edibles, and people who came in the day stayed on through the night. Friends of ours, Arthur Gold and Bobby Fizdale, the piano duo, would play, George was convinced to do one last trick with the cat, and, with our stomachs bursting, we discussed food to our hearts' content.

Dancers are always hungry. Especially the women, who are usually on diets. Laughing uproariously, Maria described a sour Pippin apple she ate once while George ate a plate of spaghetti. Diet or no, the physical nature of our art gives us appetite, and most of us think about food a lot.

Diana usually came afternoons, the winter and spring of 1965, with little Georgina. She was a quietly gurgling baby sporting a shock of exotic blue-black hair. It pained Diana to put Georgina down, but at last the baby slept wedged between pillows and her mother did prep at my side. We discussed the company. Diana was dancing again, although infrequently. All was not well. In company class, George tailored exercises to Suzanne. He'd have Suzanne demonstrate combinations and say to the others, "Do like Suzanne." He took the jumps out of ballets Suzanne danced because she couldn't do them. Natalie had reported that George and Suzanne were often spotted together at Tip Toe Inn—how appropriate—a deli at Seventy-Fourth and Broadway, or at Dunkin' Donuts, wherever that was. Dunkin' Donuts? To my knowledge, until now George had never set foot in the place, hadn't ever eaten a doughnut. For a week it was all I could do not to say to him mornings, "Cruller or glazed?" I was punch-drunk from cooking. Helpful Eddie chaperoned George and Suzanne to keep up appearances.

What did they talk about? Cats, maybe. The Bible. I had heard she was religious. George didn't mention her to me unless she came up in the context of *Don Quixote*, his latest three-act ballet. I'd known of *Don Quixote* since George began working on his version with the composer Nicolas Nabokov the previous summer. I knew Suzanne would dance Dulcinea. I accustomed myself to the idea. What else could I do? George was obsessed. Let him stare at her, I thought, let him listen to her teenaged musings over doughnuts. He had always been interested in the lives of young girls, in their problems, hair, clothes, the aches and pains of their young bodies from what he asked them to do. They were his material. If I felt bothered I parked myself at the typewriter and spun out the biography and culinary background of Alicia Alonso. I'd get on the phone and discuss borscht with Rudolf Nureyev. I revised for my preface the anecdotes illustrating dancers' appetites:

"I took such and such a ballerina out for a late-night snack and it emptied my wallet."

"All I invited were a few of the principals and, my dear, they descended upon the food like a plague of locusts."

It wasn't as if I had nothing to do. It wasn't as if George and I didn't *seem* to have a good life together, we did. Of course, much of his life he lived with his dancers. But the key word here is *dancers,* plural. His exclusive obsession with Suzanne seemed increasingly mad, yet I told myself that if their relationship stayed as it was, I could wait it out.

I was deluded, fixated on making the best of my own life and coping each day with my paralysis and life in a chair—which takes an abundance of hard, cold energy minute by minute only those who endure it can know.

I couldn't control what was happening and I didn't want to believe there was anything near me I couldn't control. Since losing my legs, I couldn't bear it. I couldn't conceive that my life might contain other grief of a comparable magnitude.

The truth was I had *not* gotten over the polio, even as I worked to simply "be me." I could not leave behind what had happened to me, as George preached in all his behavior that people should, and I was sometimes convinced that this was why he didn't love me.

Even when his finger had been heavily bandaged, he went about his life as if the accident had been nothing. For him, I think, the bandage was sort of a badge of honor. For me, it was a constant reminder of his duplicity.

My mind couldn't grasp what might come. If I entertained the thought that there existed a real possibility he would cast me aside, that I'd be *an abandoned woman,* me and the chair—well, that made it worse, so pathetic—I became furious. I did not want to play another role I hadn't chosen. I hated his power, that he could do this to me if he wanted to.

In my mind's eye I was still the beautiful girl on the Cape in the summers. Mother gave tea parties and the girls wore white gloves and all of the boys in the neighborhood were in love with me.

I'd wonder searchingly why George could not see this too. Such was my arrogance and my hubris.

He announced that for the gala premiere of *Don Quixote* he would himself play the Don. I was about to show him the dress I bought for the premiere, a swirl of white silk I alighted on in the pages of *Elle*, when he said nonchalantly, "You know, Mayor Lindsay will be there tomorrow. Suzanne and I will sit with him at his table." He took the box out of the bag.

"Give me the dress," I said.

"I didn't see it yet," he answered as if the earth

hadn't tilted and fallen off its axis. The solid room heaved. That was the nature of the experience, coming to me like labor, like birth.

"Give me the dress." He handed it over. I wheeled back into the bedroom closet and put the box on a shelf.

He did his version of babbling. "This is what he will like, the mayor, to sit with the stars."

That was not how it worked. I quietly shut the closet and said, "George, if I am not there at your table tomorrow, I won't be here."

"Here? In the apartment?" he said.

"Yes."

"Well, we are sitting with the mayor at his table. Suzanne and I," and he left the room and went to work.

He thought I was bluffing. Eddie called later to tell me that I would sit at a table with Mother, Jerry, Diana, and Natalie.

"No, Eddie, I won't."

George and I didn't speak that night and continued cold war the next morning. After he huffed off, I loitered around the apartment, finally made plans, and packed a small suitcase. I called Carl, giving him the bare facts, but by the time he came for me at six he must have heard more, because he looked crestfallen. Carl was considerate; Carl cared for me.

We silently rode to the threadbare midtown hotel I had located, one with wide doorways for the chair. I had so hoped for an upper room in the Empire Hotel, where I could gaze haughtily down at the theater out of my righteousness.

My midtown refuge stank of old carpet and bleach. I'd stayed in worse.

"Go ahead," I said to Carl. "I'm fine." With calls to make, I was anxious for him to leave.

Carl had unusual down-sloping blue eyes, and they were moist. "Do you know we took adagio class together?" he said. "Do you remember?"

"Sure." I picked up the room service menu, wanting to concentrate on what was tangible, dinner.

"It was a long time ago," Carl said. "We were teenagers."

I put down the menu. This seemed important to him. "Why don't you sit down, Carl."

He sat, mournfully. His whole bulk said mournful. For god's sake, he wasn't cheering me up. Carl hadn't danced long. I realized I knew very little about him. He had told me he lived with his mother in Germantown on the Upper East Side. His hair was always carefully combed, I thought. Such thick blond hair—why did he live with his mother?

"You were already performing," he continued. "I wasn't that good. But I was strong and they praised me for that. We got paired for a couple sessions and I thought you were great. I mean, a great dancer and a nice person."

"Thank you, Carl." I was a self-involved person. I'd seen him practically every day for years and it hadn't occurred to me to ask him a thing about his dancing. "Know what I remember?" I said. "Your striped jersey. It was nice, violet and blue."

"Yeah," and he laughed. "I didn't wear it every day, but it was my favorite."

"You weren't so . . . big then. What got you started on weight lifting?"

"I was sick as a kid. They thought I'd die. The dancing was therapy too, intended to build me up. I've still got . . . a heart. A small problem."

"And you carry *me?*"

"Oh, it's beneficial. I've been assured."

"Well, I'm glad."

He stood. "I'll go. Call me." I watched his broad back go to the door.

I didn't make any calls. Let my absence linger in everyone's mind and leave my whereabouts a mystery. I had warned Carl to keep this to himself.

Not that George would care tonight. He might tomorrow. I took a bath and drank too much wine and ate my terrible dinner.

In the morning I decided to go stay with Mother. This flophouse might be dramatic but I couldn't take it and maintain any measure of equanimity for more than a night. Mother's apartment on

Riverside Drive had fairly wide doorways and a decent elevator to travel up on.

"Tanaquil," she said when I called, *"where have you been?"*

"On the lam. I'll be over in a while."

"I tried to give him a piece of my mind, but Natalie wouldn't let me."

"We'll talk," and I hung up the phone.

Natalie said Mother had been about to march up to George at the head table with Suzanne and the mayor and say, "Mr. Balanchine, where is your wife?" On top of the ballet itself and my empty seat in the audience, the gala was the last straw for my ma. Natalie and Diana took her home.

"Did my seat at the theater stay empty?" I asked Natalie.

"Yes, being right next to Jerry's, it glared."

"Oh, goody," I said. High drama. "Did you go back to the party?" I asked, imagining George and Suzanne on the dance floor. But Natalie said they didn't want to. Nor would she say much about the ballet. Suzanne was all right; George was all right; it was a long dark ballet. The balletomanes were thrilled George was dancing.

It wasn't real dancing, it was more acting and mime, but he was almost always onstage and the part was demanding.

Diana said she wished she had sat farther back. His chest heaved at the end of his scenes. Suzanne washed his feet with her hair and he crawled on his knees to her. Like Natalie, Diana could not be objective. Nobody, including Jerry, who barely said anything, wanted to see it again.

Man of La Mancha was on Broadway that year and people associated "The Impossible Dream" with the assassination of the young president, the death of his Camelot. Emotion was blatant, full-blown throughout the culture, things bigger than life were going on in life—life was opera. Nothing seemed to be left of the fifties "cool," of abstraction, of hip. And here was the neoclassical master with his long, maudlin, grasping ballet. Well, that was a definite aspect of him too. I could just hear the reviews, but thinking of them didn't offer much solace.

Mother was in bed getting over a migraine. Why hadn't I warned her? Why hadn't I said I was leaving him? There were instances, and that morning was one, when I thought the Suzanne debacle threw Mother more than it did me. I made us hot chocolate, and the scent of it mingling with Mother's orange-blossom soap filled the darkened bedroom with sweetness and calm. As comforting was her shredding bed jacket, the yellowing thinning lace dropping away, the maroon satin ground of the jacket remaining intact and brilliant. She was always there. People needed continuity. I loved her so. Sitting by Mother's bedside, I experienced gusts of sentimental Victorian longing. Ordinarily I didn't like coming to Mother's apartment. It bulged with shrines to my career: grouped portraits and framed reviews, scrapbooks, a trunk of old costumes. But I was able to get around here more easily than at the hotel. After the polio, Mother got rid of the rugs.

"She isn't a *cultural companion* for him," Mother said on a groan.

I didn't say I hardly thought that mattered.

"Whatever you do, don't give him a divorce. You have a position, and you'll have a position when he dies."

"George isn't dying, Mother."

"No, but he will." I looked daggers at her, less upset by the thought of his death than by her self-interest. Then I softened: she was trying to protect me. Oh, god, I had begun to understand Mother's reasoning. I opened the drapes and told her I wanted to look at the water and listen to music; I'd unpack later. Sighing, shaking and nodding her head as if to a continuing voice of displeasure and counsel inside, Mother took out her knitting. I switched on WQXR and pushed myself out of the wheelchair and into the floral easy chair by the marble-topped table at the window.

One of those cold spring days: the river was gray. The trees had begun to dress in their spring clothes, but the cool light darkened the greenery, made it muddy-toned prematurely, as it would be in August from heat and exhaust. Baroque choral music, a solo countertenor; that rare kind of voice thrilled me, the sound of such high purity and still a man's, it vaulted nature. I didn't know how I had borne my self-imposed lack of music in Copenhagen. I'd listened to drips from the faucet, a distant plane, the buzzing of a lamp. Sounds of the world I had never been quiet enough to hear. They tormented me. On other days they were their own kind of music. Tiny tap-tap of a pigeon's beak outside my window and the answering tap of my fingernail on the metal bed when nothing else but my finger could move— the shift of my eyes when they were all that was left to me of kinetic expression. How nice it had been, I thought, to dance to music I'd especially loved—the Chausson violin piece *Poème* that Antony Tudor used for *Lilac Garden* was like cut glass, or Shalimar perfume.

She's been through nothing and that's why he wants her. But that couldn't be true, I thought. Nobody had been through nothing.

He called as Mother and I started lunch. Mother conveyed that he would like to see me. I closed my eyes—*go away*. But I relented, finished lunch, laboriously made a trip to the bathroom— it was more difficult here. My eyes leaped out of my face, they shone so brightly in the bathroom mirror. Red patches lit up my cheeks. I looked spectacular, as if in queenly defiance I were about

203

to go to the block. I brushed my hair and went out to the living room.

He wore the tweed jacket and brown slacks we had picked out together. These days he liked string ties and snap-button shirts, but how attractive he looked in a jacket. I felt my entirety reaching for him, almost as I had at the beginning of our relationship, and, infuriated, I compressed myself, watching him sternly.

He glanced at the living room view, the gray continuing river, and sat, turning the chair, a Queen Anne, to face me in my chair, the wheeled.

"Come home," he said.

I had been nearly convinced it was finished, that this was the point at which we would part. He suffered, was torn, but one didn't do what he had and request compassion. His dark eyes glistened with the excitement of staying out with her until midnight celebrating their performance—I knew.

"You belong home," he said.

"Why?" My eyes said, you betray me in private, in public—tell me you're not in love with Suzanne. Yet I didn't say the words, hoping the truth would still go away.

He rubbed his chin; the finger still seeped under the Band-Aids. "Tanny, we've been through too much," he said. "You married a man who makes dances, but I'm not going anywhere."

I didn't want to go home with him; I did. I wanted to be in my own apartment. I was confused.

The station wagon and Carl were downstairs on the street. Obviously my agreement was a foregone conclusion.

Five dozen yellow roses glittered the lobby at home. Second time, same note, and a note from the theater saying they'd been delivered the night before. George glanced over my shoulder and saw, *To Tanaquil, the sublime, ballerina assoluta forever.*

It seemed to annoy him; I intuited that it wasn't at all how he wished to see me.

I spent the summer and well into the following autumn in Weston. George came out when he could, for a few weekends. He was in Europe on tour; he was staging his ballets for other companies; he needed to be in New York; he was on fire with ambition for the enterprise. He was in love with Suzanne. The first stop on tour was Paris, and I imagined her receiving the Continental education, walks along the Seine, lessons in food and wine. If she wasn't a cultural companion for him he could make her one. He'd buy her perfume, jewelry, clothing, and shoes.

They were in Paris dancing while I was in the country writing about dance. The recipe part of the cookbook was done, but the contributor portraits and other connective tissue were taking forever. Father came out for a visit and I told him that masochists wrote books, now I at last understood him. Still, I worked at my kid's desk in the blue bedroom and Father worked on his Rabelais at the table outside, since the weather was fine—I didn't have Father's powers of concentration and would have been endlessly distracted.

I thought it sad that Father hadn't remarried, nor did he have any lady friend I had heard of. "I'm too selfish," he said. "I have my habits and routines, I like to work. I like my wine." He was not doing badly, didn't start before late afternoon. He had quit drinking for several years. I thought the wine had to do with the melancholy of his aloneness, chosen or not.

"Your mother was born forty," he told me. "Inside, I'm a lad. My expectations are unrealistic, so I live in books."

"Books don't hurt other people," I said.

"Don't be so sure."

Try as I might to stay off the subject of George, he colored my conversation, my point of view. George was on Father's mind too, but he only spoke out at the end of the visit, as we waited for a taxi to take him to the train.

On lawn chairs, my lovely father in his beige linen suit, leather bag and typewriter case in the driveway, Panama hat in his lap. He was born in 1899, and men of his generation dressed to travel. "I'm not taking it well," he said. "It isn't what I wanted for you, a troubled marriage. I feared it in the beginning. I hope your mother's more optimistic outlook wins out in the end, if that is what you want."

"Thank you, Papa."

"It shouldn't have been like this, it really *shouldn't*." I saw him correct himself, an emotional man, but one who also employed a good deal of control.

"I'd already had enough," I said, "with the polio."

He turned fully to me. "That wasn't my meaning. The polio hasn't anything to do with it!" He sat back, thinking. "How shall I say it? When I saw you, from the first day, I wanted everything for you—just an astonishment of joy. You'd be the finest, the most exemplary dancer, had I been able to know your abilities then." He looked at me: "And so it was. But I would have wanted you fleet into deep old age, a sprightly old lady jumping higher than . . . trees." He waved his hand at them and I laughed. "Your beauty wouldn't wane, how could it? *But*—it was your soul men would love. They would cleave to you." He smiled. "I should write a poem about it, extemporaneous speech is useless.

"You've been a blessing to me," he said. "You taught me to love someone more than myself. All men should have children. It's an unrecorded fact that men need to have children more than women do."

After Father, others came in George's absence. I liked the diversion, but I preferred being alone, in the eye of the storm. The parts of days I wasn't toiling away on the damn book, I enjoyed the peace of summer and Weston. I'd fervently wish that *I* were in Europe again, not to be with my husband or out of a dancing fantasy, but to be again in the beautiful places I'd thought, at twenty-seven, I would return to repeatedly. Then the simplicity of my house and yard would strike me, strike out the wish, and I'd be in Weston totally, calm and alert. I felt as I had mornings alone in the studio as a young dancer: fresh, quietly purposeful, flush with the light streaming in. A good neighbor brought me the *Times* in the morning and groceries if I asked. I could tell hours by the scent of the garden. Each month had its character, which I'd never noticed as fully before. With September came commotions of birds. First a blast of crows that could have been shot out of a cannon funneled over and into a copse of trees, cawing. One group scattered off from the flapping black core but got quickly pulled back, as if on a string. They were a tumult trying to arrange itself, maybe within the trees to rest. Then came the loud honking Vs of geese, and one day late in the month as I sat at my desk the sky shouted with such congregations I felt for a moment frightened—I had seen Hitchcock's

The Birds—and I sneaked cautiously outside. Beyond our driveway at the crest of a rise stood a long line of trees, and the thousand-member chorus of birds cried from inside the leafy tops: flashes of wings and tails hovered and flapped with the flickering busyness of a silent movie, heralding autumn.

Natalie came out and said I was hiding in Weston. I wasn't hiding; I kept up. I'd seen the *Life* magazine cover of Suzanne and George in *Don Quixote.*

Natalie challenged me: What happy things could I do?

Go blond, I said, and I did, in New York.

Go to Europe, as I had once planned, and I decided I would as soon as the book was finished.

She didn't have to say that with George coming home soon for the fall season I needed to close up the house and face what I had chosen; either I'd gone back to him or I hadn't.

Maria called soon as I returned, saying she wanted to see me. She came to the apartment in a navy-blue Dior suit.

"You look exquisite," I said as we kissed.

"Tanny, you're blond."

"What do you think?"

"Luscious, *very* Monroe."

We retired to the parlor, Maria on the elaborate slate-blue western couch, her navy set off to stellar effect. She wore her black hair back in a silver clip; her high cheekbones blushed with coral rouge, matching her lipstick. We caught up on subjects easy to talk about. She told me how much her daughter looked forward to Halloween. Maria had also wanted a baby and finally got one. The annulment of her marriage to George provoked headlines that read, "No Papooses," ostensibly the reason for the breakup. I'd never felt guilty about seeing George while they were still married. I did now. I told her, and she brushed it off.

"I wanted that baby," she said, "and a different type of man. You were young. So was I, and marrying George, I didn't know what I wanted." She paused, figuring out how to tell me what she'd come to say. We shared allegiance to George—he was friendly with all his ex-wives—as a choreographer and a teacher, and a person as well; his values were basically ours, and to address the area in which they weren't, or where our patience stopped short, was unpleasant.

"I'm leaving the company," Maria said. "I wanted to tell you before the announcement. Nobody dances but Suzanne. Maybe it's time for me to retire anyway, but—"

"That should be your decision," I cut in.

"Yes, exactly. But I was going to say that others might leave. He's about to lose good young dancers because they can't develop; he gives them nothing. I've never seen him like this."

"Over anyone."

"No." She lowered her eyes. "May I be frank?" she said, looking up. "When you got sick and he was planning the next season around you, you were *ready*. You could always dance, you were like a little jewel." She touched my hand, smiling her charming and natural smile that issued forth all that was exceptional in her. "But by *The Nutcracker*, the *technique* you had by then made you even better than I thought you would be." Her eyes misted. "Remember? The applause wouldn't stop the first night. I just shook. I was afraid to go out after you!"

"Maria, your Sugarplum Fairy was a triumph. You torched the stage."

"Thank you." She rushed on, "This girl isn't ready. He's giving her every kind of role in the repertoire and she doesn't have the range you did."

"I couldn't do every role either."

"Nor could I." Maria was a great ballerina. When she danced *Firebird* and hit the *triple à la seconde* on opening night I stood with the crowd backstage beating my fists in the air and silently screaming. She was generous too, giving the fledgling me helpful advice. Now she confirmed that no one was helping Suzanne: "She's despised," Maria said. "She sits in the canteen alone. I've yet to see her with anyone"—she didn't say except George—"in the hallways." My sympathy for Suzanne had dried up. Small price to pay, I thought.

"I shouldn't have come," Maria said.

"No," I answered soberly. "I'm not made of glass, and whatever you've told me I'll hear eventually." I stopped talking there.

"I miss you," she said. Her home was in Chicago. "Let's have lunch next time I'm here."

I saw her off and sat thinking. It is *my* company, he'd say if pushed, and if ten ballerinas left, he'd get ten more. I was furthermore tired of people's idealization of me. Little jewel indeed, as if I were valiantly dying. I thought of the yellow roses—it had happened again, five dozen more—and decided I didn't like them; I was not yet embalmed.

Maria's official statement in *Newsweek* magazine added a bit of welcome hilarity into the farce: "I don't mind being listed alphabetically, but I do mind being treated alphabetically."

Other dancers left, still young ballerinas of my generation and a few of the newer, promising principals. In an interview with columnist Earl Wilson, George said, "As long as I am alive, as long as I can work I will always have new dances for Suzanne." The company was in crisis. Word was Suzanne's dressing room was a hothouse with flowers from George. "Farrell is not only the alpha but the omega of his young ballerinas," wrote *Newsweek*. "The exquisite Farrell is the latest in a forty-year series of Galateas that include Danilova, Geva, Zorina, Tallchief and Tanaquil Le Clercq."

Suzanne danced twenty-eight ballets that fall, and the *Quixote* photographs were omnipresent. George didn't like having his picture taken, but whenever requested he squeezed on the skullcap and wig, glued on the beard, struggled into the tights, the gold-buckled shoes, the armor. Nothing was too much to spotlight his star, and to disperse into the atmosphere what he felt for her and the imperative of their collaboration—as if she also needed convincing.

I heard rumors that she was unhappy. People witnessed signs of discontent—tears, a bad attitude—in rehearsals. Outside the theater Eddie guarded her, took her to dinner if George was unavailable. Young she may have been, but I'd heard she was proud. Natalie said she resented excessive control.

The age difference had to be a factor. It had been substantial going back to Maria; now it was extreme. *Of course* she would adore him in the dance with the attention he lavished on her and the enormity of his knowledge in the art to which she had devoted herself. But how would she fare with his friends? His most abiding relationships were with the Russians, people of around George's age and with parallel paths. They would make her feel stupid and ornamental, a green girl at the end of his highly publicized chain of muses. And given her youth, did she possess the ability to see the great Mr. B as real, as a person—moreover, a man as he wished to be seen? Try as I might, I could not grasp his willingness to ignore the obvious drawbacks. Was he blinded by his own power? Was it as simple as that? Deep and unspoiled as he was in many ways, perhaps it occluded what reason remained.

I heard that one of the young ballerinas who eventually left confronted him, got him up against the wall in a passageway at the theater and demanded an explanation for why he hadn't cast her in a ballet she very much wanted.

I could see it. She was a broad-shouldered girl, taller than George. She must have known he abhorred being challenged, that formal distance was gospel to him. At the end of her rope, she might have been goaded along by a whole pack of girls.

"Well?" she said. "I want an explanation. Why wasn't I cast?"

The expression on his face changed. He didn't like to be pushed, but *if* pushed he dug in his heels: his mouth set.

They were formidable opponents, she brilliant in her youth, size, and audacity, he in his absolute faith that he always knew best.

"You want to know?"

"Yes." She kept him locked in place with her arm cage.

"I don't like how you look in a tutu."

This took some wind from her sails. "I'm in lots of tutu ballets," she protested, "what about those?"

"Oh, those, well, I overlook tutu because you have strength to knock over buildings and that's what I needed in those."

"I'm not the only one," she said somewhat less boldly, "who's unhappy. You ignore us, in favor of one I won't name."

"I am entitled to love." Flinty-eyed.

And out of her hurt she replied tenderly, hoping that he might hear this because it was wondrous and important how much his dancers sincerely loved him, "You should love all eighty of us."

The love part of the exchange I didn't hear for some time. Nobody would report it to me.

Meanwhile, back at the ranch, I was livid. So one night at dinner I said, "Why don't you *do* something? You know, George, I hear things. I even see things."

"I'm here, aren't I?" he answered.

"Oh, super, *thank* you." I slammed down my fork. He proceeded to eat. I guzzled wine. "You want me to say it, is that it?" I said. "You don't want to be the one? Kick me out. Go on. Coward."

I sat at one end of our long dining table and he at the other. My end was kept open so I could pull up in the chair. Quietly, he set down his utensils with a nod of regret at his plate of perfectly nice warm food that would now become cold. He scraped out from the table, came and sat in the chair to my right, pulling it close, facing me, and repeated the word "Coward," as if I were the coward, then said it again: "Coward," as if he were saying he loved me. Then softly and, strangely, without a hint of mockery he kissed me full on the lips. I laughed, *with* mockery, and he grabbed my hand.

"Tanny . . ." It was a warning.

"What? Let go of my hand." He did. He returned to his dinner. He finished, complimented the moist lamb, patted napkin to mouth, and said, "I'm going out."

Ordinarily he was just gone, he saw Suzanne after rehearsals and performances and on tour. Their affair was tucked into his professional life and didn't obviously impinge on his life with me. I hadn't been put in the position to ask "where" before.

"Where?" I said. Just a spark in his eye, and he left.

I had to make ten calls to locate Jerry in a nightclub. I'd planned to pour out my heart on the phone, but he said he'd come over.

It was a black night in December, nearing the

shortest day of the year. The cat and I watched for his car to come through the guard's gate I could see from the kitchen window overlooking the courtyard.

He wore a festive, fashionable coat with a fluffy fur collar and, as I exclaimed, "Bell-bottoms!"

"Yeah, baby!"

"Groovy." We sat on the couch and smoked cigarettes. "Were you having a good time?"

"Not really."

"Do you take drugs?"

"No." Then I put my head on his chest and cried. I got hold of myself and talked it all out.

"You can't go on like this, Tan," he said. "Ask him to leave."

"How pat," I answered. "As if that would solve everything."

"Wouldn't it?"

"God. It would be just the beginning of—" worse complications and pain. I couldn't conceive of anyone actually leaving. "If I could only see what is really going on," I said. "How can I fight what I can't see?"

"I think you see pretty well," Jerry said.

"Listen, go back to your party."

"Tan . . ." Pity any outsider who gets involved in marital discord, and Jerry could not know the density, the thickness of marriage. The death of a marriage wouldn't be as traumatic if it simply died. The process was long and arduous like a real death. Would that all of us just went to sleep and expired, but we have these bodies. And marriages too are made out of matter, are knotty rugged things crammed with bank accounts, furniture, houses, and cars, and the links of time that bound you into a sort of two-headed creature. In our case there were also the dances and the polio, which seemed to be *the* problem, or *a* problem, but was really the best part of us, the nights he sat at my bedside to help me get through. Even his past felt like mine, I was practically Russian! I felt I knew places I'd never been and people dead before I was alive. I felt I knew his mother as a young woman, in the tall beaded crown she wore on the day of his christening with its white ribbons that trailed to the ground and her pearls big as grapes in the picture George kept of the two of them under his handkerchiefs in his top bureau drawer. The baby in the elaborate bonnet stared straight at the camera. By god, he was undeniably present right from the start. His mother, I thought, looked depressed.

In the morning I knew I had to take action. I settled on a plan and the perfect setting in which to play it out. I bathed, dressed beautifully in my camel-hair sweater and skirt and loads of gold jewelry, and called Carl. When Carl arrived I called Eddie; hearing his voice, I hung up. He'd tell. I called Natalie, and a few minutes later she called back and told me that George was in his office. He had his lunch in there, so far uneaten, and would probably be in there for a while.

His office was fine. I'd been prepared to confront him in a rehearsal. People would love that. They would be grateful to me for weeks. Too bad; another time, maybe, or I hoped not.

Nice to be out, nice to be down in the good grubby streets of New York, trash blowing over the sidewalks, people shoving for space, terrible drivers in terrible moods. Carl slammed on the brakes. I caught myself from hitting the windshield with my hand.

"What was *that?*" I asked.

"Sorry," Carl said. "Psychotic cabbie."

At Lincoln Center we glided into the underground parking garage and up in the commodious elevator. Oh, how I loved modernity. We handicapped were about to become the disabled, soon ramps, bathroom stalls, and parking places would sprout for us everywhere.

Carl served as my escort. I didn't want to waste energy wheeling myself. I looked so much cooler just sitting. Carl knew where to go. I hadn't visited George's new office, why was that? Afraid of what I might find?

He had the door shut. I tapped. His nasal voice rang out, "Yes, yes, what is it?" I opened the door. "Wait in the hall for me, Carl." I entered, leaving the door gaping wide.

He was on the phone, flabbergasted.

"I'll wait," I said sweetly. Same furniture from City Center set off by a dazzling view. I went to the windows overlooking the plaza, across which he could see the theater he had built.

"It's lovely," I said, turning to him. "Hello, dear!"

"You should have called. I'm very busy."

"No, we're doing a scene like in the movies today, George. Neglected wife shows up at wandering husband's office and he must reckon with her at last."

"Tanny, don't play games." He hadn't stood up from his desk and appeared vaguely ill.

"Why not? You know, it really *is* nice here. I should come more often. I feel more myself here. I'll do that, I'll stop keeping my distance, would you like that?"

"Oh, how should I know," he said despondently. Then he noticed the open door and rushed to shut it.

"Thanks, I forgot. Now we can talk."

His face went stormy like Heathcliff's, but I was Cathy. "Enough's enough," I told him lightly. "I want it to stop."

"What to stop?"

"Oh, I thought I wasn't, but I'm very tired," I said. "May I ask you a question? Is there any possibility she doesn't want you as you want her?" Although he attempted to cover it, I saw the angry flash of masculine pride, delicate as a Fabergé egg. I hadn't the strength to take out my white curator's gloves.

"I figure it has to be that," I continued, "or it's that you love me, or it's obligation. But you aren't good at doing things you don't want to do." I could have gone on. I could have said, do you know you're acting like an ass? This is what you use your success for, to regress? In the *Life* magazine article about *Quixote* he had sketched out his philosophy of the dance and life. The dance part made sense as far as it went, defining ballet as an elevation of Woman. Unlike Frederick Ashton, who emphasized men, George was the choreographer of ballerinas. So far, so good, except then it got fuzzy, blurred into life with the comment, "Everything a man does, he does for his ideal woman. People have to have something to believe in, and I believe in a little thing like that."

The foremost choreographer in the Western Hemisphere, was he aware he sounded adolescent?

But I couldn't point out that it was beneath him. Though he was wise about so many things, this he would not understand. He would just feel demeaned, as he had demeaned me. What a mess. He was trying to have his way, as he always had his way, and at the same time not hurt me.

I'd said what I'd come to say. I was ready to lose him if need be. "It has to stop," I said once more. "And find me some new dancer to coach, will you? I'm bored. Carl!"

I opened the door and Carl wheeled me away.

He accepted my ultimatum. I didn't assume that he would stop seeing her completely apart from work, but he certainly saw her much less. I worried that I hadn't taken the best course of action, thinking maybe he just feared further scenes. But after that day, he seemed *relieved,* as if he'd been away and was so pleased to be home where he could relax and, oh, my goodness, what a surprise, there's my wife!

I'm sure he felt boundlessly grateful that I hadn't said too much too overtly; possibly we could halt the whole thing right here.

I saw him build bridges over what he had done and whom he had wanted—still wanted, I couldn't stop feeling. He brought me boxes of candy in the evenings because I'd lost weight, bought me rabbit-lined gloves because my hands were colder than ever, came home in the middle of the day as he had once done to fix me lunch, though I told him I was happy to fix it myself.

I was still grinding away at the cookbook, finishing endless little tasks, planning the layout of photographs within the text. Seeing me sometimes fed up, he decided to help me. He decided to come in and confiscate the project.

He pored over the manuscript with a red pencil

and pronounced that I had written a light, readable portrait of the international dance world, how ingenious of me. But, dear, so-and-so lied describing her family home, it wasn't a villa in Bath but a tiny bedsit in Chelsea, and the other one never did dance *Giselle* except in a student production, and I should call Jerry and tell him that his spinach with pine nuts wasn't tasty and could we replace it with his roasted turkey? *And* if we used too many photos the book would look like a scrapbook and not a cookbook and we'd risk shooting ourselves in the feet, ending up with a beast that was neither fish nor fowl, so to speak. It reminded me of my student days, when he would show up for a day or two and teach class, upset everybody, and leave—that sort of thing. I told him to back off my book.

I went ahead with my trip to Europe, traveling with Natalie, her two college-aged daughters, and Carl to England and France, bearing a long list from George of what to bring back, special condiments and tinned foodstuffs he couldn't get in the States. The trip was rather a comedy of errors. Carl and I ended up sitting out lots of sights I couldn't navigate in parking lots and restaurants. But I liked even the parking lots, with the foreign signs and people going the wrong way. I liked simply sitting on another continent, after the polio and without George's orchestration.

When I got home it was June, and we drove to Saratoga Springs in upstate New York for the ballet's summer season. The weather was perfect. We sat on the grass by our cottage in the afternoons and late nights with friends. Suzanne danced, but we didn't see her outside of the theater. I felt light and vibrant.

One night an acquaintance of George's named Jack Hooper and his wife, Mary, stopped by for nightcaps, and with animation partly induced by Calvados, I described the earliest costumes for *The Four Temperaments*. The ballet fused classical steps with an angular style and was one of my favorites. It was created out of the medieval belief that people are made up of four different humors that determine their personalities. I had originated the role of Choleric. They called me Le Choleric.

"Those costumes were miseries," I said. "I had this *immense* nylon wig that came down to about my rear end. On top it had a pompadour with a white horn in the middle like a unicorn's." I turned to George sitting beside me, butted him in the shoulder, and said, "That's my horn." To the others I said, "And the horn made it nearly impossible to do most of what my sweetie over here had made for me to do. If I swung my arm too close to my head, there was this horn. I had these breastplates and when I crossed my arms they'd go clunk." My wrist hit George's chest.

"Then there were these miniature red wings all down my arms ending up in enclosed fingers. Not even gloves—no fingers at all, not a thumb! It made it very hard to give your hand. You're doing arabesque promenade, they grab for something, and they don't know what they've got—it's just a big clomp of material.

"George finally cut the costumes, and I remember thinking he saved me." Now he was smiling. "But the premiere . . . I was so young! And it felt impossibly claustrophobic in that getup and I started to cry."

"Oh, yes, the *tears*," George said.

"He told me a thousand times," I said, "I could not be emotional if I wanted to dance."

"But she was anyway," George said, and shrugged like, what can you do?

"Well, you were trapped! If you got something in your eye or you wanted to unzip to get out, you couldn't. And George came over, remember?" I asked him. He nodded. "He cut this slit on the inside palm so I could put my index finger out, and I felt much better."

Jack, also loaded on Calvados, laughed, we all laughed, and then Jack made a bit of an inappropriate remark. I didn't care because I felt good and people often inadvertently said things to me that were inappropriate. I was used to it.

Jack, this tall jovial fellow who adored socializing with dancers and had seen me in everything and was a fan, beamed and said, "You're nothing like—forgive me, but—your energy and fun, it's—oh, what a wonderful story. . . ." He trailed off.

"I'm nothing like a person in a wheelchair?" I said.

Jack's wife, Mary, shot him a scathing glance and put her head down.

"No, I just meant—oh, why can't I say it?" he said to Mary. "I admire your vivacity," he said. "And I admire it more given your limitation."

"Well, it *is* a limitation, that's true." I wasn't upset, though I must say I enjoyed his squirming a little. But why not say it? Wasn't it as bad to pretend the chair was unmentionable, invisible, didn't sit blatantly in its undeniable mechanistic nature right in the room—or on the grass, in this instance?

"Yes!" George chimed in. "It is extraordinary, isn't it? Isn't she?" We looked at each other, the light in his eyes a balm—and I remember there was this unusual blue glass light fixture above our cottage door that tinted the grass, turned it to plastic excelsior in an Easter basket. "I've noticed it many times," George said. "You stop seeing the chair."

Those last five words, their weight and the meanings they implied.

Never mind; it was our Indian summer.

5

When I lived over the liquor store as a very young dancer, I was engaged to a composer named Richard, the nephew of a friend of Father's, a few years older than I was, enough so he seemed a man and not childish as the others I'd gone out with had—good-looking too, with big white teeth and bosky, coppery hair smelling of cedar. He had his own apartment in the Village—wildly impressive. We'd neck and pet on his bachelor bed and drive each other mad, rolling away if we got too heated and lying apart so our hearts would stop pounding, and Richard would do multiplication tables in his head and calm down.

I'd watch a redbrick wall through the window. Closing my eyes, I can see it again and it's sex, excitement, and that huge youthful sense of the most fundamental things being shadowy and mysterious. For me the mystery was especially so, since I'd been different from a young age, committed to dance, out of school a lot until I quit at thirteen. Near the ballet school on Madison Avenue in those days was a deli called Sammy's. They had a Balanchine sandwich that was *very* expensive, and on occasions I splurged and split one with a girlfriend, I thought it the height of worldliness, eating the Balanchine sandwich at Sammy's.

One night at Richard's, we'd rolled away from each other and were hanging off our respective sides of the bed panting as if we had just run a marathon. I was nineteen, I'd begun seeing George, and it came into my head that my virginity was a liability I should dispense with, pronto. I rolled back to Richard and after the deed was done and I was thoroughly disappointed, because as usual the first time wasn't swell, Richard tipped my face toward his and gazed at me with such powerful gratitude and joy that his eyes were searchlights, leveling on me their immensity and wattage. But he didn't register my disappointment. He was too subjectively agog.

Women like sex, but what sex means to men and what they do with it, ideologically and sentimentally, goes way beyond how we perceive it.

I had a pretty good idea Richard and I were finished. My objective in losing my virginity that night was prompted by the notion that I couldn't proceed with George if I was a virgin.

I suppose I used Richard. I didn't intend to. I didn't think I mattered that much to him as an individual, and I didn't love him. Compared to what I felt for George there had been little there.

Funny, then, how George was surprised that I wasn't a virgin our first time together, and I had only done it that once before George and brought no experience to it—and it didn't matter of course because we were in love.

We had been working alone in the studio after rehearsal for hours, late into the evening, and in the hallway, I agreed to show him my apartment. We went outside to snow, unexpected and heavy, white rushing against a dark purple sky. He chattered gaily, and I was suddenly, thoroughly altered from how I had felt in the studio. I thought, Shut up, shut up—don't be so happy! I couldn't stop smelling myself. I'm sure he stank too, he had worked like an ox, but he didn't care and I did, and anyway, in the studio sweat fit.

In the vestibule he brushed off a snow cape, and, shaking myself, I turned to him and saw, for an instant, snow on his eyelashes.

Two were too many going up the narrow stairs. He pushed behind me, past the door, and into my apartment: a wee shabby place, jejune, a word I'd just learned from some book, and intimate? God. We might as well have walked into a mouth. On the minuscule kitchen table in my one room reeked an open box of Loft's Nut Butter Crunch, and for god's sake Mother had put my Charles Boyer doll on the bed when she had last visited, thinking I'd like it, and I hadn't buried him in a drawer, and there—on the stained counter beside dirty dishes I'd left my hairbrush, sprouting hair. Seeing it, I felt so sad.

He sat on my couch, the one adult impressive

item but stupidly red like a tongue, in his wet trench coat it hadn't occurred to me to take, but not before a quick conclusive scan of the premises, during which, I was sure, he'd seen everything, even my messy closet, and asked me, "Sit down?"

Loud, very loud, I sat miserably down about a foot away from him, still in my coat.

"Is your first apartment," he said. "Very special." Oh, sure—the thick rental apartment paint on the door hinges, the battered trunk I used as a coffee table. "You know?" he said. "I told you about the cold and being hungry after the war. Water froze pipes and they burst. Ice floated in sinks. Once, I was with boy who stole fish. He grabbed, we ran, fish started to flop in his shirt. Caught, we could have been shot. Other times, we had to walk close to buildings not to get hit from stray bullets. . . . But it wasn't always too bad. When I joined Mariinsky, salaries were so low we formed concert troupes to make money for food. People sang, played violin, and we danced. We played resort Pavlovsk, in Tsarskoe Selo, Tsar's Village, Soviet times, so we lived in abandoned mansion of Youssoupoff prince. We set up beds and lived together, like . . . playing house. There was ballroom with mirror where we practiced dancing, and grand falling-down garden. Boys and girls fell in love.

"Well, I'll go."

He got up and I found my manners. "May I take your coat?"

He caught my hand in both of his—and my body as liability and trap dissolved, the room faded away. In its place calm, then rightness, then bliss.

People wondered about us after the polio, which struck me as ignorant, and a mite offensive. I'm not saying anyone asked me outright if we had a love life, but I felt it, picked up on assumptions, and I'm sorry to say it wasn't hard. People can't see past their own tiny peripheral visions. I'll just say this: there are cushions. We were dancers, flexible and acrobatic. We liked what bodies could do. Once George said to a male dancer who could not get the right approach to a lift, "Go down on her." I will just say, as I don't need to reiterate, that my husband was a man who loved women.

And then it crumbled and fell completely apart. I wonder if the year he came back to me was awful for Suzanne. If I think of it from her side I can imagine her confusion. More than their age difference, more than her inexperience, her religious beliefs, and his historical reputation with other women, was the fact, I can safely assume, that he didn't indicate for a long time any intention of leaving his marriage. It was different from how it had been for me in relation to Maria.

For all his public adoration of Suzanne, from the years 1963 to 1967, he seemed to want her without marriage.

I knew that during our last year together he still saw her outside of work, took her to dinner. But he went out with other colleagues after rehearsals and performances; work spilled over. I had to give him the benefit of the doubt, or what did our relationship mean?

So our summer in Saratoga ended, and throughout the autumn and into 1967 he worked on a major ballet called *Jewels* with parts for many of the dancers, including Suzanne.

But it was *Jewels* that finished us. At the time, I was coaching new girls in *Apollo*, and, hearing about *Jewels*, I knew we were through. We had a last year together, but Suzanne still ran in his blood.

The three sections of the new ballet were based on gemstones: emeralds, rubies, and diamonds. Suzanne's was the *Diamonds* section, diamonds, of course, being symbolic of marriage. She would dance it in white, like a bride. And the *Diamonds* section represented Imperial Russia—the height of ballet in the nineteenth century, its magic the ecstasy of his youth and the origin of his art. Onstage, he would crown her the queen of his realm and his heart. I didn't consider putting myself through the premiere, their public marriage, and by then I thoroughly wanted out of my private marriage, which had finally become a sham.

He saw how I felt. It could not have been any more obvious; we lived in this pall, but didn't speak of it.

We skirted each other, not even polite. We occupied, as they say, the same cage, and one or the other snapped if our cellmate came too close.

"Move out," I said, and at last it was easy to say, the harbinger, I hoped, of some relief.

He ignored me until I said it again, and then he answered that we needn't be rash. I told him to sleep in the guest room.

One night I'd been asleep and woke up with him lying beside me. It felt momentarily comforting as it used to, and then I felt invaded. His getting in bed without my permission seemed somehow violent. I didn't want him, his hands, his mouth—any of him, even as I could not have conceived myself capable of that degree of negative feeling about him. He tried to make love to me, tried to kiss this cold fury.

"Don't," I said, rigid. I lay on my back in the dim green glow of the Statue of Liberty night-light. I felt the authority of the bed frame and the furniture around us, the solidity of what had been, the inanimate charged with what I had felt for him, and he could have been a phantom. He kept lying there a little longer, and then he slowly got up and left.

I have to end this.

I wanted to stalk out and scream at him. I had to get in the goddamn chair. I couldn't stalk out in a chair.

I lay hating the chair instead of him.

Will you ever get over it? Just get up and get in the chair, which is just a chair and helpful every second of your life, and go out and do what you need to.

Or lie here and die.

He had left the door to the guest room open. From the doorway I called, "George." He didn't answer. I went farther into the bedroom and spoke his name again. Close as I could get to him, I said, "Devils sleep sound."

He sat up. I'd put on a light in the kitchen and I could pick out his outlines in its pale luminosity reaching the bed.

We were finally of the same mind. Neither one of us wanted more light; we sat in the dark. "Talk," I said, and made myself wait for silence to bloat the room.

"I feel . . . someone is holding me underwater," he said. "I can't breathe."

"It isn't me," I said.

"Tanny, if I go on with this marriage as it is, I think I won't be able to work anymore. To create."

"What did you think I would do with all this? Did you think I would just . . . absorb it?"

"Yes."

I saw he was paralyzed, but I wasn't anymore, at least not emotionally. He loved us both, wanted us both, or wanted her but couldn't bear to appear bad to himself or me or to others.

"You can't have everything," I said. "You just can't. Do you think *I* can breathe? Who is happy here, George? You're not. I'm certainly not. I hope Suzanne is happy for all of us. . . .

"This is what you do," I said. "You find an apartment. You take your things and we live separately, all right? Do as you wish and I won't have to see it."

Impossibly, still, too much remained submerged for understanding. But I felt that how he loved her, romantically, rapturously, freshly, as if he were young again and within the dynamic of creating dance for a beloved woman—he loved this more than what he loved in me; with me. He could stay with me until kingdom come, but the new love would tunnel up through the work, splash over the stage, and wing through the world—and he couldn't stay with me anymore because I would not let him.

Do you want a divorce? I asked him the next day.

No, no divorce.

I could have insisted, I suppose. Maybe I should have insisted. Each step felt monumental, and I couldn't take another.

• • •

He didn't have much that was exclusively his, clothes, a few books and scores. He left me the furniture, the kitchen equipment, even the two pianos, since he hadn't room in his apartment and I would need them when I entertained—oh, *definitely,* I was planning a season of parties.

Natalie and Diana came over the night after he and Eddie moved out his belongings, and helped me rearrange the closets and drawers. The gaps, I knew, would unhinge me.

We opened two bottles of wine and doggedly emptied them. Natalie rubbed my shoulders.

"You're good," I said. "Strong hands." Not his hands anymore; girlfriend's hands; hairdresser's hands; Carl's and Jerry's platonic hands; Mother's and Father's hands.

"You'll meet a perfect American man," Natalie said. "Russian men are trouble. I was smart, I found an American man."

"Don't," Diana said. "He just left. Anyway, they're all trouble."

I felt a cool draft from the window I'd cracked; felt dampness, smelled food we had cooked over the last weeks. I pushed Natalie off and checked the cupboards to see whether he'd taken his condiments; he hadn't. I stared at a row of them over the stove: olive paste, brown mustard, evil-looking pimentos, and pickled mushrooms. "I still don't understand," I said to the room at large, "he still didn't want to go." He'd even cried, said please, and I had to look at that face I hated and loved and did not understand and say again, go.

"Diana," and I turned to her sitting at the black-and-white Formica kitchen table, saw how she was beautiful, more fleshed since the baby, always elegant and timorous around the edges despite her sophistication; a foil to Natalie's bluntness. "Why did you?" I asked her. "With George?"

A sharp quick inhalation: her initial response. Natalie, who had been standing beside me, sat down at the table exhaustedly, as if already there'd been a knock-down, drag-out—which didn't come. Surely Diana had always expected the question and knew what I wanted was insight, not apology.

She drained the dregs of her glass. "He said the two of you were fine, and although that strikes me presently as absolute nonsense as a justification—well, I heard no guile in it. . . . Oh, how do they get away with, oh, god, the whole spectrum?" The future of Diana's marriage also looked bleak. She didn't feel up to generosity toward men. "They walk the earth as if it's their backyard. They think: It's mine. We say excuse me, and may I, and will this be all right? What chance do we have? How will our way of looking at anything ever get over? And it isn't just Russians, Natalie."

Diana turned back to me. "He said he couldn't help falling in love with me, as if it were a force outside of himself he couldn't control. I don't think that's original," she said dryly. "He is just smoother and, oh, boy, does he believe it. He believes he is as right about the things he is wrong about as the things he is right about. . . .

"And, Tanny, you were sort of detached from him then. You wanted something he wasn't giving you—"

"Not to lose him!" I said.

"It didn't seem that you *would*," Diana said. "I felt convinced, or I *wouldn't* have."

"George is so disappointing," I said. "He is so ravishing and so dense. Nobody can have him, really. Huge aspects of him exist somewhere else. And as you say, he can be so very gracious and reasonable about being unreasonable—well, he's impossible."

"Know who I love?" Diana said. "My little girl."

"I love my girls *and* my American husband," Natalie said firmly.

The summer of 1967 was called by the hippies "the Summer of Love," an irony that was not lost on me. George stopped by the apartment and puttered or cooked in the kitchen as if we were great friends. It was the one summer I didn't want to go to Weston. He complained about having more than his share of chores at the house and I said, "Tough." Anyway, Eddie did most of the chores. One day I had been out with Carl and came home to find George in the kitchen dumping bowls of the bright red-orange berries from our mountain ash trees into pots.

"I'm making the jelly," he announced. "You look hot. Shall I turn on the air-conditioning?" He had installed the units himself, as he did every year.

"I like to sweat," I said. I'd come to the doorway of the kitchen and sat there sweating.

"May I get you a cool drink?" he asked.

"There's a pitcher of tea in the icebox."

He got it and set a glass of it on the table. "Snack?" he asked.

I didn't answer and he recommenced cooking. I went to the alcove in the living room to watch TV. I watched a lot of TV in the Summer of Love, which was also a summer of violence, of the Vietnam War escalating, and of riots in Cleveland, Detroit, and Newark.

I put on the news and watched the black-and-white jungles blast open. Soon the bitter smell of the cooking berries merged with the sight of burning buildings, of kids running through American streets fast as the running soldiers halfway around the globe. Why do you watch it? George often asked. Because it's important, I said. He found the Summer of Love stuff festive, but the dreadful things that were happening in this wonderful country were anarchy, he said, and the antiwar protests would lead to more. This country has problems, I'd say, why do you suppose people are angry? All would be well, he maintained, if the government took care of the poor and supported the arts, and free love was one thing, but going against the troops was another. "It's an unjust war!" I'd say. "You cannot let the Communists win," he said. "George, they're winning." The smell thickened, filling the apartment. The jelly was used for meat or game. Each year we saved some of the berries to flavor vodka. Put a handful of berries into a three-quarters-full bottle, place the bottle on its side for two to four weeks, then remove the berries and serve the vodka ice-cold. A car on a dark street burst into flames.

He came out from the kitchen, walked through the dining and living rooms to the alcove, blinked at the TV, and with his arms folded across his chest he asked, right on cue, "Why do you watch it?"

I didn't answer; he turned it off.

"I'm watching," I said.

"It isn't good for you, staying in always," he said.

"I've been out today. I don't stay in."

"Tell me about your day," and he sat down beside me. Silence; smell of the simmering jelly; a crouched soldier running across my brain.

"I hate you," I said.

"Would you like to come out to Saratoga for the weekend?"

"Did you not hear me? I said I hate you."

"You shouldn't," he answered.

"Don't treat me like an invalid. That I can't abide. If I say I hate you, the proper response would be 'I hate you back.' It is not to ask if I would like to come out to Saratoga, which, as I said, I would not."

"You'll sit here all summer?"

"It's none of your business what I do this summer. But if you must know, I'm adjusting. I'm taking my time to adjust." We sat as if trapped in a viscous substance—the jam, the past, the angst of those who have once loved.

6

*P*ain dilutes in the extension of time. Like ink in water it blackens, and then the water stays clear and the blackness whirls. Days come when it's a single black thread swirling about. *There it is. Hello. There you are.*

The Ballet Cook Book was released in August and eclipsed by the headlines. There wasn't review space for light fare, and the tone of the book seemed antiquated. Ballet itself did that summer. I dutifully did my author interviews, requested, I am sure, because the Suzanne uproar still hadn't died down in New York even while the world burned. The polio was old news, but me as one side of the triangle made for good press. I brightly told the reporters that George and I lived separately, but he was at the old apartment all the time. Then he incensed me. He told a reporter in Chicago that Suzanne was the next Mrs. Balanchine. He was crazy, truly, refusing to admit to me whether or not he actually used those words.

"It's over," I told the press. "He wants somebody who can dance, that's what it comes down to." My pride compelled me to say more: "When I married him everyone said I shouldn't, that he was too old for me. Perhaps they were right. Anyway, now I'm living *my* life, not his."

I felt some satisfaction going public, as he had been publicly courting her since he moved out. I would see pictures of them at Le Cirque, the Four Seasons, and our place, the Russian Tea Room.

"Oh, what do I care?" I said in one of the countless conversations I conducted to the air. "You're an old man and that's why you persist in this, you're desperate. I'm not. I'm young and I'm free."

Although not in the habit of appearing alone on the street, Miss Freedom went out to the newsstand on Broadway to read all the junk. We weren't on that many covers, so if I was unsure, I bought everything we might *possibly* be in, scanned them for evidence, and threw out the batch. I couldn't leave them around the apartment, since Mother was enraged enough at George that giving her any further ammunition might have endangered his personal safety.

Here was a bingo: "Do you know he and his wife, former ballerina Tanaquil Le Clercq, are secretly divorced? So much for the pas de deux—and the faux pas."

I called George at the office: "It's good you don't want a divorce, because I wouldn't give you one. Remember, I won't."

Young, sure, I was turning into Mother.

I threw a big party for Jerry's forty-ninth birthday in October. Gold and Fizdale again played the pianos; people came and went until four in the morning. Jerry, the King of Broadway, had walked out on Broadway, and by this date he was running an experimental theater company. He brought the troupe—fabulous creatures in spangles and jeans—to mingle with painters, writers, musicians, actors, and most of all dancers. I renewed my dance contacts while writing the cookbook and anyone from anywhere who was in New York that night came to my party. It made the *Post*. In the morning I felt I had reclaimed the hollow five rooms I'd rattled around in. I opened the windows to let out stale smoke and, humming, cleaned up the mess by myself. The long glass and wrought-iron dining table was a landscape of fish bones, candle stubs, empty wine bottles, scraped plates with cigarette butts sticking out of leftover gobs, and Mourka sat in a sliver of space amid the clutter, tail flicking a basket of demolished bread, observing the ruins.

Jerry had split with his long-term lover, Mark, and with more time on his hands, we frequented outdoor cafés together that balmy autumn, commiserating, talking for hours. He'd taken to wearing a navy-blue Greek fisherman's cap I loved; the beard he had grown was there to stay, more white now than black.

And then he disbanded his troupe and abruptly decamped for Rome.

November 30, 1967
New York

Dear Jerry,

Do you plan on staying in Rome forever? I need you. If I say desperately, it's insincere. I'm loveless but busy. I'm planning to write a book for children. It will have cats and ballet. (Surprise.) Another very interesting development is I got a call from American Ballet Theater to coach. Should I? Cross the plaza and double-cross George by sleeping with the competition? I don't want to add murder to separation but I must say I considered it. . . . Oh, well.

I went and saw *Jewels* with Carl. I said I would, right? I didn't think that much of *Diamonds*, to tell you the truth. Too Russian for us, it doesn't really work. Patty McBride and Villella were smashing in *Rubies*. But *Emeralds* is by far the finest. It has some of George's most beautiful patterns, not just for the corps. Long walking diagonals for one of the couples are hypnotic and echo the music delicately. They take their time, they seem to go on and on and somehow become time. He pushes it just enough. Then there is the prettiest intricate port de bras for Violette. Very French, a woman at her toilette.

As for George in his personal life . . . it isn't good. Apparently Suzanne decided to stop seeing him outside of work. He stopped eating. Really. Completely. Lost, I heard (we've gone two months without meeting), ten pounds. She gave up.

She dances nonstop without any understudy, driving the folks in the office to tear out their hair. He no longer necessarily watches the programs straight to the end. When she is through dancing, they leave.

A rumor: One of the corps girls cornered her backstage and asked why she couldn't just sleep with him. Would it be such a big deal? I guess she thought if she did, it would make everyone happier. Enough. I told myself I had checked out of the saga.

Miss you and kiss you,
Tanny

December 10, 1967
Spoleto

Dear Tanny,

Back in a place where I was contented. Not really. You were still in the hospital when I was first here with Ballets: USA. I felt sick myself with worry about you. But I was contented in work, relatively. You know me. I've never regretted leaving the musical theater, but what is next? I think it's the dance, I think I keep knowing that it's classical dance. How would you feel if I went back to NYCB? I won't if you don't want me to.

Rome made me more depressed. Hot breezes kept blowing up Mark. The two of us didn't go to Spoleto. So here I reside. Waiting. (To know what to do with my life. To stop missing Mark.)

George saddens me. Remember, it doesn't have anything to do with you. I've told you repeatedly, and you don't believe me. OK. Take it on, if you insist, but it won't help. I know you can't be happy, but you're a hell of a lot happier when you let it go. I mean the responsibility. Baby, there's stuff you can't control.

Take it from one who keeps trying to learn that damn lesson.

Misses and kisses,
Your Jerry

December 20, 1967
New York

Dear Jerry,

What you say isn't true, I feel I can be happy and almost have/had been lately. Then I saw George. We lunched at the Oak Room. Silly me, I wanted to be seen. He looked unwell. But he's sixty-three. What does sixty-three look like? Hell, I'm thirty-eight. How'd we all get so old?

Anyway, George asked whether I wanted to spend Christmas together. I said I'd think about it. I've thought. I won't. I'll spend it with Natalie and her family. And on New Year's Eve Diana, Georgina, and I are going to Weston, snowstorm or no. (Ronald left, and Diana and I are two gay divorcées. Chuckle.)

Remember last year, that day in January at Snedens Landing? It's the best of your homes, albeit I haven't seen the one in

Rome. I felt incredibly comforted by you and Mark. I don't mean to hurt you by bringing him up. . . . But I keep seeing the river, the Palisades across the way through your windows, the three of us goofily crooning, "the naked river, the naked cliffs, the cringing clouds, the blanched vulnerable sky, the sad wet naked trees, and the bark is crying . . ." It was that kind of day, nature looked so exposed. There'd been all that snow for weeks, then it melted, leaving everything out there as if its skin had peeled off. . . . And I was distraught, and you and Mark were so caring, being there with me and making me, finally, smile. . . .

No snow here this year as yet. I'm all right. Just the first Christmas, first New Year's without. . . . Go back to NYCB with my blessing. You told me once that the classical vocabulary would say what you needed to say.

Love,
Tanny

December 30, 1967
Rome

Dear Tanny,

I'm back. OK now, feels good being back. Hope you got the gift. Another's coming for New Year's. The slippers and robe are soft as bunnies, and you didn't forget my new favorite color! Yesterday I didn't get dressed. . . .

Tell me about your Christmas. Pretend your head's on my shoulder, princess.

Loads of love,
Your Jerry

January 2, 1968
New York

Darling,

The earrings! Nothing so beautiful ever hung from my head. Such old gold. I feel certain the first pagan Tanaquil actually wore them. Someday in the not very distant future (I hope?) I'll visit you there and you'll show me Rome, every cranny.

The tapestry . . . how do I tell you how much I study and admire it? I tried it everywhere in the apartment and I can't decide where it is best. (Near the pianos probably.) You can help me decide. I'll wait. For now in majestic splendor it graces my bedroom wall where my eyes can caress it from bed.

Do you want me to come? Would you like company there? Write soon. I must get away. . . .

Love and Kisses,
Tanny

January 15, 1968
Rome

Dear Tan-tan,

In a rush. News is I've met somebody! Only a fling, but nice. I'll show you Rome later. I don't think I'll be here much longer. Do this: Come out to Snedens for the weekend when I get back. We'll write more bad poetry.

Can't wait.

Love,
Jerry

January 25, 1968
New York

Dear Jerry,

Remember what you said about Mark at the end? That you felt you were putting too much of your life into him, trying to live through him almost? I think I'm doing that too—with you.

I love lots of people, but I don't feel quite the same about you as I do about, say, Arthur and Bobby. . . . So thanks for the weekend invitation, but I won't come.

As ever,
Tanny

7

$\mathscr{S}$ train showed in Suzanne onstage. The somewhat exaggerated quality she brought to many of the dances went over the top. "Vulgar" was a word someone used. Her own mother, Edith's spies reported, begged Suzanne to come to her senses and give in to George. "So what if he's old?" the mother maintained. "He's a genius." She stridently took Balanchine's side, and Suzanne moved out of the family apartment.

She started seeing a young man in the company, a dancer George had also nurtured. In an effort to break up the relationship George was gruff and abusive to the boyfriend in rehearsal, and he offered Suzanne marriage, saying—the coup for a person who didn't desire it—he wanted a child with her.

And this coup: he was planning for her a *Sleeping Beauty*.

In the fall of 1968 I got a call from him over crackling wires. He'd gone to Mexico for a divorce. *I'm sorry, I'm sorry, I'm sorry.*

When the divorce came through the following February he came to see me, his black eyes burning, and softly explained that the apartment and the house in Weston were mine. He would provide; I wouldn't want for anything.

Then he flew off to Hamburg to stage *Ruslan and Lyudmila.* In a modest ceremony in New York that same week, attended by a scattering of New York City Ballet employees, Suzanne wed her youth.

It had all been for nothing.

He wouldn't come back to New York, he said. He would stay in Europe and Lincoln could have the company. Eddie and Lincoln flew out and tried to reason with him.

One morning I got a call from a woman who worked for him, someone I didn't know well. Would I talk to him?

I refused, carefully put the receiver back in the cradle. You could say I hung up on any chance of rapprochement. But it had died long ago.

He was convinced to return. If he saw Suzanne in the hallways he spun in the other direction. She would not be the only one anymore. She taught her dances to other girls. Her husband was stripped of his roles. Dark chords rolled out from behind George's closed office door.

At last one night when the husband should have gone on, as he had before in a role vacated by an injured dancer, the role was assigned for the night to another dancer. Suzanne said if her husband didn't dance they were leaving the company.

They were both fired.

They had nowhere to go. Nobody wanted to hire

her and anger Balanchine. Of the choreographer she ended up working for in France, the less said, the better.

Three moments.

The first: His calling from Mexico where he had gone for the divorce. The crackle; it was hard to hear.

You're in Mexico why? *Why?* I see. Chills running over me, they were his fingers and I his piano.

Nothing felt real after that for a long while. Blunted, filed down, slow-motioned, muffled, sounds muted so even music was barely audible. I couldn't hear other people's voices on the phone. I'm sorry? I'm sorry again, excuse me? Pardon me, I didn't hear? The grief felt like fear. If Mother arrived five minutes late I was sure she'd been crushed in the street.

My body was overly tender, easily bruised, any sore spot a portent of disaster. One week I didn't go out because I didn't trust myself. I would miss something and die—miss a curb and spill onto the pavement and crack my head open. I could hear it, see it, and almost feel it: the knock on the skull and the warm fluid leaking like oil under the knees of a stranger who came to help.

I was a target, a vessel of some inexplicable aura or vulnerability that would draw the worst.

Freak accidents, thieves, and the destruction of people I loved beyond George.

But it had been ending for years. Hadn't I lost him in bits and pieces? Hadn't I braced myself since Warm Springs to lose him?

I hated to look in a mirror; combing my hair, I averted my eyes. If I caught sight of myself in a public place, that woman I saw looked far away just like everything else, another stranger.

I couldn't be rational, I was too unhappy for logic. My logic had fled with him, it seemed. I dropped the children's book I'd started writing. The activity was too solitary. I didn't want to go out and I didn't want to be alone. Mother tried to teach me to knit but my fingers wouldn't work, I was suffering neurological damage related somehow to the polio, a delayed symptom. This could not be, a doctor told me. There wasn't anything wrong with my fingers. Then it was my brain. It explained why I couldn't read new books. I could read books I had read before, as if the first readings had been rehearsals—and I could sleep. I slept twelve hours a day and didn't dream. I'd nestle into the bed like warm snow, soothing, covering whiteness of bed and the soft insubstantiality of sleep.

The second: The divorce was final.
He came to me. *You'll be all right?*
I'm fine.

I was Medea. I wanted to murder his unborn child. Had I been able to stir from the chair, I'd have prowled nighttime streets, taking it in—it was over. Feeling it, being it, myself alone. What the sky, what the buildings looked like, being alone. How things smelled and sounded and how other bodies I passed on the street related to mine. Perhaps I'd step into a bar and pick up a guy. People did that now more than before. Jerry did it all the time. Jerry claimed he wanted real love, true love that lasted, but he didn't, and anyway even if he had he could not have coped with loving someone in my situation. Too bad, I knew he was sorry. Everyone was so very sorry. The black waters of Venice came up and engulfed me in waves.

Dip of the finger.
Fresh.

The third: He was in Hamburg and wouldn't come back. She had married. I carefully put the receiver of my white kitchen phone into the wall cradle not far from my window post. Morning. I could see through the window a thin stretch of sky between the rooflines. Within it were silver-edged dusky white clouds of an indeterminate day, clouds swollen with rain or about to part, revealing soft light. But all in the moment was stillness, and for a long minute, from the shock of how it had played out and the full realization that the end of the story was here—I thought I'd black out. Without George, it seemed I would fundamentally cease to exist, because who would I be without him understanding me, loving and seeing me? And where would it go, all we had been to each other? I breathed deeply, steadied myself.

How could I ever have imagined that he *hadn't* seen me? Saw the beautiful girl in Woods Hole in white gloves on the lawn near the glowing white sea of the Cape. Saw the child dancer as if he were viewing her from the wrong side of a telescope, already a ballerina, just small. Saw my power, my chic, my love of humor and wit, saw the jazzy Tanaquil in *Ivesiana* and the wild tender spirit I'd been in *La Valse.* Every dance he had made for me was seeing, was adoration and attention. He had given me Paris and the Wild West to dance. He had given me my first sight of La Scala filled on that day of our honeymoon with pink carnations, and Vienna before I got sick—*how I had danced,* so well it rained blown kisses and roses onto the stage until there was nowhere to step without trampling flowers. When in the hospital they let him into my room, pronouncing me out of danger, he said he had prayed night and day, but his prayers had confronted emptiness until the evening before: a vision of his mother had come and told him that she would look after us; he felt great peace, and next thing he knew they had removed the quarantine.

I didn't die, but my dancer's body was stolen so abruptly it had taken us years to adjust. We had managed a lot together. I could have gone on, he couldn't. He tried. You could say he constructed a new life for me, created my possibility: brought me unreasonable hope when I couldn't continue without it, built me a shelter of spacious rooms where I could heal; widened the doorways, built the ramps out in Weston, loved me again.

It had happened again for us, which made it better and very much harder. . . . Whom would I love now? The clouds outside held, with tremulous light.

You're free, I thought. There wouldn't be any more waiting, any more dreading that he might leave, would leave. God, could I not have been wrong?

I sat alone in my chair in the empty kitchen. I thought of the people who had come to my party, winging through the world. I thought of Jerry and George, their lives an array of possibilities that only the mobile and luckiest had.

What happy things could I do?

I missed Weston. In the spring I'd plant trees: a silver spruce and a Japanese maple. I'd watch them grow. So I would begin.

It took me ten years to decide not to die, but I decided.

Venice came up and over me in a black wave, and receded. I closed my eyes: in my mind I held on to him, afraid that if I let him go he would disappear, float away into the atmosphere. I gripped his beautiful forearms, held fast to his fine wrists, my fingers digging the turquoise and silver bracelet into his skin, that Russian skin.

Part Three
The Body
1972–1983

Nothing has changed.
Except the run of rivers,
the shapes of forests, shores, deserts,
  and glaciers.
The little soul roams among those
  landscapes,
disappears, returns, draws near,
  moves away,
evasive and a stranger to itself,
now sure, now uncertain of its own
  existence,
whereas the body is and is and is
and has nowhere to go.
                    —*Wisława Szymborska*

1

Three years after the divorce, George phoned to blackmail me into teaching at Arthur Mitchell's Dance Theatre of Harlem. Mitchell and cofounder Karel Shook had established the company in 1969 as a response to the death of Martin Luther King, Jr. It was the first major ballet enterprise to ensure that all American dancers would have the opportunity Arthur did at New York City Ballet in the pre–civil rights era.

"I'm delighted to hear from you," I said—tone: effervescent, I'm fine, I am fabulous—"but teaching's a big commitment."

"What else you've got to do?" He was just being George, and he was right. Relatively healed, relatively sanguine in the wake of our own shattering 1960s, I had put writing aside, happily. But life in the country and occasional coaching in the city didn't take up enough time. He needed a teacher steeped in the neoclassical style. Arthur's were good dancers, he told me, but he couldn't feed them his repertory—he had promised dances in support of the new company—if they weren't trained.

"You don't do it," he said, "what will I do? I give my pledge."

"George, there are plenty of people you could ask."

"No, I want you."

Silence. "All right, but only if you show me how to do it. I request a private lesson." He agreed to come to the apartment in two days.

It was April, the cruelest month, and on the appointed Wednesday the sky opened up with spatters and splats, raining and sleeting huge clots of gray mess. I cringed for the early plantings Carl and I had risked over the weekend. Carl was still my primary mode of transportation, but now he also took care of the grounds in Weston and worked with me on the gardens. The flowers and vegetables flourished, and with Carl I hung bird feeders everywhere, attracted all manner of feathery friends. Maintaining Weston—plunging my hands into soil, partnering with sun and rain—was my recovery from the ending of my marriage. But I couldn't have done it alone. The spring of the divorce, I made good on a vow: I bought trees, small scruffy things that would only provide gratification in years. At the time, all of life had seemed scruffy and small. Carl, in his physical immensity, in his strength, tending to those tiny trees like a protective father, brought me a foretaste of renewal.

George arrived dripping wet in his trench coat; laughing at Mourka, who leaped, whirled, paced, slinked, rubbed, meowed until we didn't think he would stop—little catch in my throat—but we couldn't bring ourselves to confine him. He thankfully settled, an eye slit watching his long-lost love.

I gathered George's coat, spread it across the bench by the front door, and went back to him standing beside the blue western couch, near the tea and molasses cookies on the oblong table.

He took my hand, said I looked lovely, what a beautiful blouse—my silk ice-blue, like his heart—and pressed my hand to his lips: so warm.

Over the last three years he had sent gifts for my birthday and Christmas. Sometimes he called, as he had to thank me for the olive oil I bought for him on my recent Italian trip. My coaching assignments came through assistants, but once in a while he showed up at a studio when I was working and watched. We collided twice on the street. He invited me to rehearsals of dances he thought I'd like, and I'd gone to one. But these public sightings and formal acknowledgments were scraps, thin gruel compared to agreeing to meet in the old homestead, scene of our strife. The dense air seemed extra private and the medium in which I could really *look* at him again: see how he'd aged.

He was grayer, his hairline farther receded and thinner on top, skin pinched and more lined around his eyes and mouth—but oh, the mouth, his hands, the iridescent black-brown of his mutable eyes. He wore different cologne, a touch floral, and that seemed *wrong;* or it was simply a whiff of estrangement.

He inspected Jerry's tapestry draped on one of the pianos. "How was Italy?" he asked. Back at the couch, he surveyed the cookies. "Did you make them yourself, dear?"

"No. Babka's."

"Aha!" He approved. Nice Russian cookies.

I had also put out a decanter of whiskey. Oh, go ahead, be yourself, I thought, eat the whole plate of cookies, have a couple quick shots. He sipped tea and nibbled a sweet. I poured us both half inches of spirits, drank mine, watched his sit.

"Hairline fracture to my tibia," I said.

"When?"

"That was the trip."

"Oh."

"Up and down we went over the cobbled streets and one day, not far from the Spanish Steps, we hit something, and boom, knocked me out of the chair."

"Oh, Tanny."

"Oh, yes. I was fine in the end. But Jerry thought he would faint at the hospital, he felt so guilty. Everyone made a fuss over him, the sensitive plant, and I nearly fell off the X-ray table."

"Jerry," said George. "Jerry, Jerry, Jerry," and he giggled.

"Jerry, Jerry," I said, a conspirator. Pause.

"George? I'm sorry about Stravinsky. Did you get my card?"

"Yes. He isn't gone." He didn't just mean the music. He believed in continual life, in contiguous planes. His mother's death many years ago had also left him serene. One more for me up there, he'd said. For Stravinsky he would host a musical celebration, a triumphant week of premieres in June that would put to rest talk that he was finished, after the creative slump since Suzanne: that April day Balanchine was about to rise yet again.

"Number one," I said, pouring myself another nipper of whiskey, "your credo: get up and show. I can't, obviously."

"Dear, it will be your own style. When you are coaching you don't show. I've seen you and you're fine with gesture and speech."

"But teaching's different, I'd think," I said.

"No, the same. Don't forget, neoclassical barre is conventional barre with intensity, that's it."

I had *never* seen him conduct a conventional barre; he drilled steps, one day tendu, another glissade. But he worked with dancers he extended and tested. My dancers would first need a basal understanding of the technique inside their bodies.

We talked about energy, attack, articulation, and the problem—for dancers who hadn't come up in his school—of his minimal preparation

265

between steps. We discussed how he wanted the weight on the ball of the foot, "Like pussycat," he said; "and landing without heels; no bent knees, pas de cheval. Then try," he said. "They must try. You watch. For teacher everything's watching. I say show, but I *watch*."

"Then there are the men," I said wanly.

"You know men," he insisted. "If you could stand up, you could partner me, easily." His eyes flashed; the thought seemed to intrigue him. "But for company class it's same for both." The cookies were gone. He poured himself a fresh shot.

"I can't give corrections," I said despondently. Of course, I *had,* coaching, but I so loved the hands-on Russian style.

"You can with words! Sometimes, anyway, is better. I give images. I would give more if I thought of them!" Softly with the heel of his hand, he tapped his forehead: "Not much in here. But elephant trunk for the turnout they like, they understand. . . . Here's one: I say present heel. Enough rotation, the heel could balance glass of champagne."

Mourka stirred as if awakened by trace memories of George's inflections. "You taking notes, cat? I'm famous man. Is funny. I don't trust words and everyone wants them from me. You know, I can't explain things," he said seriously, in a shift. "Not with words."

"You do pretty well." I put down my glass. No more, or I'd get emotional.

"How is Mother?" he asked.

"A force of nature."

"Oh, yes," he said sagely. "Father?"

"The same, in his fashion."

"I always liked him."

"I know."

"Tanny, bring Father to the Stravinsky Festival!" Discreetly he added, "You can bring Mother another day. It runs a week. We're shutting down, to prepare, for ten whole days. Lincoln couldn't believe. He'll see. Big success, oh—so exciting. I have new danseur noble! A Danish boy with immense head, hands like sides of trucks, and I put big Danish pastry in pas de deux with skinny Kay." He lifted a finger and sparkled. "You'll see."

At the door he said, "You have trouble at Arthur's, dear, call me. I think you are going to love it." We kissed cheeks. "They say I'll be remembered as a choreographer, but I think as a teacher."

Mourka dragged himself over to say good-bye, but he was an elderly cat now and as a result of his earlier exertions he would sleep for the rest of the day.

"My, my, my, my," I said out loud to myself, observing the damp ghost of a coat on the bench. I should have hung it over a kitchen chair. How

267

long since I'd seen him expansive and charming? How lovely—how awful, given that I had promised myself I would never be vulnerable to him again. Well, it was done. I would teach. We'd become friends. He could disarm anyone if he had a mind to. Not one of the ex-wives had succeeded in total estrangement. Just be mature, I counseled myself. A terrible bore about getting older was that at a certain age—I was forty-two—it seemed incumbent upon one to be mature.

But I couldn't help feeling the excitement of change and new possibility.

"Energy's endless," George had told me long ago. "You think there isn't any more, and then there is."

At Arthur's I confronted twenty bright souls in fresh, glowing skins the colors of rust, milky cocoa, dark peat—all of the mingled shades of gray, brown, yellow, tan, and red. They stared at me with mild curiosity only. On a trip to Paris in 1949, the dancer Betty Nichols and I had performed in an artist's studio for Merce Cunningham. The audience sat on the floor and in a balcony above us, and sun through a skylight lit us. Alice B. Toklas and Giacometti were there—people said Betty and I were Giacomettis. But Betty had subsequently traveled an unfair, daunting road as an African American in classic ballet. Though I knew little of them, Arthur had faced his own battles.

So this studio and the dancers before me were eminently hopeful in an extraordinary way. I had prepared for today by writing down classes of George's from memory. I began by talking about his approach, the differences and the emphasis. Dancers sat on the floor, others leaned up against the barre, and they danced questions: Like this? This? I demonstrated with a hand. My right arm had never regained much strength, but I was right-handed and the hand itself was my more expressive: so I propped up the right arm by the elbow with my left hand and, using my right hand, showed what they needed to do with their feet. It was a fortunate substitution, I told the class, since Balanchine wanted the feet to have the energy of hands. The talk evolved naturally into larger movements. Afterward people lingered, asking more questions. Soon Owen, the young man who had picked me up and brought me to the school, stuck his head in and told everyone to leave, as we had agreed. Out of sight of the dancers he carried me down the stairs while a secretary brought down the chair.

That first day, back at home, my head jumped with ideas and plans I wrote in my notebook. As inspiration, I wrote down what dancing had taught me and what I still believed: that chaos could be mastered, life and ourselves made capable of order, and that order and beauty could be one.

Then I called Carl and asked if he would come over. I wanted to share my enthusiasm. We had drinks and ordered Chinese and I yakked and he listened in our lovers' microclimate of absorption, of freedom, and then we got into bed and watched TV while we ate.

I had realized one day that he was in love with me. I unearthed a shopping list he had tossed into the trash, recognized his handwriting, and knew. We were in Weston, the summer of 1971. Out in the yard weeding, I'd felt his eyes on me in a way that was familiar, yet different. I looked at him curiously and he looked away, embarrassed. I had been in close physical proximity to Carl for years, nearly back to Warm Springs. We became friendlier later, on the trip to England and France while George and I were still technically together. Then, as Carl began doing more for me, I thought my feelings for him were those I would have felt for a brother.

Yet there we were out together in the dirt, after years of him seeing me at my worst—distraught, disarrayed, needy certainly, and in senses other than the one that involved not having the use of my legs—and he suddenly didn't seem like a brother at all. It wasn't possible, I thought. Then I thought harder, pretending that I was just weeding one of the raised beds along the drive.

With nonchalance that turned out to be less than convincing, I wheeled into the house and dug through the trash in the kitchen and found it. I turned, and Carl filled the doorway. I held the list out to him.

"This is your handwriting."

His down-sloping blue eyes filled with tears. Strange, then I understood that he was moved. His emotion and his exquisite masculine beauty entered me—my pores seemed to open to him. For a long moment, we watched each other cautiously. He was several years younger than I was, and mobile. I was terrified something would happen, and that it wouldn't. I was afraid I'd invented what I'd felt outside, afraid I misremembered previous moments between us that were suddenly stark and no longer enigmatic—moments in which I had felt rich, prismatic sensations, being with him, and the same wafting from him to me.

He came to the table and pulled out a chair, turned it around, and sat facing me. "I'm crazy about you," he said. "Full-out, head-over-heels in love. Are you angry?"

"Angry?" I wanted to laugh, to simply froth over with joy. Instead, I got stern. "No," I assured him, appearing quite angry, I'm sure.

So, feeling that he had nothing to lose, probably, having already proclaimed himself, Carl spoke of what he had not been able to say before, of his feelings for me as a dancer, and for the person I was after my dancing was finished. Carl spoke of things I hadn't imagined could lead to romantic love. I'd seen what I'd had to do since the polio as necessity only. Carl saw, and admired, what I'd done as me. No matter how prideful I had once been or pretended to be, since the polio I had often felt glossed by shame. Carl, as he spoke, rubbed the shame away.

Had he not spoken, I wouldn't have had the courage to say what I did. "Touch me?"

He covered my hand on my lap with his. I clutched it, almost rocked from the chair by the spark of how it made me feel. "I think I feel the same," I said.

"You think?"

"We could do some investigation," I said, which I couldn't *believe* I said.

We went to the bedroom, and he lifted me from the chair and onto the bed and unwrapped me slowly and carefully, but I couldn't doubt his impetus because his hands burned.

He kissed me, and he took off his own clothes and got into bed. I had been certain I wouldn't again be touched as he touched me. The box I had lived in since George, not such a bad box but a box all the same, fell away.

"God, I feel young," I said.

He laughed. "Are you old?"

"Oh, I was," I told him. "Yesterday I was ancient." A panel slid back, and we were together.

· · ·

It was such fun to watch people discover us, not that we flaunted our relationship. I preferred secrecy for many months. I had lived such a public calamity, then a public betrayal, and privacy felt essential, felt lush.

I loved going with him to the ballet, acting as though relations between us were as they had been, and then going home and pulling the blinds and lying nude in his arms as if we were the only creatures on earth, as if whatever the world was and did were inconsequential.

We never did let on to anyone outside a small circle—Mother, who try as she might remained perplexed by us; Father, who was very fond of Carl; Diana, Jerry, and Natalie, the one I most worried might spill the beans.

He was unlike anyone I had been close to. He worked part-time shelving books in a library, and the rest of the time he lifted weights at the gym or shuttled me. His clothing was fragrant with where he lived, with whom he lived—his mother: mothballs, lemon Pledge, and soup, a concoction I craved.

Little was strained between us. We talked openly, like children. We didn't go on and on about our wounded psyches, as Jerry and I tended to. Questions were asked, answers supplied, no thorny protections interfered. Nothing seemed inexplicable, incommunicable, and Carl listened less in an effort to comprehend meanings and locate significance and more to dwell in the sound of my voice, the sense of my spirit animating the sound.

One day he asked what the polio did to me, inside.

"Carl! In ten words or less?" Had it been anyone else I'd have stopped there. But I said frankly, "What was it like to be destroyed? I was in the smallest possible prison, with nothing I could do to get out. You fight. You think you will die. Part of you does die. Then you come back alive."

Of course he understood desecration himself, as George did, but their experiences were an ocean apart. I know that an aspect of my relationship with Carl, our easy sympathies, derived from our shared knowledge of illness and our continuing perspectives as outsiders, since ours were illnesses we didn't entirely recover from and had to carry through our lives. Carl's heart had been damaged by rheumatic fever at age twelve. To go on living was Carl's raison d'être. His dancing and the weight lifting were vehicles to more time. He took marked pleasure in breathing, in stretching—and I appreciated this. To me he was rather a beautiful, sculpted, blond gorilla, an animal I thought divine, and in the flower beds at the house in Connecticut, in the vegetable garden, trimming trees, pushing a full wheelbarrow over the property, he was a sight to behold. It was impossible not to marvel at the sheer gorgeousness of his body, which as he worked in the country appeared as if it had sprung whole from the soil, instead of from illness.

He was my consolation prize, and I don't mean what the phrase implies. I really mean each of the words separately: Consolation. Prize.

His overdeveloped body hated clothes; they were uncomfortable for him. Indoors, he liked best underwear, or his pajamas if he felt cold. It was how he lounged about at home with his mother, and in his life with me I didn't mind. I never met his mother. I just couldn't. There were limits to our affair and, though I would live to regret that, he accepted them.

"What did you most like about dancing?" he asked me.

Where were we? Probably stretched out in bed. We were wonderful bed partners, indolent friends.

"Three things," I said. "Dancing's so much from the gut. As a source of good cheer, it's endless. And I was drawn to the structure, the discipline of being a dancer. And onstage your emotions become so heightened that what you feel afterward by pushing through the fear and exhaustion is thrilling. When I performed well, afterward I felt . . ." Linguistically, I chose my example from him. "I felt like a giantess."

Carl was sun sliding into the sky, there on the sidelines in plain sight while I couldn't see anything but what was impossible—such a good man, so good to me. George had always said he didn't worry, didn't plan ahead much because you couldn't know what would come along. Carl proved this true for me better than anyone or anything had, more than the polio. Carl was a gentle lesson, a *jubilant* lesson, lest we persist in our contention that suffering is the one school.

On the first day of my teaching at Arthur's we turned off the TV, cleared the take-out cartons, made love in the Chinese-restaurant-scented sheets, and then we lay on our sides in the gloom of the evening, watching each other.

"Who are you, Butch?" Looking into his downward-slanting blue eyes—the far edges sloped subtly toward his cheekbones, unlike any eyes I had ever seen.

"I'm nobody, Toby." Why we called each other Toby and Butch, don't ask. Being nobody was the type of thing Carl said. But you have to interpret it from a Zen point of view.

"You're Toby's boy." My hands in his thick blond hair, I kissed his blunt nose, his broad cheeks, and the ridge of his brow.

"Don't stop," he said.

"No." My hands on his hard chest, I thought of his heart deep inside. What was Picasso's phase, those rose, beige, and dusky white paintings of heroic women with limbs thick as pillars? He could have been their cavalier.

To add to the intricacy of my affair with Carl, I suspected that I might not have recognized him, felt about him as I did, without George.

One day in Paris, I had been clomping along in new pretty white shoes with George when he stopped before a patisserie window, because he must have those rolls: golden brown with perfect clefts, buttery light.

We ate the rolls from the bag on the steps of a church, and easily plowed through half a dozen. "You see, because always so hungry in Russia, we Soviet Dancers saw on the ship crossing the Baltic the baskets of rolls and we couldn't believe."

He pulled one apart and studied its delicate innards. "Work of art," he said, "this roll."

Not long after I started at Arthur's, Father grew sick. We quickly received the diagnosis and in two months he was gone.

His last words to me were, "You're tired, go home."

"No, Papa."

Mother transformed to a weeping bundle of hysteria from the day we heard he would die. Why now? I thought, how can you? I sat in the hospital room taut and resentful, as if the wound of my fading father could be retroactively healed had the original wound, the divorce, never happened, and my father, his still dark hair framing his narrow face, would get well. The color drained from his cheeks as if color itself poured out of the world. I convinced Mother to come to the hospital to see him, and he stared up at her with such openness, almost hope!

"How are you?" she asked.

"Not too bad," he said reassuringly.

She didn't sit, stood clasping her purse as if it would protect her from the poignancy of the occasion. "I had a letter from Beryl Brown this morning," she said. "Evidently the children were forced to sell the business." Father clearly couldn't remember the Browns.

"Lamps," she reminded him. "They were in lighting." I'd made a mistake; whatever had brought my parents together initially was so inaccessible to Mother that only by poking about in the area of their common past could she even begin to approach the terrain. "I've been shopping for a couch," she said, and he graciously arched his eyebrows. "Nothing decent to be found." She described a Biedermeier settee from our apartment on Madison Avenue in the 1940s she should not have given away, should have reupholstered. They didn't make decent couches anymore and a Biedermeier lasted forever.

She wouldn't come to the funeral. I wanted my family together one final time. Livid, I took my place in the church at the end of the first pew, beside Jerry, Carl, Natalie, and Diana, who pointed out dancers from my class in Harlem and a row of people from New York City Ballet. But lodged in my mind was Mother, crowding out other thoughts, and I couldn't take comfort in my supporters. As the minister entered I felt a change in the church, and hoping for Mother I turned to see George standing just inside the doors. From down the long aisle he caught my eye and nodded, and I was put right. Father's body in front, George in back, antipodes of my existence, beginning and destiny, shaper and outcome, and the reverse: indelible poles.

2

In 1974 George received a note from Suzanne, who had been to a summer performance of New York City Ballet in Saratoga:

As wonderful as it is to see your ballets, it is even more wonderful to dance them. Is this possible?

He called and asked my permission and I agreed. In truth she was fantastic, and I thought he needed her. Their romance was long over, but she enlivened his already fine ranks and enriched his choreographic imagination.

One day Suzanne would insist that she and George never did consummate their relationship, true to the rumors that flew while they were involved.

But by 1975 she was back in the company and George was back in my life, although our bond wouldn't strengthen for several years. We had dinner together every so often, and he came to one of the parties I threw for my dancers. Very late that night I found him and Carl in the kitchen discussing methods for staking tomatoes. They sat head to head, the older man and the younger, George telling Carl to come to the prop department at the theater and pick up scraps, they had good wood, and use *rags* like the Italians for tying up the tomatoes, using strings dented the flesh. "Trim lower leaves," George stressed. "They will not get tomatoes and you want energy going up to the fruit." Carl in his blondness, his big body, listened carefully, acting amazed by George's fairly pedestrian gardening knowledge.

The tomatoes that summer were plentiful and delicious. We did as George said, stopped at New York City Ballet for wood to take out to Weston. George met us in the prop shop and helped load the car. As a result, we ended up with enough lumber to stake a whole forest of tomatoes.

George stood on the loading dock seeing us off, grinning from ear to ear.

"He likes to help," I said to Carl.

"We could build a deck," Carl said, and we laughed until we choked.

That August Carl brought George a box of tomatoes each week. In the cool of autumn—we stayed in Weston longer each year—and at New Year's, when I always got out of the city, we used the New York City Ballet wood for fires.

Especially in the cold weather, Carl and I liked watching sports and animal shows on TV, because we liked watching things move. What a pair, Carl and his heart, me in my chair, both equally rigid with excitement as a cheetah tore up the veldt in pursuit of an antelope.

In Weston, we lay in bed watching the birds outside clamor and swoop. We often lay in the bath together. To be in a bath with Carl meant not much room for me, but it made the experience interesting.

On warm enough days in spring, we got up early in the morning and sat quietly in the yard, hoping to spot deer that grazed at the edge of the woods. One morning a group of five frolicked just inside the woods, sheltered by the scanty leaves. They playfully knocked horns, their hooves beating the hard-packed ground. The yard felt electric, primeval. It was misty out, fuzzy with green. When the deer vanished as magically as they had come, Carl picked me up from the chair and carried me inside and we made love until we got hungry.

"Get up," I said, "I'm crushed."

"You like being crushed."

"Truth's out. Roll off me." He did, but neither one of us could move and we lay side by side on our backs.

"We'll lie here and starve," I said. "Fucked to death."

"Marry me," Carl said.

I looked at him. "What?"

He pulled me in to his body, surrounding me with his strong flesh. "I want to marry you, Tanny."

"I hadn't thought about it," I said.

"So what do you think?"

I kissed him, I smoothed his mussed hair, I smiled, and I sighed.

"I guess not," he said.

"No, I mean—"

"It's all right," he said.

It wasn't, but I couldn't say anything, go into muddled explanations of feelings I didn't fully comprehend.

Ironically, at about this time I noticed changes in him: a little less appetite, more need of rest. We had discussed what could happen just once. There was nothing to do except live.

But to my annoyance, Jerry had to pick this same time to undergo what he termed a nervous breakdown, and I wasn't in the least sympathetic.

"Trouble in work? In love?" I said to him. "Is anything different?"

"Yeah, it is. I can't handle it anymore."

Against my advice he committed himself to a fancy rest joint and was incensed to be told, three days later, that he couldn't leave.

"That's what committing yourself *means,* Jerry. The ball's in their court."

He put on his best behavior and was released in two weeks. It made my head spin, how fast he regained control.

Years later I told him, "Looking back, committing yourself was a damned good idea. Set you straight immediately."

"I hadn't envisioned a sterile locked ward," he said. "I'd pictured a haven, very genteel, with deep verandas and polished tables. . . . I needed a rest."

There is no rest. Life can be beautiful and full of meaning, but rest is rarely in the offing.

Carl died in Weston. One early but flourishing June, he left me after breakfast to inventory the grounds and didn't return.

Beyond lunchtime, his absence felt ominous. My calls for him from the lawn meeting silence, I crossed by the side of the house leading to the back property, called at the rows of mountain ash trees that disappeared into dense green, beyond which I couldn't see.

Carl. Stillness. Mute nature: dumb birds, twitching leaves. Nothingness. I decided I could go farther, pushed hard, arms straining against the resistance of the rough ground maybe ten more feet, another two—it was impossible. *Carl*.

Don't explode, I told myself, for I thought I would burst now for sure out of my body, since I couldn't run for my lover.

I turned and wheeled back and called my neighbors, two elderly painters, who came at once and set off through the mountain ash trees, their white hair swallowed by green.

Carl had fallen and hit his head. The old men could not bring him out. An ambulance came and the paramedics brought Carl through the trees and over the clearing across the grass, covered by a blanket, to where I waited at the side of the house. He had died of a massive coronary, but he fell hard and initially they assumed the blow to the head killed him.

I said I wanted to see him and, kindly, they carried him around the house and put him on the outdoor table, seeing that I could not have knelt down on the ground.

One of the painters went into the house for a damp cloth and I washed the blood from Carl's face. I kissed his brow, his cheeks, and his mouth. He had died fast, on a perfect sunny day.

Natalie came out and stayed with me until a storm cleaned the bloodstain on the table: it was a sign saying that I should go back to New York.

Carl's mother made the arrangements and, as it happened, a large extended family mourned him at a Lutheran church in Germantown.

He was forty-four.

Time collapsed, and expanded again because of teaching. I took on other classes at the Harlem school, besides the one for the company. I told George that it was another way of dancing. Flying away. In Weston, I would look hard at the cardinal flitting red through the leaves, the bats in the dusk doing a tango across the yard.

Jerry helped me sometimes in Weston. The cooking and physical labor were good for him.

Then in March 1978—and was this middle age? years just gone, blurs—George suffered a mild heart attack at his apartment.

The air jangled loud with mortality; I felt besieged.

"But he's all right," I told Mother. "A week or two in the hospital, rest, medication, he's going to be fine."

I didn't care for hospitals, to put it mildly, because of my lengthy hospital stays, and visiting Father I was twice mistaken for a patient proceeding illegally to the exit.

I went to see George at Roosevelt Hospital, four blocks down Columbus Avenue from Lincoln Center. Sitting up in bed, on the phone, he put his hand on the mouthpiece and exclaimed,

"Darling!" He finished the conversation: "*Après moi, le board*," and hung up.

"What was that?" I asked, situating myself to the hospital whiteness, relieved by a chaos of color in mixed vases jumbled across a low shelf, a single bunch of purple tulips set on the windowsill.

"Lawyers. Can you believe? To this man already I'm dead. Tanny, I feel much better! The dizziness? Tiredness? Now I know why and I'm fixed."

"You look good," I said, distracted. "After me, the board," the single stunning articulation I'd heard of his thoughts for the future of the company beyond his lifetime. He had probably said them to placate the lawyer. His complexion was excellent, ruddy and bright.

"I'm Georgian," he said, "we're long-lived. What the lawyers don't know is they told me in 1933 I had optimistically three years. How are you, dear? That's a pretty Italian dress."

"Thank you, but it's French."

"Then the material must be Italian."

I laughed. "You may be right."

"How is Choleric?"

I was coaching a dancer in my *Four Temperaments* role. "Coming along."

"Good ballet," he said. "I couldn't have done my *Stravinsky Violin Concerto* without it." He considered the latter ballet his finest work, and hated missing a single performance.

"She's a fan of *Orpheus*," I said, "and I told her it's like the Bacchantes, *kick, bam, fast, hard*. You have steps to do in a given amount of time and you can't interpret or you'll be late. You won't be with the music."

"That's good. What else?" he asked.

"It should look maximum, one hundred percent everything, move a hundred percent, turn a hundred, and stop dead—nothing slow, no ad-aahgio."

"That's right."

"What beautiful roses." Velvety crimson against the white wall rising sheer as a cliff. I thought of the two of us under the sky tending our garden, double lilacs, double mock orange, our best roses—hot pink and dense as a cabbage.

"We had beautiful roses," he said. "Do you still cultivate roses?"

"Certainly. You should come out and see them."

"I could come?"

"Of course."

"You know, I have little patch of dirt at my house, but I haven't done with it anything. A shame. No time." He had recently bought a condo in Southampton, Long Island.

Time. If it was conceivable, he was busier than ever. There was no possibility he would slow down, as his cardiologist suggested; medication could only do so much. But the company topped a hundred dancers, frequent travel continued, and a dance boom—in a broader sense than earlier in the States at the start of NYCB—was on with the popularity of the new émigré dancers. Mikhail Baryshnikov left Ballet Theatre for the privilege of working with Balanchine that year. In response to his general physician's concern about his intake of alcohol, rich foods, and sweets, George told her a Stravinsky story.

Late in life Stravinsky developed a serious affliction that in the opinion of his doctor precluded booze. Stravinsky arrived in New York shortly thereafter and summoned Balanchine to his room at the Pierre and suggested a celebration, caviar and champagne, shots of scotch. Balanchine reminded Stravinsky of the doctor's orders and Stravinsky said, "Yes, I'd better call him." He told the doctor about his good friend Balanchine. They were happy to see each other and wanted to celebrate. Might he please have champagne? Absolutely not, said the doctor. "But we see each other so seldom," Stravinsky said in a tiny sweet voice. Champagne is bad for you, the doctor insisted. "Please, Doctor," pursued the composer, "just one bottle of champagne and—"

"I wash my hands of you!" the doctor replied. "Do as you wish."

Stravinsky hung up the phone and, turning to George, he told him, smiling angelically, "He says it's all right."

. . .

It wasn't long before George again became dizzy. He was occasionally unsteady on his feet, and he had angina. In January 1979, while he was in Washington, D.C., to accept an award at the Kennedy Center from President Carter, the angina hit him with a pressure pushing straight from his back through the front of his chest: "Punched out a hole," he told me. An assistant helped him to a bench. Straightened out by a hooker of vodka, he went on to the ceremony.

Tests were inconclusive. An angiogram would show the extent of the blockage, the doctors said. Surgery might very well be recommended. But George was frightened of anything intrusive and determined to cure himself of what ailed him, as he had in the past, by home precautions and folk remedies, the nature of which even those of us who had lived with him could not define.

He dragged through the spring. He called me more often, telling me what he was thinking and feeling in his new state, his parallel life. We had been through my illness and now we would go through his together. Many nights he was awakened from sleep, his bed plunged into a fun house of tilting floors and distorting mirrors: his vision was dulled and hallucinatory from cataracts and glaucoma, and in the darkness, tipping from his dizziness, amoebas in electric green morphed to blasts of angular splintering gold. It could turn out to be a glare from the window he had forgotten to cover. It could be the Statue of Liberty night-light. It could transgress a dream's borders and paint colors onto pitch-blackness.

If his chest was free of the terrible squeezing, his eyes adjusted and motion stilled, and he would lie thinking of the mountains in the days of his tuberculosis, the heady thin air and permeation of pine. He thought of the dust-rain in Copenhagen streaking his cheeks, the wet soot embossed on the skin as if he had spent an hour in a mine. He heard the iron lung, saw my encased body and my head on the cushion, my eyes open wide in the dark; saw himself telling me stories, trying to ease me. Deeper back, in the white nights thieving sleep, he would go see the sphinxes from Egypt three thousand years old, the eerie night whiteness and the stately stone cats in his memory fused, attached like damp rot and the hologram picture he carried of his family's dacha in Finland.

Vertigo tricked the senses, and I encouraged him to have his eyes examined again very soon. But his heart was the primary concern. I hadn't said a word to George about Carl; our conversations were centered on dance and his health. But I didn't want George smashing suddenly down on the stage, his heart burst like his night-vision's exploded stars.

"Please," I said. "Have the angiogram."

"I know what they'll say."

"Then why wait?"

"I don't want to be cut. . . . I think of the knife."

"*Don't* think of it," I told him. "If the thought comes, blot it with another thought."

Then I couldn't stop thinking of it myself. Touch of scalpel on skin, beading blood, the hot throbbing interior opened, birthed into harsh exterior life—an action, an event unintended for nonmedical, civilian contemplation. I too practiced blotting the thought.

Several more months and he couldn't walk without pain, couldn't cross from his bed to the bathroom to brush his teeth.

He had the surgery, and in the ICU just a day afterward he was again himself, unafraid. I just shook. Outside the room I sat gripping my armrests, whispering, *steady, girl.*

"Here," he said softly, "do you see nice straight green line?" I did, on the EKG monitor. Then nodding at the machine that displayed his heart and breathing rates, he explained how it worked. "My nurse told me. She's young brilliant girl. Science. We should bow down. Art isn't everything."

I laughed. "I know!"

He slept; I watched the green line.

Stay, I thought. *Stay,* and I let memories wash over me that day.

London in 1950, George wasn't traveling with the company at the time, and then—unannounced—he was there. Maria had a sprained ankle and, while she rested with an ice pack one afternoon, I met him at a pub.

Blackened gray London, bombed London, my beaming anticipation: strange, the vicissitudes of this world.

Every night at the Sadler's Wells, ordinarily disinterested stagehands watched us from the wings, for despite rotten reviews they had never seen anything like George's dances.

The dim pub, dark as a basement, canceled my sight. Just inside, excited and blind, I groped to the bar, where someone who looked like George sat. He grabbed my gloved hand and pulled me with the strength of his physical teaching and partnering to his side, and said ever so gently, the barest fingertip-touch on my cheek, "Do you know I'm in love with you?"

Recuperating from the surgery in his apartment, he requested I visit. "Big building, big lobby, no steps," he said. "Wide doorway into my apartment and there aren't any steps down inside." Levels, sunken living rooms in vogue in the sixties, were problems.

Everything in my life was harder since Carl died. Now I kept a complicated appointment book and depended on eight or ten people instead of a few. I had employed Owen, my Dance Theatre of Harlem chauffeur, to stand by on Mondays and Wednesdays. The visit to George fell on a Monday. The downside of Owen, a sweet young man the color of milk chocolate, was his enthusiasm. In all my born days, and by now I had lived half a century of them, I hadn't met anybody so smitten by the dance scene in New York. Handsome and wiry, Owen started dancing late and had not yet made it into the company. He took classes on scholarship at the age of twenty-two. I didn't trust that, sweet as he was, he wouldn't gossip about me. He asked questions constantly in the car. "Sorry!" he'd say if I declined to answer. But a minute later he'd ask again. They were too frequently personal questions about someone I knew. Try as I might, I could not convey to him that certain inquiries were inappropriate.

"Look," I finally said one day, "I like you. I don't mind talking with you about dancers if I'm in the right mood. Here's what we'll do. If I don't feel like talking I'll just say, 'Bad day,' when you arrive. Otherwise, you'll know the coast is clear. Deal?"

"Deal."

Well, the poor child looked so unhappy and even physically uncomfortable on the bad days that I seldom said it. I got cagier, dodged the questions, or lied.

"Balanchine lives here," he said as we pulled up to the place on West Sixty-Seventh.

"Common knowledge," I answered.

"But you're *visiting* him."

"Um, could be that I know somebody else here, Owen."

"You don't," and he laughed. "You're friends again?"

"Bad day," I said.

"Sorry."

"It isn't as if we're rock stars."

"You're rock stars to me."

"We were never not friends."

"I don't believe that."

"Owen. You are veering into the realm of the insensitive."

"*Sorry,* I wouldn't—gee, man, I'm sorry. But you can—I think you're too touchy," and he said this openly and without the least bit of malice or judgment—it was as if he were trying to help me—and I couldn't be that annoyed with him.

"Come around and help me out of here," I said. "And get the umbrella and the towel." Damn, one of those summer drizzles, and I wanted to protect my hair. I had to look as beautiful as possible for George; it made him happy.

My inquisitive employee opened the chair on the passenger side, toweled it, and then, while he held the bag of deli food and the umbrella, I shifted into the chair, banging my hip; damn again, I was distracted, didn't get the right angle, and I'd felt a small twist in my arm, catching myself, that I would have done well to avoid.

"Onward," I said.

Inside the cold lobby, cold aesthetically and overly air-conditioned, I asked the doorman to announce me and told Owen to go back to the deli and read—he read dance biographies, naturally—until I called. I didn't know how long I'd be, and the deli proprietor didn't mind.

"I'll just see you up," Owen said.

"No, George isn't well, as I'm sure you know. Go."

"Okay, boss, worth a try," he said, grinning. "See you."

The doorman told me to wait; the nurse had come late today. I pulled over to the waiting area, my feet and legs damp. Through the picture window people hurried as if in a deluge, newspaper hats, umbrellas popping, shouldering hard to get by.

Holding the bag of warm food in George's building, it saddened me that we each lived alone. It made sense. George saved his energy for work, and I saved mine to cope with the disability in order to *have* energy for the rest of my life. It wasn't as if an aging man and a cripple could take care of each other.

A guy on the sidewalk dropped his briefcase

and it opened, spitting papers into the gleaming gutter. I heard him curse.

"I'm old man," George had said, already years ago now, after Suzanne, "and nobody's going to get me anymore."

He could do any amount of work, he said in a recent interview, but he couldn't cope with complicated human relationships. True. Sad. In a way, he probably hadn't wanted a wife, not one, not five. On the other hand, lately he was ambivalent. In another interview he said, "Sometimes you only wanted to be alone, it solved everything. Then there were times the aloneness was almost unbearable." I understood the ambivalence, but after Carl my opinion was, if people were difficult, so be it. George had recently spoken to me of the pride and comfort he took in the good relationships he had with *all* his ex-wives. The "all" was to designate me, since I'd come around. He didn't see Maria or Vera Zorina much. Tamara lived in New York and Alexandra taught at the school, and they were Russian; he had depended on them as confidantes for years. Was I competitive? Whom did he love most? Or *had* he loved most? Suzanne? My spine stiffened. Oh, get over it. Trouble was, you couldn't stop wanting. Wanting and wanting was the human condition. A little girl sashayed on the sidewalk, tongue out catching rain. I wanted to do that. In dreams, I always walked, never wheeled.

My legs were dry but freezing. I put the bag on the nearby table and rubbed them vigorously, making my right shoulder scream.

People weren't meant to live alone. In primitive days we banded together against threat from the wilderness. What remained were the invisible threats, viruses, heart attacks, and immortal desire. Father's apartment hadn't felt in the end as it had—monkish and whispery, hazed by his alcoholic elixirs. It only felt hollow, and the jugs of red wine were cheap. I got a headache just looking at them. I tried to be patient with Mother. At her age, friends and relatives dropped off like flies. The texture of her horizon—culture, politics, style, the city—had so drastically changed since the days of her youth, her defining beginnings, she didn't know where she was anymore. That was what it was like, getting old. And she hurt here, *here,* and *here,* couldn't see, couldn't sleep, couldn't get used to the dentures.

My legs hurt. What was that nurse doing up there, performing a second surgery? I wheeled over to the doorman and asked whether the air-conditioning in the lobby could be turned down. No, it couldn't. I wheeled back. Cold bothered me due to my legs' lack of muscular protection. Old story that lately had gotten worse. Other things were worse too, or diminished, as if through overuse of some parts of my body in compensation for others I was wearing out at a faster rate.

It could be my imagination. In 1969 after George killed me—I often phrased it like that in my head, overwrought as it sounds, because anger and candor propel, release, and to say that he killed me resurrected my fighting spirit—in 1969 I had experienced those intense physical symptoms, which turned out to be nothing.

Absolutely nothing, *I'm sorry, Papa,* not your death, not Carl's, compared to losing George.

It had stopped raining. I could look and look at the sidewalks and streets and I would never see Carl. No Carl in the multitudinous comings and goings would ever walk out there again.

Carl's special quality was that although he had plenty of hurt, he had such a small portion of the usual response. Carl didn't tighten; instead he let go.

I could hear his voice, its rounded notes, how the words blended into one another and didn't land in strong stops at the end of a sentence.

George's door was a portal into the past. He opened it, and I could see glowing candles in a darkened room.

"Are you all right?" he asked.

"No. What were you doing up here? It was freezing in the lobby, I'm wearing a skirt—"

"Come in, come in. I made a nice pot of tea, snacks."

"I told you I'd pick up food from the deli—oh, shit. I left the bag in the lobby."

"Leave it."

"It's cold anyway," I said. He started to the kitchen so slowly I realized the nurse could have left ages ago—I hadn't paid any attention to people going through the lobby—and he was up here making tea and lighting candles, slow as a snail.

"I didn't expect you to entertain me, George."

"It's nothing," he called back. "Go to the table."

I was shivering. I almost said hurry, but I stopped myself. The dining table outside the kitchen was set against a beige wall. There was an open ironing board near the windows, a spinet piano, and a couch. Through a doorway I glimpsed his bedroom, a tall shelf of books—they would be science, religion, Shakespeare, Chekhov, Tolstoy, Pushkin, and Akhmatova. Not much, his abode, nondescript rooms in a nondescript building; he lived at the theater. Above the table was a rectangular muted landscape by an artist I couldn't quite place. I imagined the candles were soothing, restful. By the one on the table an icon in a gilt frame glittered: St. George. He put a plate of delicate cucumber sandwiches down in front of me.

"You were up here slicing cucumbers?"

"No. I made them this morning."

"Can you get the tea? Can you control the air-conditioning? Can I have a blanket? No, look, give me your sweater." He took off his cardigan and I wrapped my legs.

"Control's over there under the window," he said. I went for it and he went for the tea. Now we were in sync.

"Better," I told him as he sat at the table. "Tea. Tea."

He poured. I gulped two cups while he watched, then took an enormous breath and said, "So. How are you feeling?"

"Better than you are."

"I'm fine. No, I'm not. George?" Just out of the hospital, soft, rumpled, in his chest an unimaginable hurt, fuzzy on pain medication, and here I was—oh, to hell with it. "I had a companion, a lover, he died."

"What happened?"

I couldn't say it had been his heart. I put my left elbow on the table, forehead to hand. "It didn't just happen. It's been three years since—"

"You miss him."

"Yes."

He got up and pulled his chair next to mine. "Sit back," and he gingerly put his arm around me and I rested my head on his shoulder. "Poor girl," and he kissed my hair. "There." No cologne, just him, clean, slightly astringent, warm meadow, carnations. "Do you want to tell me about him?"

"No," I said. He held me, then we disengaged

and he silently served me sandwiches. He didn't eat, he watched me.

"Scrumptious," I told him.

"Good," he said. "You're little skinny in the face. They love you at Arthur's."

"I know. I love them."

"How is your arm?" I had confided the new weakness I'd noticed.

"It's there," I said. "I think it's inevitable. I overuse my arms. I overuse everything to make up for the legs."

"It could be on a subtler level," he said. "Nerves were destroyed. Have you talked to doctors?"

"They'd probably think it's psychosomatic."

"I'll give it some thought," he said.

"George, there's nothing to *do*."

"There's always something to do. Warm?"

"Yes. How are you coming along?"

"Oh, me. I'm slow, but it's the recuperation. It's nothing, because to walk without pain is such a relief. I'm like old car they give new engine. Soon I get new headlights and"—he zoomed his hand in a jet arc—"we are off!"

"Ow. Doesn't that hurt?" I said; he had done it so vehemently.

"Nothing hurts." The fluid retention was down, his features emerging from puff.

"What did you want to talk to me about?" I asked.

"The will. Don't worry, I told you. Petipa"—the great choreographer of the imperial era—"lived to ninety-two. I'll do the same. But if I get hit by a bus, Lincoln says, and the lawyers confirmed it, my brother's the heir. My dances to Andrei! To the Soviets, so I make will."

"And is it what you think you want twenty years from now?" I took his hand on the table.

"Yes. I am leaving you the American rights. You will look after."

"You just won't let me fade into obscurity, will you?"

"I trust you," he said. "That's that." He hated the subject, was already on to something else, working it energetically in his busy brain. I poured myself more tepid tea. "Did I know him?" he asked.

"Who?"

"Your lover."

"Why?"

"I can't believe I didn't know. I never heard anything." Good for Natalie, I thought, she didn't rat.

"What, you keep track of me?" I said.

"Of course I keep track! Who was this man?"

"Oh, George. Really."

"Who?"

"Carl."

"Carl the driver?" Biggest scoop of the year, of the decade, that's what his face said; he slapped the table. "How'd you keep it to yourself?"

302

"Well, I didn't *entirely*—oh, don't." His expression had changed. "Did my stock just soar in your estimation?" I asked. "He's dead, George."

"Yes, sorry. Sorry. I thought he just drove you around and planted tomatoes. But I'm glad for you, dear, you had someone."

"Thank you."

"Big strapping man," he said. "You just never know. . . ." Then he looked hard at me and asked, "This didn't start when we were still—"

"For god's *sake,* George! You have the nerve to ask me that?"

"Yeah." Didn't seem that he got the connection at all, and from his stare I could tell there was no way I couldn't answer.

"It started later."

"That's good."

"But he loved me when we were together." I couldn't resist telling. "He used to send me dozens of yellow roses."

Drew a blank. He didn't remember.

3

Late one night, I picked up the ringing phone at the side of my bed to George calling at the end of his very long day. His routine by this time, in 1981, was to leave his apartment midmorning, have lunch in his office, and then dinner at the Empire coffee shop with coworkers after rehearsals and performances. No longer conflicted about his living arrangement, by this period in his life he wanted to be alone. He was too tired at night to do anything but throw off his clothes and rest. I accepted his preference for aloneness. One must, given no choice, and I had made a pact with myself back while he was in surgery, vowing that if he could stay a few more years, I would be fine.

"The dancers voted to strike," he said. The mere possibility had been an outrage. Who were these sixteen-year-olds expecting comfortable apartments and looking ahead to a secure old age?

"Ingrates, materialists," he said. "I haven't the strength, but I will find it. We made five companies and we'll make a sixth. Did I tell you Princess Grace of Monaco wants a company? I will go there." I had loved Monaco on tour, the tidy, minuscule dressing rooms and the expanse of picture-postcard perfection outside. George first worked in Monaco for Diaghilev. Once in those days he was reprimanded by Diaghilev for dismissing a rehearsal early—unusual for Balanchine, and it was good for me to know that, like me, in his youth he had wanted more life, wanted out of a dark rehearsal hall. "I tell them go to John Clifford," he said, "Canada, Ballet Theatre, Europe, nobody is forcing them to stay here. Why aren't you arguing with me?" he asked.

"Because you won't listen," I said. "May I make one suggestion?"

"Aha!"

"My one suggestion is talk to them reasonably. Arrange a meeting and tell them why you can't go higher."

"Yes. . . ."

"Then go a little higher."

"That's two suggestions."

"Ignore either one."

"I haven't enough to do? I have to go everywhere—give interviews, attend receptions. It's terrible, it's tiring, but, I think, it's for the theater. Without the company there's no ballet. Without the audience we don't dance. I have to do everything and I always have."

"They know this," I said. Diana now had the job of running the school, Natalie was still in the office, and the company dancers, they had both said, drooped in the hallways, whispered guiltily to one another about the demands of the union. They were torn. Worried about Mr. B, concerned for his health, they didn't want to upset him. But the fact was the company wasn't a family anymore, it was fully an institution. It had grown too large to be held together and run by one man. Since the heart attack he taught company class only sporadically. A number of the principal dancers had no relationship with him and minimal contact at best. Still, to the dancers he was a god. They danced for him, didn't care about anyone else's opinion. Anxiety spiked the air, nights he stood in the wings. People thinking it didn't go well cried as if their whole family had died. A soloist threatened to jump off the roof. So said my various sources. The current dancers were under tremendous pressure. New York City Ballet was a harsher place, the ballet master a cultish distant figure. It was nobody's fault. It was simply the price of the passage of time and success. But he couldn't expect dancers who'd beat out thousands of others to work for nickels.

Nevertheless, it was George I cared most about and wanted to support. "How are you feeling?" I asked him.

"What does it matter?" he said. Then, "Don't you remember with the polio everyone asking you always how you are feeling?"

"I do."

"Don't ask always how I am feeling!" He was right. A person got lost in that repeated questioning.

"All right." Of course, if I didn't ask, he acted hurt. But the unspoken was if we didn't speak of the recurrent symptoms and the new symptoms, they'd go away. The doctors continued to insist that the bypass had been a success. They said the present symptoms derived from other, and mostly mysterious, causes. Everyone had been bowled over by his renewed vigor for more than a year. In

London the autumn following the surgery, he shunned cabs and walked everywhere. New dances flowed from him in the spring, and that summer in Saratoga he washed all the cars—six—in his row of cottages one early morning. He had treated himself to a Mercedes he doted on, "And if it was having a bath, why not the others?"

Eddie told me about the cars on the afternoon they came out to Weston that summer for lunch, and George strolled the property, approving the roses, the young trees, and noting the bird feeders Carl and I had installed. He proclaimed, "You've done a nice job, dear, just too many birds." They were one of my obsessions George didn't share. He didn't remark on how I'd let the vegetable garden go. He patted my hand and said, "Rest. It is what you need. You come to the country, be with your trees and birds"—little giveaway sniff of disdain—"and rest." He had discovered documentation to support a hypothesis that polio survivors living long enough were susceptible to recurrences of their original symptoms, pain, fatigue, breathlessness, weakness, and his advice was for me to slow down, save my energy for *la danse*, for teaching: "Go easier," he said, "on the mat. Get the boy, Owen?" I had allowed Owen to meet George, and Owen, meeting *God,* was temporarily rendered mute. "Get him to do more for you," George said. "Don't get out of the car by yourself. Don't shift into chairs. Stay in

Lenore." Lenore was *the* chair, and I had just named her. It had seemed appropriate on the cusp of our Silver Anniversary.

But given George's symptoms, showing up quite emphatically by then, I was sorry I had mentioned my less significant problems. By winter and the time of the strike—in late 1980 and early 1981—George weakened and we didn't know why, and his Tchaikovsky Festival, doomed if the strike lengthened, was nearly upon him.

The strike was resolved quickly. Management conceded slightly more than the original offer, similar to the strategy I had suggested. What he needed, I felt, were friends who could offer advice. If I didn't have any advice, why, then I made something up.

At Angelo's, equidistant from where we each lived and met in those days for dinner, he ate sparingly, plain pasta with cheese, a glass of red wine. But he still didn't look like a dancer should, he said—*slim*—as a result of drugs and less physical activity. He had to choreograph from a chair, although I'd heard he was always jumping up. He bemoaned the loss of his *bella figura*.

He toted an umbrella everywhere, rain or shine. He often required a prop for balance and would have been mortified by the suggestion of a cane. He wore jackets again, knotting a scarf at his throat, and I complimented him on his apparel.

"More formal is better, as I'm not much to gaze upon." Smile. Sigh of regret. How wrong he was: I gazed on him surreptitiously with unappeasable thirst, I noticed his every glad gesture, weary step, the slight totter that had attached itself to how he arose to stand, the press of his long, still elegant fingers against his tired eyes, and the silky white hair that grew from certain parts of his hairline as it always had and that he so carefully combed, making the most of what was left. With all of the changes, at Angelo's in our booth under the yellow light, our voices, our sudden loud barks of laughter, sounded exactly as they had in the beginning, in the middle, in all of the restaurants in all the cities, same as here at the end.

Balanchine's late-period work was full of angels and gypsies, dreams, visions, and portents. He began to go every week to services at Our Lady of the Sign, a Russian Orthodox church on the Upper East Side, and was friendly with the priests. His uncle had been a priest. In Russia, priests were called white clergy and black clergy. White priests could marry. He witnessed the ceremony of his uncle advancing to black priest, the level of a monk. His uncle lay facedown before the altar, arms stretched in the shape of a cross. George described to me the jewels of the priests' tall miters, the candlelight in the dark like the light of a stage, the swaying censors spewing streams of smoke. They covered his uncle with black crepe to signify he was dead to the world, and led him away. He returned garbed in glorious golden vestments.

"You know those men in Tibet up in the mountains?" George had once said. "They sit nude in the cave and they drink only water through straw and they think very pure thoughts."

"Yes, the Tibetan monks. The lamas," Ruthanna Boris, a choreographer, said. They were sitting together at a rehearsal.

"Yes," he said. "You know, that is what I should become. I would be with them." And then he looked around at the dancers. "But, unfortunately, I like butterflies."

He retained his excitement over new dancers even as he lost the ability to shepherd them all. At the time of the heart attack he rhapsodized over Maria Calegari: "Red hair, so beautiful. . . ." He made virtuosic dances for Merrill Ashley, of the incomparable technique. For the very young Darci Kistler he again spoke about mounting a *Sleeping Beauty*. "But not bargain-basement. Only if we can afford to do it right." Then there was Suzanne, with whom there existed complete dance understanding. No need to explain, expend extra energy he didn't have, he was able to give her the briefest of instruction and she took it from there. Peter Martins, his danseur noble from Denmark and Suzanne's current partner, was one of three or four men he created dances for and repeatedly cast. Peter would one day run New York City Ballet.

Karin von Aroldingen worked her way up through the ranks and into the circle of his attention and trust. Karin listened, as Suzanne had done, and her talent for acting and using a stage made her increasingly valuable. It wasn't until George and I were again close that I learned of his closeness to Karin in his personal life. He bought the Southampton condo to be near Karin and her family's vacation home. Married, with a child, nonetheless she was his woman after Suzanne and until the end of his life. Though it didn't negate our relationship, it hurt with a pain that was unsurprising but deep. Sometimes the most obvious things are so. I understood then—as I couldn't when we were still married and I didn't fully want to understand—that sensuousness for George was movement. He had been ripped from his mother when she was the age of all the women he was drawn to, and if he couldn't live without a young dancer even in old age, this last one, both young and maternal, had very nearly his mother's maiden name: von Almedingen.

So—Karin, my apologies for the resort to Freudianism, but there it is.

Diana said, "His main interest is dancing. People come in and out, but for Balanchine dancing's the thing. This doesn't make him an

311

unfeeling man. It's how he is. What interests him is to see somebody move, and this produces in him an idea. It helps him create. I don't fault him for that. I think that is what his life is about."

"I like being married to a dancer," he once remarked to a reporter. "You always know where she is, in the studio working." As a boy asleep in the barracks at the Imperial School, rising each morning and donning the blue uniform with the lyre on the lapel and the cap, he was taught that all that—the barracks, the classes, the regimen, the performance—was home.

Balanchine had his Tchaikovsky Festival. The strike resolved, and he went to work in the studio, pushing through his physical limitations. The festival closed with his ritual staging of the *Adagio Lamentoso* of *Symphony Pathétique*, its atmosphere shaped out of Byzantine iconography, wings on the gowned angels aimed straight up at heaven, and black-robed monks in the posture of his uncle's investiture. At the end a boy blew out a single candle.

If the work seemed to some an acceptance of death, I knew he hadn't accepted death, he wanted to live. He kept searching for answers, conferring with doctors, and though they could only say that his problems were neurological, after what he had already been through with his circulatory system, he wasn't discouraged, he said, "We will get to the bottom of this."

"You know," he confided to me, "how I'm supposed to choreograph last movement of *Pathétique*, with balloons?"

In a dream he roamed through his New York State Theater, through the house, glancing up at the boxes, the tiers, the studded lights big as serving platters masquerading as jewels that I hated, used to tell him belonged at the opposite ends of a Chevy's front grille. He gazed at the magnificent gold curtain. He paced the stage, the good floor with wooden joists he had ordered for buoyancy and give, and the deep and wide backstage. He wandered the passageways by the storage vaults, by studios and the rehearsal space for the orchestra; rode the elevator up to the shops and the dressing rooms and sat down at one of the mirrors and smoked a cigar.

"A cigar?"

"Yeah, was good, was congratulations. I wasn't young man again, but I was better. Everything worked as it should."

"Listen," he said to me one night as soon as I picked up the phone. I knew the news wasn't optimistic. He couldn't disguise the especially nasal twinge, the strain in his voice. "How are you? Were you asleep?" he asked, recalling himself, for he had been about to jump right into whatever he had to tell me.

"Fine, I'm awake, what is it?"

"I have rushing sound in my ears, like wind very fast in the wheat, or you know how in open car going fast you can't hear what somebody's saying. Then it gets worse and I can't play piano, I can't hear the notes, is a roar."

"When did this start?"

"Oh, weeks ago. I didn't want to worry you."

"George? Worry me. Please."

"Well, what are we going to do? More tests. Maybe I go deaf."

"I don't think that's how people go deaf."

"Me either." I held on to him through the wire, intently aware of the dark shapes of my bedroom around me, the table he used to sit at by the window, the rooms looming beyond, the kitchen and the pianos and the foyer and downstairs the lobby; the eleven dark blocks of Broadway between us; I pictured him sitting in bed, the Bible beside him, an icon, a burning candle; the stark room, the tall shelf of books standing watch. "I think in a year I'll go to Monaco for good," he said. "I like Monaco. There's always too much to do in New York. Maybe I should settle down. A company there wouldn't be as much work. Maybe I should eat good food, sit in the sun, and work a little. I could have nice life. I could be buried there someday. You come. You come and teach. We'll live up in the hills and the sun will be good for your muscles. It's always warm and

314

sunny. It's nice to breathe sea air. Nothing dies there, you know. It's flowering all year long like California.

"Are you there?" he asked.

"Yes."

"What do you think?"

"It would be good."

"A year," he said, "that's all I need. Then Peter and Lincoln and Jerry can run the company."

The months stumped along. No one could figure out what had taken up residence in his body and wouldn't stop trashing the place. People commented that his interviews didn't always track. Well, he would prop himself up with a bolster in his office so dizzy he couldn't sit up straight and guess at questions if the sounds in his head overwhelmed words coming from the outside. Maria worried about the too-bright lights she encountered at a rehearsal when still, she said, Balanchine thought the stage was too dark. Braced against a box of equipment in his spot downstage right, he watched his dancers zoom in and out of focus until he felt sick and had to sit down.

At Russian Easter 1982, he attended the late service at Our Lady of the Sign, and in the ritual churchyard procession his candle went out. Another worshipper lit it for him and again it went out. The third time Balanchine said to leave it, that it wasn't supposed to be lit.

A new complaint: trying to pirouette to the right from his left foot, he couldn't. To the right on the right foot his balance worked fine. This bothered him incessantly and the cause, as with everything else, was unclear.

Another festival to honor the centennial of Stravinsky's birth was slotted for June. Rehearsals were sporadic, dependent on how Balanchine felt. One piece of choreography, a solo he wanted to do over again for Farrell, wasn't ready in time and was performed only later that summer at the end of the season. But it made him content—he had such a lovely contented look on his face, speaking of this dance. "The first time I did it, I didn't have it right," he said. "Now it's exactly what the music calls for." His impulse was simplify. "Too busy," he'd frequently say of earlier dances he reworked, "must simplify."

In Saratoga, he seldom felt well enough to leave the cottage he shared with Eddie. People said he was losing his mind and that it was Alzheimer's—this wasn't true, he had been tested—or some other form of dementia. At the festival George's third wife, Vera Zorina, with her beautiful speaking voice, had been the narrator of his *Persephone*. She said that in a production meeting he screamed, "Only *I* know what to do—nobody else knows anything!" She was sometimes afraid to go near him. "At times," she said, "he looked as if he did not know who I was."

He did not want to die. He was fighting the revolution of his body. He struggled to cut through the barrier that whatever had happened had erected between him and the outside—first of mist and fog and then of steel mesh, it seemed, and rightfully, he was enraged.

In September, after George underwent a cataract operation that didn't work, Jerry visited him at the apartment. George answered the door in Jockey shorts and an unbuttoned shirt, his hair mussed and eye bruised. He looked, Jerry said, like his own Don Quixote come off the stage. He spoke of his plan to retire to Monaco. Perhaps doctors in Europe—in Switzerland, the clinic he'd gone to for the TB—could tell why his motor functions had broken down. "My legs won't hold me up. No muscle. Some choreographers work from a chair, not me. I must *show* them."

Then in October, rushing to answer the phone—he couldn't remember to go slow—he fell and broke four ribs and a wrist. It wasn't the first fall. I couldn't take care of him; Karin had a family and a career. Eddie wasn't equipped to serve as a nurse.

So Eddie checked George into Roosevelt Hospital on November 4, where he would have constant care. Switzerland was discussed, but it was felt he would be better off where his dancers and friends could visit.

"Very tired," George said. "They will have me right here for tests. I don't have to show up for appointments."

He had a bright corner room with windows on two sides on the top floor of the hospital. I kept hearing his voice, back when I was a dancer.

"Come," he had said. "Give me your hand. This way, you see? I will show you. We'll stay until you see what I mean. I'm not in a hurry. There, yes. Again. No. Try again. Why always so frustrated? You have everything you need to do this. You have everything. There, yes. Again. Yes. Again. You showed them beautiful girl could also be funny and now we will show something else."

4

*P*eople helped me from the time I was born, Mother and Father and then George. I sailed forth into adulthood, though it didn't always seem so then, with the wind behind me. I was blessed with fortune and opportunity. George liked to acknowledge how fate smiled on him at the Imperial School. You could see how he felt about his childhood watching him work with children in rehearsal, very gentle, very much on their own level, quietly anxious to impart to them something of what he had experienced. The chances George and I had, the luck, you can't cancel it out by what else came along for the ride, by lives that if you step back and look at them nearly whole were admittedly lives of extremes but extremes on both sides of the coin.

On the days I taught I arose early, bathed and got dressed, and sat for a while with Mourka before Owen came. After class and lunch, I visited George. Today Jerry was stopping by, and I got up earlier than I usually did.

"Come, boy," and Mourka, who had been solemnly following me and awaiting this moment, crouched next to Lenore as if he could still jump, and purred as I lifted him into my lap. "Big old ginger cat, you are just skin and bones," I said. I rubbed his old joints, his shoulders and hips, and it soothed him; the loose skin pushed easily back, the fur was bristly and dry. At night I brushed out his dandruff and anointed him with baby oil. We sat at the front window post by the pianos, where there was so much to watch with the street and traffic island and stores. But in the still dark early-winter mornings the view was peaceful, quietly humming in tandem with the rub, with purrs.

The buzzer rang. I greeted Jerry in his navy-blue fisherman's cap and a red muffler against his white beard. He kissed me and petted Mourka, pressed like a hot furred rock into my lap and determinedly anchored throughout the commotion of taking Jerry's coat and going to the kitchen, where I'd brewed coffee.

"You're looking good," Jerry said cheerily.

"Hell I am." I hadn't slept well.

"How is he?"

"Still trying to run the company from bed." I poured coffee.

"I'm going over this evening after rehearsal."

"Don't go too late."

"No." George faded early. "They haven't said anything new?"

I shook my head. On his chart it said he suffered from progressive deterioration of the brain and nerve centers, but why remained unknown.

"It isn't fair."

"No."

"Do you have any food?"

"Um, no."

"Toast?"

"I forgot to buy bread."

"Tan—"

"I'm fine, I forgot."

He picked up a folder I had on the table from a real estate agent. "What's this?"

"Florida properties. You know, the cold. I'm thinking of buying or renting for a couple of months in the winter. Maybe next year."

"Why not this year?"

I pushed over the sugar and cream.

"So I think you're too wrapped up in George," he said, "so what?"

"So it's none of your business." I suspected we were brushing against history here. Something was always disturbing it these days.

"You're a relatively young woman, you're—"

"Jerry! I am not a young woman by any stretch of the imagination. If you want to pretend you're a kid right up to your dotage, go ahead."

"Thanks."

"Here, have cream, it'll fill up your stomach."

"It's just—you cut back on your classes, your thing with George . . ." He backed off but it was too late.

"I cut back on my classes because I *hurt,* understand? My body gets sore and tires easily, and I don't like to spell it out." He scowled into his coffee. "What 'thing' with George?"

"George's illness is arduous. You aren't married."

"I visit him once a day, big deal, if there were anything else I could do, I would do it."

"Why didn't you marry Carl?" he asked.

I looked away from him to the kitchen window. We were all losing George. Jerry was losing his colleague, his idol, and, essentially, his father. "Don't beat me up, honey," I said.

He stood and opened the refrigerator.

"You're starving," I said.

"Not really," and he sat again; he had not touched his coffee. "Tanny, I want the company."

Breath left me. "Oh."

"I want you to talk to him."

"One minute I'm too involved, and the next you're asking me to intercede. . . . Why? If I was disposed to a debate on the subject I'd take Lincoln's side." But George said don't give it to Lincoln. "When have you ever wanted to run anything, Jerry? The few times you've tried, you got sick of it and quit." He had the dogged set to his mouth, the pained eyes.

"I will not be humiliated by having Peter appointed."

"Ah. Talk to George if you're so determined. He isn't dead yet, pal."

"You talk to him."

Unbelievable. "No, and I mean it. This isn't a business meeting, don't grab on to me like a bulldog. Anyway, it won't do any good because I don't give either."

"No kidding."

What did he want, for me to go against George's obvious wish not to appoint a successor? The board would eventually muddle it out, and Jerry would be given every consideration.

"Are you analyzing my character?" I asked. "Or are you being ruthless? Or both?" He was red in the face but wouldn't yell at me, although I didn't particularly care if he did.

"What do you know about the will?" he asked.

"Nothing." Cool liar.

"I'll go," he said.

I knew he intended to stir up my temper since I would not take his side over a trifle, a waste of energy, ghoulish—and the crack about not being married, and Carl.

"Go," I said. "Mission isn't accomplished but you said what you had to say. Nice visit. Thank you for your concern about my welfare."

He didn't move, weakened. "Don't hate me," he said.

I didn't answer.

"I'm all—"

"Confused? I hope so, Jerry. I really do."

"I'll see myself out."

Mourka meowed and I took him back in my lap. Sitting dully, depressed, I waited for Owen to ring. I realized that it should be Peter. Lincoln and Jerry were, frankly, too old.

"Bad day," I said to Owen. He didn't mind as he used to. He was in love and his interests were finally varied. I put on my fur jacket, got my bag, said, "Good-bye, cat." Mourka hit the basket as soon as Owen walked in the door, dead giveaway of imminent desertion.

Outside, I let Owen lift me into the car. The uniformed man in the guardhouse rushed over and folded Lenore. It was freezing. Owen handed me the wool blanket and I put it across my lap, down my legs. I wore fur from October to April but it wasn't enough, partly because I remained vain: woolen tights instead of silk stockings had been suggested by a doctor, but so what?

Today Owen wore a dark knitted hat pulled low to his eyes that made him look like a thug. I snatched it off.

"Hey, man!" His hand jumped to his head.

"Oh, dear. Owen, I'm sorry." He'd colored his hair an undoubtedly mistaken orange.

"It was supposed to be dirty blond," he said.

"Who did it?"

"Me and Woolworth's."

"You want to go to my guy?"

"You mean it?"

"My treat."

"I don't exactly want your shade—"

"Just tell him," I said. "I'll give you the number."

Different generation. I liked them. Mother said I should have been born twenty or thirty years later, but I had been born just right.

We were early this morning and I chose the longer route up the West Side Highway along the river, the calming but invigorating way I liked to go before class. In the water small icy floe islands bobbed beside the few chugging ships, and in the distance New Jersey squatted in chalky white air. The blank sky, the brittle trees against the remembrance of grass in Riverside Park streamed by, and then, cutting over on 152nd to Broadway, we entered bleached Harlem—it appeared paler than my nearby neighborhood, not in the sense of lacking robustness but in its lack of the simple infusion of money that painted more prosperous parts of the city with stateliness, clean modernity, or the funky charm of the Village. "Morning in America," indeed; Ronald Reagan, how amazing; soon we'd have Bozo the Clown running for mayor of New York.

We cut up the alley by the side of the building and parked in back. Someone had strewn white Christmas lights all down the zigzagging fire escapes, and a pair of pink tights were tied to the iron railing just above the back door—they'd been there on Tuesday, waved in the breeze like a welcoming flag. Now they looked frozen, stiff, shriveled, tarnished by dirt.

I sat in the stairwell while Owen fetched the secretary for Lenore. The old-building smell, the thrill of getting out, superseded the unsettled feeling I had brought with me and couldn't transcend, what Jerry had set off in me. Strong Rebecca crashed through the door—what I wouldn't give for ten cents of her vigor—and I floated into a sort of elation. It wafted me up the stairs, as Owen gripped and hurt me a little and Rebecca told us my dancers were all in a company meeting and we would have to start late today.

It was nice. It gave me the opportunity to be alone in the studio. Rebecca bustled out and Owen left to get tea. Sweat, rosin, creak of the radiator, a heating smell of warmed wood embraced me. A slight chill emanated from the double-hung windows and the mirrors looked cold. Strange how over the traffic chatter and clash of city studios, spread like the blanket I drew from my legs, there was always a hush. I breathed it in. I bent down and took off my left shoe and, holding my left foot, I stroked my sole across the smooth floor. Comfort, excitement, even sensuality, come in diverse forms. My foot remembered. My skin remembered.

"Tea." Owen handed me mine and sat down on the bench and opened his, let the steam breathe up at him, smiling, blew, blew again, tried to sip, and, puckering, put the cup down beside him to cool. He hoisted his bag off his shoulder and dug inside, coming up with a magazine. "Article on Balanchine," he said. "You want it?"

He handed stuff off to me when he finished; he was one of my lines into the dance world.

"Oh, gee," I said, taking it, "another retrospective of the career. . . ."

"A couple of pictures of you. Gorgeous ones."

"Yes, Owen, those always capture my interest."

"Even if he wasn't in the hospital," Owen said, "they'd do these articles. When somebody's old . . . They interviewed him for it. Good quotes."

I flipped through, worried he'd sound confused, but I didn't see anything alarming. Things he'd said before, about arms and legs contrapuntal to the body, about his conviction "that dancing is an absolutely independent art, not merely a secondary accompanying one. I believe that it is one of the great arts. . . ." To illustrate, he spoke of staging *The Bat* to the music of Strauss's *Die Fledermaus* for the Metropolitan Opera in the 1930s. He had given over the stage to his dancers, relegating the singers to the pit with the orchestra. Fired. Banished to Hollywood.

Owen sat closer and turned the page to a photo of me on the backstage steps of City Center in 1950: a gazelle fluffed up in tulle. I hardly recognized her. What mattered to me was the quote from George underneath: he said I had been born with artistry, and that when I got sick we were just getting started.

One of my dancers strode in.

"Hi, Charlie," I said, looking up. "Thanks," I said to Owen, and I stuffed the magazine into my bag and greeted two of the others entering quietly, with their exaggerated splayed ballerina's feet, their tight hair—Jahala and Rune.

I drank my tea as the room filled and activated with stretching bodies and voices and the *tock, tock, tock* of toe shoes against the floor as girls tried things. Darling Joel the rehearsal pianist entered and sat.

Today we would work on petit allegro.

But first the best part, and the dancers gracefully formed lines, taking their places at the barre.

People from nearly all epochs of Balanchine's life came to the hospital: Russians, ballerinas back to his earliest years in America and through the Ballet Society years and City Center, to the New York State Theater dancers beginning in the 1960s, and up through today. The youngest had never in their lives known ballet without Balanchine as its foundation, and they wanted to see him and be with him in his illness; their concern was touching, as was their utter belief that he would recover.

The women and girls came and came. A clerk at the desk on Balanchine's floor said he had never seen so many beautiful women. Sensitive to his frailty, the visitors instinctively siphoned one or two at a time in and out of his room. It wouldn't last, all the people, with the impress of winter, the duress of his condition, and as the excitement of crisis wore thin. I felt him leaving us only in moments that December, in sudden confusions, the veil that would draw over his eyes, in a few bursts of rage—similar to what Vera described—in his tendency to drift back to the past and a willingness to speak of things he would not have ordinarily. He experienced trembling he couldn't control, and his vision worsened. At first his vision was better—everything was better, bed rest did him good. But then he got worse. He didn't speak directly of death. He patiently doled out what people needed, a talk with one of his young male dancers about fifth position, acceptance of an apology from a musician with whom he had quarreled. Business details were ongoing in the beginning, and more loose ends even after it became clear that whatever the outcome of his hospitalization he would not be home soon and could not participate in this year's season.

One day I encountered Suzanne stepping briskly from the hospital elevator in a voluminous Mexican poncho, her face shadowed by a slouchy felt hat. She was quite famous in New York, and I pegged the outfit as a disguise. Diana told me knots of corps girls, seeing Suzanne approach in the hallways, disassembled and parted in awed respect for her like the Red Sea. She had matured splendidly. Her beauty was deeper, her dancing clean and masterful. There weren't many who fulfilled their early promise; Suzanne exceeded hers.

She spotted me, and acted flustered. I stopped where I was a few yards down the hall and let her come to me.

"Hello, Tanny."

"Hello, Suzanne. How is he today?"

Her eyes were red-rimmed. She put a flat hand

to her mouth, turned her face away. "He asked about my knees. My *knees*. He had been praying for them."

"Well," I said, "a couple of prayers can't hurt. He's always asking about my arms—I have this—" I began to explain. But, interrupting myself, I said, "Your knees and my arms seem inconsequential, don't they?"

"Yes," turning back to me gratefully. Offstage, Suzanne was shy. She wiped a tear with a knuckle.

"I'm sure he was so happy to see you."

"Yes, I—I hope." I took her hand and pressed it good-bye, and then she walked off, regal again, in command, even the hospital hallway a stage.

Well, baby, I thought, good thing I'm not shy. You couldn't disguise Lenore. I noted the edge of bitterness and the hearkening back to the urge to stay inside to avoid putting myself on *display,* as I'd seen it. I forgave myself for the minute of weakness. On display, ha. Nobody gave a damn.

Owen dropped me at the smooth ramped emergency room entrance. Hi to the girl at the check-in desk—what a job—stop at the fountain to take a couple Excedrin—prophylactic measure for long days—and head for the elevator to the main lobby, another one to George's floor. Having to go through emergency provided a dose of perspective, bloody-toweled secrets, fast stretchers, expressions eloquent of pain, and the poverty I could read in the postures, the clothing of some people waiting. Then here came the wheelchair lady in mink, part of the New York carnival scene, our bursting-with-all-of-it town.

I found George in his top-floor room sitting up and expectant, fairly bristling in the quiet, no WQXR today. For a person who had been so active, inactivity was a trial. His shoulders and head jerked toward me at the door. He had probably heard Lenore, but the jerk I identified as an adjustment to a block in his vision. Winter afternoon light shyly clung to the windows; a tall amaryllis rose up from the floor, a small blast of joy. Most flowers people carried off, he was sickened by their scent. He could tolerate violets, and I tended a little collection on his bedside table. A New York City Ballet calendar was tacked to the mirrored front of his wardrobe. December featured Heather Watts in Jerry's *The Cage*; Heather was astute and riveting in *The Cage* and a dancer Jerry especially liked. Someone had made a mistake and put *The Nutcracker* on November.

"Tanny, you just missed Volkov." Solomon Volkov was a Russian musicologist conducting a series of interviews with George that he would collect in a book called *Balanchine's Tchaikovsky*. I'd happened in on them one day. "Solomon Volkov, may I present to you Tanaquil Le Clercq," George had introduced us in formal style. They'd switched from Russian to English for me, continuing their conversation about old St. Petersburg.

We kissed and George said, "I don't want Volkov here anymore."

"I thought you liked talking to him," I said.

"I've had it." I had heard it before. All of our visits began with similar statements.

"Did you have a walk today?" I asked.

"Yes, Karin took me this morning. We marched. Twenty miles, thirty, I couldn't tell you." He scratched his soft wrinkled neck, which looked so exposed and vulnerable in the limp collarless hospital gown; over it he wore a beautiful forest-green sweater.

"I love your sweater. Is it new?"

"Somebody brought it, I don't know who."

"You don't remember?"

"No. It was sent here by somebody I do not know, Tanny," he said sternly.

"I see. I'm sorry."

"It itches."

"Then take it off."

"I'll be cold."

"I'll get you another sweater." He shrugged: Go ahead, I don't care one way or the other, and I opened the bottom drawer of the chest beside his bed and took his gray cashmere from the stack.

"There's a package in there," he said. "Get it out." I found a small brown paper packet and held it up.

"This?"

"Open it," he said, changing sweaters.

A small Byzantine cross, two inches tall, studded with tiny garnets like bird eyes.

"Was Mama's," he said. "She gave it to me to take to school. It's for you."

"Oh, no, George."

"Are you atheist now? I thought agnostic."

"Pantheist, secular humanist, worshipper at the altar of art. I mean I think you may still want it."

"One thing I've got is plenty of crosses." The Russians and priests kept bringing them. "And religion and art are separate, but I wouldn't try to convince you. I just thought you'd like the cross."

"I would, thank you," and, following the dense creases, I rewrapped the precious object and put it carefully away in my bag. Would like the cross, need the cross, what didn't he know?

"Is something wrong?" I asked. He was slightly off, and his eyes wouldn't quiet. "What's going on?"

"I can't read." His ability to read was unsure; pulsing lights obscured what he tried to see, wavy colors flowed off the pages and onto the bedcovers. Even on good days he confronted letters smeared with Vaseline and straining to decipher them was painful. Now I noticed the absence of books he kept on the bedside table and along the windowsills.

"Where are your books?"

333

"I had Volkov put them away in the closet."

"Don't give them up yet," I said. But he was generally right about the downward trajectory of his impairments. Arriving here, he planned to watch TV and read. He could think of better pastimes, but they'd be okay. TV went, and now reading. So far the radio, played softly, didn't set off the loud noises in his head.

"I could read to you," I suggested.

"I lied. Volkov took the books."

"Where?"

"To a library, I don't know."

"I have books in my bag," I said. "Mysteries and—I know, I know—"

"Big bore."

"*I know.* I have *War and Peace.*"

"You're reading it?"

"Yes, I'm reading it again. I just came to the part where these soldiers on horseback, scores of them, jump into this river to impress Napoleon, do you remember? This treacherous river and they're drowning, the men, the horses, swirling away and going down in the water that's too difficult to cross."

"It's terrible."

"Yes."

"Did you come to the part where Natasha dances?"

"Not yet."

"She goes to the peasant's hut, the beautiful

young noblewoman. The peasants are having celebration and she hasn't danced Russian dances before but she can and does. It's in her blood."

"I remember. I could start over from the beginning and we could read it together some every day."

"I don't care," he said.

"Yes or no?"

"I'm a captive audience. Suit yourself."

I opened the book and began, "'*Eh bien, mon prince*, so Genoa and Lucca are now no more than private estates of the Bonaparte family.'" He closed his eyes and lay back. In a while I thought he was asleep but in my pause he said, "Go on." I didn't stop again for an hour.

A faint smile lit his mouth. "I was thinking of Léon's." Léon Barzin had been a conductor for New York City Ballet, and he and his wife continued to invite the dancers to their estate just outside of Paris; there were formal gardens with decorative ponds, fountains, and even a grotto. "I was there just last year," he said.

"It's the same?" I asked.

"It's beautiful, yes, but it isn't the same. What day is it, Friday? You had two classes today, you must be tired."

"We'll read again tomorrow if you like. Jerry will be here later, after your dinner."

"Jerry's the best American choreographer."

"You're not?"

He remained lying back against the pillows, and he looked steadily at me now. "Best American choreographer," he repeated.

"You're the best international choreographer, then," I ventured.

Of course, he answered me with a nod. "Jerry's *very* good," he said. "Best American."

"Tell him. It would make him happy."

"I have to do everything, don't I? Tell people things if I can't do anything else."

"I guess that's just part of being who you are." I put the book in my bag. "See you tomorrow."

Without telling me, Mother made a pilgrimage to the hospital around the holidays.

George reported her visit.

"How was she?" I asked him. "Did she behave herself?"

"Was fine. We talked about Copenhagen and Venice."

Testing the soil of the violets for dryness, I looked at him and said, "Venice, why?"

"We took gondola ride, the three of us, you, me, and Edith. I hadn't remembered." He was lying on his side deep within the sheets and blankets, pressing his trembling hands to the mattress; it was not a good day but he wanted to talk, he welcomed the distraction. The top blanket shivered as if mildly electrified. I recalled the luminous quality of Venice in the cold that

September, after the blistering heat just one week before. I remembered Mother and I with George in the middle setting out on the canal for dinner one evening.

"You know we were close sometimes, Mama and I," George said. "She is cultured woman and not really foolish."

In the cold, the virus had already entered my body. His mention of Copenhagen and Venice in combination unnerved me.

"Waiting together during your illness," he said, "such closeness lasts. I was glad to see her. I told her she was good mama.

"Why are you quiet?" he asked.

"I'm not."

"Would you like to read?"

"Yes."

He said nothing else about Venice and I felt secure again in my belief that he didn't know. I felt I couldn't bear it if he knew. Mother may have heard what I'd done and told him. Another visitor could have decided to impress him and confided the act, which would verify his suspicion that I *had* contracted the virus in Venice, but not in the way that he assumed. Even the thought that Mother might know jacked up my heart and doused me with heat as I sat with George, reading.

Unable to forget it, I spoke to Mother the next day to be sure. She said, huffily, that she and

George had their own past, their own relations, and why should she tell me what they had discussed?

"I hate to burst your bubble," I said, "but George already told me."

"Everything?" she asked. "He told you he said I was good mama?" I heard the small spear whistle by.

"Mother, I tell you." She was silent. "You are good mama."

"Thank you."

"You talked about Venice."

"Yes, we took that lovely gondola ride."

"You talked about Copenhagen."

"He was kind to me in Copenhagen. He brought me those open sandwiches I liked, and coffee. He brought me American magazines. I didn't forgive him for leaving you, though," she said. "I didn't mention it, but I'm sure he knows," and again my heart beat and heat rose, the old heat of shame.

And then a few days before New Year's, which was always a difficult day and more so this year, I went to the hospital early one morning and Karin sat beside him holding his trembling hands through the covers, trying to still them, speaking softly to him in German, her light brown hair flowing over him like liquid gold. They didn't see or hear me, and I sat in the doorway fully a minute before turning and going away down the hall.

I knew her, I had seen her with him, we were part of a small group who spent Christmas Eve in his room, a dreaded night that turned out to be festive and hopeful; George in good form, a sense that, *after all,* answers were near and he would recover. But two days later he hadn't known Lincoln, and he cowered seeing me, his hands to his face like little paws as if I were about to strike him. "George, it's me," I said. Relaxing, he still looked distressed. "Do you want me to leave? I don't want to make you unhappy." I had left that day too. The nurse told me I should. The next day he was fine again, as fine as he could be in the thinned weakened catastrophe of his body, and obviously, I thought, after finding him with her as if I had discovered them together thirty years ago naked, I had begun to unravel myself.

Today, at the elevator I stopped uncertainly, recalling a story I'd read in the *New Yorker* about a woman who seemed on the surface commendable and beneficent, but underneath was a vampire who fed off the fading strength of ill people she visited and administered to. I went to the emergency room and waited the long ninety minutes for Owen.

Jerry had turned on a light in one of my little dark rooms—*you aren't married.*

No kidding, when I had warned him that I didn't give in—I didn't give. I took. I clamped on. In my little room I taught my dancers in Harlem, where

I was fulfilled, because George had plotted that it would be better for me to be active; he would leave me dances after a horrible lingering death because, still, he was responsible for me, and the rights meant money.

I had so hoped, I thought, glancing across the worn speckled linoleum floor, that he was proud of my abilities, faithful in his estimations—a hope he had seemed to assure me of up until now. I studied feet: dirty red Keds with bedraggled gray laces, salt-faded splotched workman's boots, navy pumps run down at the heels, shoes alive with feet inside shifting, scrunching their toes, tapping the floor to awaken a foot fallen asleep. They said he wouldn't walk much longer. He already walked hunched and was too tottery to be led by one person. Two nurses aired him together in the hall. It often happened in neurological cases, a doctor said, that the patient walked like a toddler, then a baby, and then not at all, curled into a fetal position at last in the bed, in the cold white hospital womb. These patients slept, fell into a coma, machines trundled in, and then finally one day, perhaps because of pneumonia, horribly a result of immobility—*immobility*—they were carried off. Before this the pain, a world of hurt, stiffness, spasms, the trembling, the eyes, and panic as the brain shot off flares in the dark. It was probably very dark in there, in his mind, already. Though he didn't often show it, he was afraid. *How dare I? Envy. Regret.*

Owen came in with his dirty blond hair, a tiny diamond sparking his ear, his pea-coated strength, and asked what was wrong. Tired, I said.

I called Diana and told her I had decided to go to Weston for New Year's as usual, and I hoped she could come. I hadn't thought to leave him for even a day, feeling my daily visits provided routine he depended on. Now I didn't know whom the visits were for.

I slept in the night and dreamed I had set the table in Weston but there was no food. It was summer but a single tree shed its leaves rapidly, a pile lay on the grass turning color from green to brilliant red and gold, as the leaves should have before they fell. The stripped tree revealed strange red-winged blackbirds lined along branches as if they were books on shelves, immobile.

Then, almost exactly as it had been in life, I was in the studio with George the day he told my partner Nicky to leave, and, alone finally, we laughed.

"You think I don't mean it?" he said. "Again," and I knew what I had to do again. I danced; he watched.

Stopping, I saw something else in his eyes. I glistened, I heaved with excitement in my wonderful flesh, I was beautiful, wasn't it grand?

"You want to go someplace with me?" he asked.

"Where?"

"To the moon?"

The next morning, I awakened with a conviction of Carl's presence. I wouldn't get hard, Butch, I thought, I wouldn't get bitter if your arms were around me.

I got up and rolled to the kitchen for coffee. I had to buy food. I knew from Father's illness that grief began while the dying lived. I could feel my bones against Lenore's seat, and this would not do.

The phone rang. "Where were you?"

The voice of complexity yet again, *he was still here.*

I looked about the kitchen for an answer and said, "I didn't feel well."

"That's what I thought, I was worried. How you feel now?"

"Better."

"Then you'll be here later."

"Yes."

"See you then," and he hung up.

When? Had I said when? Then. Anytime. There weren't schedules any longer.

The new drugs tore up his stomach; he felt sick today, but his muscles were calm. When I came to the end of the chapter he said, "Tanny, tell me the Chekhov."

"The governess?" I closed my eyes, *used to travel about to fairs and give performances . . . I used to dance* . . . For the life of me I couldn't remember. "If you like," he said, "I can recite the whole thing," and he did. That was how it would be until the last weeks: with shreds of his diminishing strength and his powerful focus and will, he grasped all he was losing once again. He could also be sad and despairing, telling Volkov he had no hope of his dances surviving: "A breath, a memory, then gone." The changes in him produced distillations that could be poetically funny: "Women sleeping curl up like cats, and awake they walk like horses." If you arrived while he was listening to the radio, he would give you a disquisition about the music. His kinetic responsiveness to music didn't falter: listening, he continued to see people dancing. Later this winter, Maria entered his room to see George lying in bed with his hands up over his head, twisting and signing. "You see, Maria, I'm making dances."

Today as I got ready to leave, I told him that I would be gone for a few days to Weston.

"Yes," he replied, recalling that I always went. "I don't like New Year's," he added. I could see him linger over the words, and, looking puzzled, he told me, "I thought we would stay married."

"Me too," I said. "Can you see me?" His face was turned to me on the pillow, but his eyes scanned this way and that; they met their mark.

"Yes."

"George?"

He lifted his chin and brow in his watching and listening expression, and I was about to say something impulsive.

"In Venice . . ." I hesitated. "Before Stravinsky got sick," not *I* got sick, I could not say it, "I went out one night with Shaun on the canal, I was drunk, and I was—"

"I know."

"You know? For how long?"

"I knew forever, twenty-six years, but so what? It isn't conclusive, only one possibility."

"How can you say that?"

"Easy. I read books. People swimming in pools, sharing a bag of popcorn, more exposure it seemed to me than a lick on the tip of your finger. Odds would be slim."

"Why did you suspect Venice, then?" I asked.

"Last place it was hot, but I don't know either. You don't think about it, do you?" he asked.

"Yes, sometimes."

"Do not dwell on what you can't know." I remembered what he had recently told Diana: always be patient and optimistic.

"I should have talked to you about this years ago," I said.

"If it was bothering you, yes, you should. What else?"

"What do you mean, what else?"

344

"Oh, sickbed confession. I listen to everybody, why not you too?"

I wiped at my eyes and laughed. The scene I had witnessed between him and Karin didn't matter anymore, had dissolved. "I made a mistake with Carl," I said.

"What?"

"I should have married him."

"Why? What would be the difference?"

"He wanted it. I could have done that for him."

"Never mind. You were good to him."

"How do you know?"

"I know." He reached for my hand.

"Can you see me, George?"

"See you fine."

Liar.

"You're pretty," he said, and just as I figured he was more or less seeing the young woman or girl me, as I would report to Natalie later, he added, "You're still pretty woman. Seeing you does me good."

"In that case, I suppose I won't go to Weston."

"Not this year," he said. "Come by for more shameless flattery and we will read."

For us both, all this, not one or the other; there was no such thing as one or the other.

Only an autopsy would reveal what had taken his eyes, his pirouette to the right on his left foot, his ability to show, his *bella figuera*—his everything.

345

Under a microscope his brain was pocked like a sponge, like the word for what killed him, the spongiform encephalopathy disease called Creutzfeldt-Jakob. We would learn that it is caused by an infection that invades proteins. As protein cells die, the patient loses coordination related to visual-spatial perception. Changes in the cerebellum produce hallucinations and alterations in other mental functions. The course of the disease from onset of symptoms to death is typically rapid. Considering Balanchine's symptoms, a disease that usually kills in a year, took five.

Polio also invades the nervous system in perhaps one percent of its infections. The virus enters the body through the mouth and binds to receptors on cells, where it multiplies quickly and is absorbed into the bloodstream and widely distributed throughout the body. It commonly stops at the outermost layer of the brain. Only a few infections go farther, spreading along nerve fiber pathways and destroying motor neurons; if the neurons controlling muscles die, if muscles no longer receive nerve stimulation, they weaken and paralyze.

Much less is known about Creutzfeldt-Jakob disease, and it is invariably fatal. It is shockingly rare, and while one form results from internal mutations, the spongiform encephalopathy version derives from external sources and is related to what in animals we know as mad cow disease. In people the virus transmits by exposure to diseased tissue. Balanchine, we learned, had probably been infected by rejuvenating injections of sheep-placenta extracts he received in Europe. Famous men of the influential generation preceding his—Charlie Chaplin, Winston Churchill, Cole Porter, and Somerset Maugham—routinely sought out the treatment, called cellular therapy, to enhance their virility. George's infection could have occurred many years before his death, since it is believed the disease has a long incubation.

As George would not settle on the cause of my infection, I didn't linger on his. The tragedy was his death, not the cause. We are creatures locked in our time and culture, tiny units of fractured comprehension. We are impulsive, or we are assured of a thing being safe and only later do we learn that it is not. When George entered the hospital in November, Jerry wrote Bobby Fizdale, who was attending the funeral of Vera Stravinsky in Venice, "It's unfair that Nature, having no regard for the soul, genius & contributions of that man, wreaks a swift & rather specially horrible natural destruction on his body, unconscious of the *who* which is contained within it."

While George lay dying, one day the density of the body struck me forcefully. I had noticed the softness of his hair, the life of it against his grayed face and the process of death. I touched it; he wouldn't have minded; he slept. *Such life still in this room*—white hair, soft as a child's. And while his cheeks were sunken and bloodless and unshaved because of the delicacy of his skin, his head itself, so solid against the pillows, seemed to epitomize substance. How else but with violence and fight could the materiality in which we exist leave, transform?

But go back.

Not yet.

One night at the end of April just after Russian Easter I would wake up at midnight, having gone to bed early. The cat at the foot of the bed would lift his head. I didn't get up, I lay waiting for the light and the ringing phone.

And before that, on January 22, 1983, it was George's seventy-ninth birthday. I was fifty-three.

5

The trumpeting red amaryllis had died, and I brought in another, rich pink, and set it a better distance away from the radiator. Sun lit up the flower in the extending afternoons; bright rays struck the thick waxy petals diaphanous pink, like an ear can look outdoors; funny tender ears, they amused me.

I made George get out of bed with the help of a walker and one of his very good nurses, Ida, and look at the amaryllis in the sunshine one day. Turning and tilting his head, he was able to see it.

"Remember the wild turkeys?" I asked him. "Their wattles? Wattles, I think it's the silliest word in the English language."

"You're silly, why you see wattles? It's silk, it's jewel, not a wattle."

"I'm a barbarian," I said. "You're an aesthete."

"Maybe pink Chevy convertible," he countered.

On the new calendar, January's ballerina of the month was Melissa Hayden, a photograph ten years old of George's dance for her retirement gala. He used to moan that Milly would never retire, but he knew her worth and she danced for him until she was fifty.

The violets on his bedside table were pushed aside to accommodate the recently published catalogue of his works. "There it is," he told visitors, "the bible." Its preparation completed before his memory grew unreliable, it listed his more than two hundred ballets, his occasion pieces, films, revues, musical comedies, dances for opera, choral works, and plays; and six pages were required to enumerate all of the companies performing his works throughout the world.

On the morning of his birthday I brought to the

hospital three bottles of Roederer Cristal, his favorite champagne, which Ida would chill in the staff refrigerator, my contribution to his birthday party this afternoon.

"Can't drink it," he said.

"You'll have a sip and the others will drink it." I could tell the party was a pressure to him. I fantasized sitting together on a sunny hilltop in a salt breeze, days running seamlessly, banishing time until we and the landscape enclosing us faded—as in a film, as if color, life, could float in the dark suspended indefinitely, concluding only in people's intangible inner visions.

I wouldn't come to the party. Today was a teaching day, and in the afternoon I had a rehearsal. But Baryshnikov, Karin, and a few of the others were bringing Russian food from Brighton Beach.

The mood in the hallways among groups of people I met coming and going or waiting to see him remained hopeful. A holiday atmosphere lingered, and my dancers in Harlem, his extended family now that they were practitioners and acolytes of his style, always asked about him and wanted to hear my Balanchine stories. I described him teaching Mourka to do entrechat-quatre, pas de chat, and grand jeté. I imitated his indictment of French dancers: lazy, always take time out for lunch. Of Russians: arms good, but feet are abysmal. By now my dancers knew that while technically his demands were precise, every inch of his choreography was not set in stone. He gave you the leeway to do it with a little personality, which some people might find surprising, since he was so often accused of eliminating the personality. The dancers' respect for him had widened as they experienced what he taught in their limbs, felt how he changed the way dancers moved, understood that for Balanchine, music itself was the story.

Owen sensed, as Diana and Natalie could—and as Mother and Jerry could when they tried—whether I needed to talk or be quiet, through the long ending of winter and freighted holy strenuous spring while I carried on in my life but was not really there, while everything lived and died in the hospital room; their behavior spoke to me their knowledge that my love for George was as it had always been.

I loved him as a woman loves a man and a wife loves a husband, and on that subject there was nothing else to be said.

The birthday party was too much. He couldn't eat. He attempted to reassure them that he felt fine and—he may not have been thinking clearly—he lunged from the bed and crashed to the floor. Paper plates scattered. An opened bottle of champagne fizzed out its contents. Unhurt but shaken, he lost his composure completely. The nurses settled him into a chair, but, vibrating with jagged nerves and disoriented, he waved a protective warding-off hand at each person who knelt down trying to talk to him.

For days he thought his room swarmed with St. Petersburg street urchins, that postrevolution desperadoes hid in the wardrobe and under his bed, stinking, shouting, and kicking their rotting muddy boots at his bare shins. Then, mercifully, they were gone.

We continued *War and Peace.* If we came to a disturbing section, I wasn't sure it was good to go on. But all of it seemed to help him coalesce, to regain himself, and he said it sounded fresh because he didn't know it in English. Sometimes I read a passage and he spoke it back to me in Russian. He corrected my faulty pronunciation of the French.

Days came when he slept through visits and I read silently on, marking the spot to return to when he was awake.

One day I met his first wife, Tamara, in the hallway, a beautiful Russian-Swedish woman of nearly eighty. She told me that he was agitated, clutching an icon and chanting, "Must believe, must believe." But going in, I saw he had fallen asleep—I could tell at once by his position in bed and his breathing. The St. George icon winked in his palm, the silver and turquoise bracelet polished by Ida set atop the thick catalogue where he could see it; wearing it hurt his wrist. Soon he wouldn't be able to see it at all, and before he died somebody stole it.

At home in bed, I began holding the cross he had given me, fingering the tiny garnets like bird eyes. Charged with him and his mother, it helped me relax. Nights I was stiff and sore and angry that sleep wouldn't come so that I could dream and escape from my worries, I put the tiny cross up to my nose and sniffed its cool brass, and then I lay pouring all my attention into the object until it poured back and into me. It gave me a sense of restoration, of feeling that nothing we had lived that was important to us could be lost. I would be filled with an urgency to tell George that I knew now what I had learned since I lost my legs. I understood his belief in continual, contiguous life, in the past, present, and future running on parallel tracks, as I did years ago thinking I wanted to die and asked him to help me. Holding the cross, I stopped being afraid of his death and even my own death—different from the one I had wanted when I was desperate and young. I stopped being afraid of the inevitable death that would come in the not too distant future, whether I wanted it or not—and I didn't want it, because I so valued life, but I wasn't afraid. On the night I held the cross after seeing the icon glitter green in George's white hand against the sheets, I thought of his *must believe, must believe,* and I realized his faith wasn't a foregone conclusion, just there in him like an inheritance from his believing family and country, but was more like a desire he fed and struggled to bring to fruition in the same way he had created everything else in his life. I thought I had never known anyone as brave. For myself, I didn't know who I would have been in this life without his example.

"I saw the czar."

"In your sleep?"

"No. I met him as a child." He had forgotten which stories I had already heard. "People say the czar's box was in the middle, but it was on the side, on the right. It had a separate entrance, a separate foyer, with a large private driveway. When you got inside, it was like a colossal apartment: chandeliers, the walls covered in light blue. The emperor sat with his family—Empress Alexandra Feodorovna, the heir, his daughters—and we would be lined up by size and presented: Efimov, Balanchivadze, Mikhailov. The czar was not tall. The czarina was a very tall, beautiful woman. She was dressed sumptuously. The grand princesses, Nicholas's daughters, were also beauties. The czar had protruding light-colored eyes, and he rolled his *r*'s. If he said, 'Well, how are you?' we were supposed to click our heels and reply, 'Highly pleased, Your Imperial Majesty!' We were given chocolate in silver boxes, wonderful ones! And exquisite mugs, porcelain with light blue lyres and the imperial monogram. I didn't save any of it. At the time, it was all rather unimportant to me." Again he closed his eyes. He had delivered the story nearly verbatim to how he had told it to Volkov. The interviews were finished; I thanked Volkov, saying their conversations had been bracing for George. I felt that recalling and finding words for his youthful experiences and his feelings for Tchaikovsky would shore up the landscape inside—that his mind, undisturbed by clashing signals, independent of sensory input, would tame down, turn to a fortress.

He seemed to withdraw into the bed—the loss and concavity of flesh, hours spent in sleep, startled flutter of eyelids, and squint meeting light. We kept the blinds open in daylight for the nurses' duties and an approximation of cheer, but Karin draped a dark scarf over the lamp on his bedside table. It was our wish now that he would lapse into unconsciousness, take the next step in leaving, anything, as one learned in this situation, to bring smooth passage.

And yet when I knew he had spoken his last words to me, I frantically scanned the room as if to find him and pull him back.

It was late March and outside black pitted banks of snow, shoved to curbs and petrified after a heavy storm, had begun to break off in chunks and New Yorkers, exhausted by winter, were grumpy as hell. In the room the cherry scent of lotion Ida rubbed into his skin to keep it supple offended me. Cherry cream just didn't work. I'd brought a bottle of the cologne he used to wear to the hospital and rubbed the scent from my hands to the sheets. Today I had forgotten and left it at home.

Five days ago we had read a little. Prince Andrei was dead, Moscow burned, and the French were about to be driven from Russia. George had fallen asleep and, awakening, asked me to read him the death of Petya, a boy falling sideways off his horse, and a man, Petya's companion, recalling the boy's love of raisins, turning away and gripping a fence in his grief.

Today I read on alone, and at the part where Pierre comes home from the war and finds Natasha, I knew George would never speak to me again. I panicked, felt gagged on the cherry lotion, and, my old sense of physical entrapment returning, I started to cry, my elbow on Lenore's arm, my forehead pressed to my hand. I knew that George might be able to hear and I should control myself, but I couldn't help it, I'd held back too long and *how could this be?*

I heard myself cough. I looked at the bed and he had opened his eyes. Fool. Bringing him back. I was at a loss about what to do. I could stay at a distance and hope he hadn't heard me.

He'd heard. I went close. I took his hand. I felt the slight pressure of his hand talking to me.

"I'm fine, George. Really. I'll be fine."

He did not open his eyes again. I read silently to the end of the novel and then, sitting with him, I reread his favorite passages. Finally I put away the book and imagined his dreams. I believed they were good ones: Telling Lincoln that with twenty girls and five men he could accomplish wonders. He dreamed of his ballerinas, Maria in her prime and Suzanne, and the young Tamara, and the girl who had drowned, Lidia Ivanovna, dancing and free. He heard the rattle of droshkies' wheels on the wooden Petersburg streets, saw the circus pony his father had purchased by mistake, uninformed of the pony's illustrious background; the poor lost fellow, pulling a cart, reared up in an attempt to perform and tossed out the cart riders. He heard the church bells of High Russian Easter, the rushing fountains tumbling water down the steps of Aurora's palace under the rapturous hot lights where he'd been enchanted and realized what he would do with his life. He was back at the piano with his mother in the family dacha in Finland before the money was gone and the children were sent off to state-supported schools. His mother put him to bed without supper if he failed to practice. He wanted to run outside all day and night through the trees. But one day at the piano, picking out a Beethoven sonata that was beyond him, he perceived in a flash of apprehension and joy the shape of the music he couldn't yet grasp, and it never bored him to practice again after that flash, which prefigured all he would do.

In the dream catalogue of his life he came to the day I decided enough was enough, I would have him and have him now. I appreciated that he was a gentleman, but I was ready and this was it. I knew he would keep me after rehearsal. I was disastrously distracted, my solo was a shambles, and the partnering was a wreck because I was too tense.

He kept me alone. He knew. He knew it all. My love reached him in beams across rooms, heated the air between us as he came near so that it thickened and seethed and coiled around him like a rope.

Come to me.

Again. Outside the heavy snow started but we were oblivious, I traveled across the smooth floor and he counted out beats, just the tap of his foot and the numbers until I was dizzy, hung limp, hands gripped on my strong thighs, head dumped to the boards. I flipped back my hair and a sweaty mess smiled at him in triumph.

Better.

Wasn't it grand?

You want to go someplace with me?

Later, I said. I wanted to dance with him. I held out my hand. He came to me, full of desire.

We went into motion, and it began.

Author's Note

*T*anaquil Le Clercq lived to be seventy-one years old. She retired from teaching shortly before or after Balanchine's death but remained an advocate of his work in her position on the board of directors of New York City Ballet. She never remarried. Her close friendships and the time spent in Weston, Connecticut, were constant pleasures. In 1998, New York City Ballet held a 50th Anniversary Celebration Tribute to Tanaquil Le Clercq, which she attended. She passed away two years later.

As I began research into Le Clercq's life and her relationship with George Balanchine, I quickly saw that the basic facts were corroborated across a wide variety of sources. But because Tanny never wrote a memoir, unlike Balanchine's other wives, I had to imagine the private drama the public record implied. Tanaquil Le Clercq, George Balanchine, Jerome Robbins, Diana Adams, Maria Tallchief, Suzanne Farrell, and other people who actually lived or are living appear in this novel as characters who are inspired by the public record.

It was, however, my goal to stay as close to the true story as possible. I used available resources for jumping-off points, from which my imagination took over. Only a few of the secondary characters are entirely fictional. I occasionally reordered timelines of events and slightly altered aspects of how the story occurred for clarity's sake, and I created the dialogue among the characters. I did not include some of the relationships in Tanny's life, in order to maintain the focus on her relationship with Balanchine. Otherwise, I was informed by my sources—books, films, videos, articles, and what people said who were there.

Shaun O'Brien danced with Le Clercq and was present during the fateful 1956 tour. He was among the group who went out on the canal with Tanny in Venice, and I depended on what he told me about what happened that night. His stories of backstage life at New York City Ballet in the 1950s were also invaluable.

Virginia Johnson, who is currently artistic director of Dance Theatre of Harlem, shared her stories of taking class with Le Clercq at the DTH school in the 1970s, and she described the glittering parties Tanny threw at the Apthorp.

Many books were helpful. Of the biographies, I should cite *Balanchine: A Biography*, by Bernard Taper; *All in the Dances: A Brief Life of Balanchine*, by Terry Teachout; *George Balanchine: The Ballet Maker*, by Robert Gottlieb; *Somewhere: The Life of Jerome*

Robbins, by Amanda Vaill; and *The Worlds of Lincoln Kirstein*, by Martin B. Duberman. Of the memoirs: *Maria Tallchief: America's Prima Ballerina*, by Maria Tallchief with Larry Kaplan; *Holding On to the Air*, by Suzanne Farrell with Toni Bentley; and *In Balanchine's Company: A Dancer's Memoir*, by Barbara Milberg Fisher.

For anecdotal material, two other dance books were fascinating and useful. *Striking a Balance: Dancers Talk About Dancing*, edited by Barbara Newman, contains a transcript of Le Clercq talking about dance and Balanchine. *I Remember Balanchine: Recollections of the Ballet Master by Those Who Knew Him*, edited by Francis Mason, contains many poignant observations not only of Balanchine but also of Le Clercq. The comments in the latter book range from those by Balanchine's earliest dancers to doctors who cared for him in his final illness.

Balanchine's Tchaikovsky: Conversations with Balanchine on His Life, Ballet and Music, by Solomon Volkov, translated from the Russian by Antonina W. Bouis, increased my knowledge of Balanchine's youth in St. Petersburg and opened a window into his state of mind during his last days. *Balanchine's Complete Stories of the Great Ballets*, by George Balanchine and Francis Mason, was an essential reference.

The Dance Division of the New York Public Library was a resource for video and for print in the form of reviews of Le Clercq's dancing, newspaper accounts of her illness in 1956, and articles about her, including many photographs of her in all stages of life: in childhood, in costume and rehearsal clothes, with Balanchine, in the pages of fashion magazines, and in Weston, Connecticut and New York after the polio. The collection holds prints of her portraits of Balanchine. Of the articles I read, those in *Ballet Review* were especially helpful. The writing of Holly Brubach, Nancy Lassalle, and Pat McBride Lousada, three people who knew Le Clercq well, greatly enhanced my understanding of her connection to Balanchine.

Jane Klain at the Paley Center for Media in New York helped me find tape of Le Clercq on television, including the complete television play *A Candle for St. Jude*, in which Le Clercq danced and acted.

Balanchine, a documentary first aired in 1984 for the *American Masters* program, was an early resource and one to which I often returned. I was also inspired by a newer *American Masters* documentary, *Jerome Robbins: Something to Dance About*, and by the film *Dancing for Mr. B: Six Balanchine Ballerinas*. All of these are available on DVD from Kultur. Over and over again, I watched the Balanchine ballets telecast during his lifetime and supervised by the choreographer; these come as a pair of DVDs called *Choreography by Balanchine*, put out by Nonesuch.

Tanaquil Le Clercq's books, *Mourka: The Autobiography of a Cat* and *The Ballet Cook Book*, gave me funny and valuable information, as did an article she wrote on becoming a ballerina, and her responses to interview questions. Although she was usually reticent on the subject of her private life, a few times she spoke quite frankly about her divorce. I often drew from her published comments for that part of the novel. Also, what she and others said about her mother and father provided the details out of which I created those characters in my fiction.

My portrayals of the other major players in the story grew out of research as well, whenever possible from their own writing.

My treatment of polio and disability had several sources. My late father was a polio survivor. I am indebted to his personal knowledge of the illness and its effects. In addition, he and my mother were active in post-polio support groups and shared with me what they knew about how polio may return in a survivor's later years.

Joan Swain, who lost the use of her legs as a teenager in the 1950s—and who is also a fan of New York City Ballet and saw many of their early performances—generously explained what it is like to live with a disability similar to Le Clercq's.

I was grateful for *Black Bird Fly Away: Disabled in an Able-Bodied World*, by Hugh Gregory Gallagher, and for *Warm Springs: Traces of a Childhood at FDR's Polio Haven*, by Susan Richards Shreve.

Nearly all of my research attested to Tanaquil Le Clercq's beauty, intelligence, and exceptional artistry; to the courage and verve with which she approached her life after polio; and to how she never stopped loving Balanchine. She called herself a "one-man woman" and died on the anniversary of their wedding.

Acknowledgments

I wish to thank the Department of English and the Division of Research and Sponsored Programs at Kent State University for their support during the writing of this book.

Thank you to my agent, Joy Harris, for her literary acumen and uncanny sense of what authors need. Thank you to my editor, Whitney Frick, who was perfect for the novel because of her dance background and editorial skill. Thank you to everyone at the Joy Harris Literary Agency and at Scribner and Simon & Schuster.

For their help I thank Maggie Anderson, Julie Barer, Risa Bell, John De Vito, Frederic Franklin, Anna French, Erika Goldman, Virginia Johnson, Jane Klain, David LaMarche, Phillip Lopate, Jerome Lowenstein, Norma Michaels, Shaun O'Brien, Jonathan Rabinowitz, Janyce Stefan-Cole, Daniel Stewart, Joan Swain, Louise Varley, and Lynn Varley.

For their enthusiasm and encouragement I thank Carol Dines-Rothenberg, Rhoda Huffey, Richard Millen, and Mary Morris.

And without Michelle Latiolais, Katherine Vaz, and Joel Wapnick there would be no book. Thank you, my brilliant, faithful dear ones.

Center Point Large Print
600 Brooks Road / PO Box 1
Thorndike ME 04986-0001 USA

(207) 568-3717

US & Canada:
1 800 929-9108
www.centerpointlargeprint.com